Stormy

Legacy

Written by Nancy Clarke

Illustrations by Penny Muire

Strategic Book Publishing and Rights Co.

Hardcover version published in 2011.
Softcover version published in 2014.

Strategic Book Publishing and Rights Co.
12620 FM 1960, Suite A4-507
Houston, TX 77065
www.sbpra.com

For information about special discounts for bulk purchases, please contact Strategic Book Publishing and Rights Co. Special Sales, at bookorder@sbpra. net.

ISBN: 978-1-63135-412-0

Design: Dedicated Book Services (www.netdbs.com)

In memory of my mother, Betty Bodine

Contents

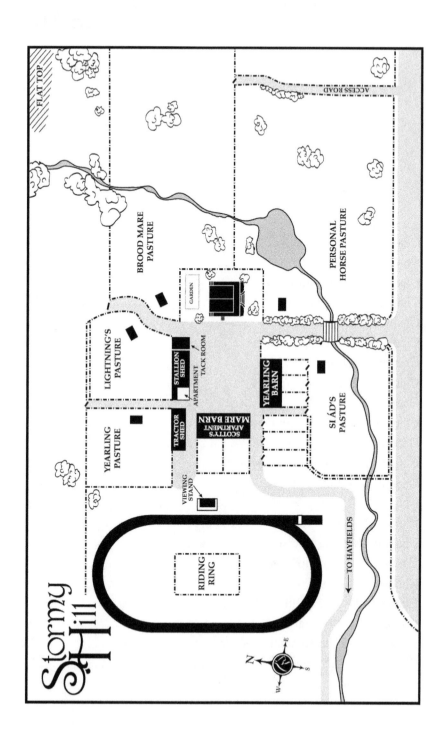

1

STORMY HILL

The bus had barely come to a stop before two very elated teenagers burst from it and chased each other up the long tree-lined drive. Their laughter rang in the air.

"Exams are over!" shouted blond-haired Ted Winters to the slender girl sprinting beside him. "Freedom!"

"No more school!" Ann Collins shouted back as she tossed her head, her long, black hair flying out behind her like a cape. "Summer!"

They both stopped and looked at each other. In one breath they voiced the thought on both their minds. "Riding!" they screeched together, and then laughed as they realized how well they read each other's minds.

"Let's go!" Ann was already in motion.

"Race you!" Ted challenged, flying after her. "First one ready gets to ride his horse."

"You're on!"

Quickly their competitive natures took over. Gravel spewed from their flying feet as they raced up the long driveway, frolicking like two young colts on a summer's day. They flew into the yard, scattering the farm's shepherd dogs dozing in the sun. Their arrival set off a volley of barking, announcing their presence. Ted dashed off to the left toward his single-room apartment in the stallion barn. Ann ran in the other direction, toward the big, southern-style, two-story house, set off to the right of the drive and surrounded by stately live oaks.

1

She ran up the steps and across the wide verandah that circled more than half the house, then burst into the kitchen, banging the screen door in her wake. Her mother looked up from her baking and smiled. Jessica Collins was a slightly built woman with pale brown hair tucked tidily into a bun, just beginning to gray at the temples. She was a quiet, unassuming woman, the antithesis of her often volatile, usually intense daughter. Yet she was the rock upon which this family depended. No matter how big or small the crisis, they all relied on her.

Right now she turned to her daughter as she flew past. "Hi, Hon. Exams all done?" she asked.

"Oh, hi, Mom. Yep. Going riding with Ted…" The last was spoken from her bedroom, a small room off the kitchen that had once served as a den. Ann, books thrown in a corner, forgotten, hastily donned her old riding jeans and a cast-off T-shirt that had once belonged to one of the boys. Seconds later she was racing back through the kitchen, stopping long enough to snatch a couple of large chocolate chip cookies Jessica had just removed from the oven.

"Gotta hurry," she said by way of explanation, "or Ted will get to ride his horse." Then she was gone, the screen door once again banging in her wake, dogs barking as they chased her across the courtyard. Jessica, used to the habits of her "kids," only chuckled and returned to work. Though Ann was the only one she'd birthed, she thought of the two boys who also lived there—Ted and Jock—as hers too.

Meanwhile, Ann sped the length of the courtyard, intent upon beating Ted to the tack room so she could get saddled first. She was too late. Si'ad, Ted's grey Arabian stallion, was already standing tied to the hitching post as Ted worked at tightening the girth to his light racing saddle.

"Oh, no," she groaned. "How'd you beat me?" she asked, taking a bite out of one of the cookies in her hand.

"Slow poke," he grinned. "I'm just quicker, that's all. Looks like you're stuck with Banshee. Too bad." But he didn't look at all sorry as he slid the bit into Si'ad's willing mouth.

"Too bad for *you*," she countered, taking another bite. "Mom just made chocolate chip cookies, and I brought you one"—she knew Jessica's cookies were his favorites—"but if you're going to be nasty, I'll just have to eat the other one, too." She held up the cookie enticingly. Ted lunged for it, but Ann was faster and slid her hand behind her back. Ted recovered and grabbed her arm, and they wrestled for a few moments until he triumphantly came away with two pieces of slightly crushed cookie.

"Thanks," he mumbled as he popped the pieces into his mouth.

"No fair," she pouted. "You're stronger than me."

"You bet." His blue eyes twinkled. "Now you'd better saddle up, or I'll leave you behind."

"You wouldn't dare!" she shrieked, heading for the tack room.

"Just watch me," he teased, making her hurry faster.

Moments later, Ann had the dark brown, almost black gelding tacked up. She swung into the saddle and moved alongside Ted on Si'ad as they headed their horses for the lane that ran behind the house. Rivalry forgotten, they were both silent, sharing the contentment of two people doing what they loved best—riding. Ann was very aware that she bested Ted in these mock contests just as often as he won, but that didn't stop her from complaining. After all, Ted grumbled just as much when she won.

It was a shame, she thought, that there had to be this competition at all. It all stemmed from the fact that Si'ad was a stallion born of the desert and, due to past circumstances, still half wild. Ann's horse was his beautiful, black two-year-old son, Stormy Lightning. Once a gentle, hand-raised orphan, Lightning had changed considerably after he was stolen. Though the details of the time he'd spent away from them were not completely known, Ann and her family found a much different horse when he did return. He had become unruly, with many fears that were only now revealing themselves. Now neither stallion would accept the presence of the other, so Ann and Ted could not ride them together.

Unfortunately this left them with no choice but to use Jessica's hunter-bred gelding, Banshee, as the other horse. Nowhere near as fast or as exciting, at least he was a mount. The result was this game they played to decide who would get to ride his horse.

Yet as they swung down the lane in a comfortable silence, Ann could not help but admire, once again, the picture Ted and Si'ad made. With or without a saddle, the boy sat his stallion with a grace and smoothness that made him one with his horse. On the ground he still may have had the gawkiness of a skinny, half-grown youth, but on a horse—especially this one—he was a natural.

Si'ad himself was no ordinary horse. Only partially tamed, the desert-bred stallion moved across the earth like a superbly developed athlete. His muscles rippled beneath his steel coat, a coat that shone with health and vitality. He ate up distances with ground-eating strides, and as they neared the end of the lane where a gate led to the vast field beyond, he swung into a light canter. In silent agreement, Ted led the way over the four-foot obstacle, leaving Ann to follow.

Si'ad cleared the gate with ease as he rose on his powerful hindquarters, his dark silver-tipped mane whipping out like a banner, his long tail of the same color—a flag carried exceptionally high, as typical of his breed. His long arched neck stretched out, topped by a finely chiseled head that tapered to an almost delicate muzzle.

No doubt about it, Si'ad was a beauty. And Ann never tired of watching him in motion, regardless of how she teased Ted about his horse. Theirs was a friendly rivalry, born of a mutual love and understanding of one special horse. For Ann it was Si'ad's firstborn, her wonderful Lightning. Because she had a unique bond with him, she could relate closely to Ted's with Si'ad. Though Ted had only been a member of their Stormy Hill family for barely a month, they had become such close friends that at times she forgot what life had been like before he'd arrived.

"Race you to the base of Flat Top," Ted suddenly called back to her, breaking her concentration.

"You're on," she replied, urging Banshee to his top speed, well aware that nothing on their farm, short of Lightning, could catch the fleet-footed Arab. Even so she pursued him, trying to stay at least within visual range of the pair. She knew things would be reversed when it was her turn to ride Lightning.

The stallion sped over the ground, across the fields and in and out of the woods, leaping anything in his path, Ted clinging to him like a burr. Ann managed to keep him in sight, but there was never any contest. When at last she caught up with him at the base of the hill called Flat Top, Ted was sitting coolly atop his horse. Si'ad was in such superb condition that he'd barely broken a sweat.

"What kept you?" he teased.

"Boy, what I wouldn't give for a horse that could keep up with either of our boys," she sighed. "Poor Banshee was never meant to be a racehorse. This is plain humiliating."

"I know, and I'm sorry. What say later you ride Lightning, and I'll put up with Banshee? Deal?"

"Sure thing."

They turned their horses toward the narrow path that led to the summit of Flat Top and started their climb. It was gradual enough for both horses to cool down by the time they reached the top. From there the view was spectacular. The highest spot around, Flat Top was a plateau from where a person could see in all four directions. Spread out before them was the heart of the Kentucky Bluegrass Region. Everywhere one looked, one saw gently rolling fields dotted with the Thoroughbreds for which the area was famous. Each field was surrounded by miles and miles of white or creosoted fencing, mostly a four-board design. Amid clusters of trees would stand the main house, often a southern-style mansion from which well-maintained showplace barns sprawled. There was usually a training track and other cottages, all surrounded by manicured lawns with beautifully kept flower beds. This was the grandeur that was Bluegrass Country.

Sloping off to the south side of Flat Top stretched their own Stormy Hill. Less prestigious and less grand than her wealthier sisters, the Collins farm had suffered a series of setbacks over the years. Ann's father, Michael, ran a feed store in town to help meet expenses, while the two remaining members of Stormy Hill's family, widower Scotty McDougal and his son, Jock, two years Ann's senior, worked part-time at the Garrison farm next door to earn spending money. Both Jock and Scotty had been raised on this farm. When financial reversals had forced Michael to make some drastic changes, including letting all the help go, they alone had remained. The farm needed them, Scotty had stated flatly. Over the years he'd officially served as their trainer, raising his young son to follow in his footsteps, but unofficially they were much, much more.

But Ann's thoughts were elsewhere as she jumped down from Banshee and flopped on the soft, thick grass beside Ted, who'd already turned the stallion loose, and was lying there, enjoying the view. Neither spoke as they beheld it together in contented silence.

Ann once again relived the events of the recent past as she watched the handsome grey. Though everyone referred to Si'ad as Ted's horse, it had not always been so. Once he'd belonged to her.

Si'ad had originally come from the desert. Through a lucky set of circumstances, Michael had acquired him to breed to his most valuable mare, Dawn of Glory. One stormy January night two years ago she gave birth to Lightning. The mare's subsequent death left him an orphan, but Ann had hand-raised him. He was a yearling when Michael, in order to pay a debt, had been forced to send Si'ad on lease to an Arabian stud farm in Arizona. Even now, Ann remembered the pain she had suffered seeing him go. He had been her horse. She alone had gentled him and known the joy of riding him. The lease was for three years, but he'd barely begun his second year at stud when word came that he'd been lost in a disastrous fire at the ranch. She'd turned to Lightning for comfort, the bond they then developed overcoming the loss of what she'd shared with Si'ad.

But even that seemed destined not to be, for in the fall of his yearling year, Lightning had been stolen from them. While the complete details of the next few months were not known, they did get some facts and could conjecture much of the rest. He'd been part of a group of horses taken to Oklahoma to sell at auction. There the thieves had been caught, but not before Lightning had escaped from them into remote hill country, where search parties were unable to locate him. He seemed to have resurfaced a month or so later on a ranch located far to the east. Its very remoteness contributed to the failure to make a connection with the missing Collins horse.

Lightning remained there for several months, becoming the favorite riding horse of the young daughter of the owner, possibly because she resembled Ann in looks. She'd chosen to take him on an overnight trail ride in the Ozarks, where something spooked him and he escaped, bolting once again into mountainous country.

From there the trail grew hazy—until Derby Day, one month ago. Ann had chosen not to go with her family as she usually did. Instead, feeling depressed over the loss of her colt, she'd chosen to ride a new mare they'd just gotten. It was right here, on Flat Top, that a clap of thunder had caused the mare to bolt, and Ann to fall off. Then she'd looked up and, miraculously, there was Lightning. Even now, remembering, she glanced over at the spot where he had first appeared, and smiled. How he got there, she had no idea, but later another piece of the puzzle was solved when her family replied to an ad placed by someone who'd lost a horse. The lost horse turned out to be Lightning, who'd been purchased at an auction two weeks earlier.

The day Ann found Lightning, none of that had mattered. She had only cared that he was back. With the impending storm, it seemed only logical to ride Lightning back to the farm. So bareback and sans bridle, she'd done just that. What a ride! Though she'd ridden him many times since, nothing could compare with that first time. Such speed and power! An exhilarated Ann had burst into the courtyard, coming to a half-rearing halt when Lightning spied Si'ad standing beside an unfamiliar van, being held by a stranger. Both stallions wanted to fight, and only the quick action on everyone's part had prevented an equine brawl. Only much later, after both horses were settled in their stalls, were the details pieced together by Ted, the stranger, of what really happened to Si'ad.

He told them he'd been working at the stud farm when the fire occurred. Because Si'ad was one of his charges, and he'd developed a special rapport with him, he'd saved him first, putting him in a distant pasture. But when Ted went to find him after the fire was out, he was not there. A grey fitting his description had been spotted, and it was believed he'd jumped out, only to return to the burning building. That was the news the Collins family had received.

Later a witness came forward to relate that he saw a grey horse running toward the mountains beyond the ranch. Ted begged to go after him and was given a mare and supplies for a couple of weeks so he could search the Superstitions for any trace of the stallion.

Details of the trip were rather sketchy. Ted had merely stated that he tracked down the stallion and caught him, bringing him safely back to the ranch. But Ann's perceptiveness where horses were concerned made her sense that there was a lot more to the story that Ted wasn't telling. Something happened up in those mountains that belonged only to the two of them, something strong enough to bond them for all time. When it was decided to send the stallion back to his rightful owners, Ted had asked to accompany him. Through accidental miscommunication, Stormy Hill was not aware of this until he actually arrived, surprising them all.

Ann, upon witnessing the silent interaction between Ted and the stallion, felt a pang of jealousy at first. After all, Si'ad had been her horse before he left. Then remembering she had Lightning back, she was instantly ashamed. Instead she understood the bond this boy could share with the beautiful stallion. It was not unlike the one she'd felt for her own black colt. She also sensed the real reason Ted had escorted Si'ad back to them, along with the pain and fear he was experiencing that they would soon be separated. She could not let that happen. She approached her father, begging him to let Ted stay.

The boy was given a home here at Stormy Hill, much to his amazement and undying gratitude. A room was fixed up for him in the stallion barn, and he was made the official stud manager for Si'ad. This was not without compensation—he would receive a percentage of the stud fee. He would also join Scotty and Jock working part-time for the Garrisons during their busy season. All in all, it was an equitable arrangement. But for Ted, getting to remain with his beloved stallion, it was heaven.

It did not take long before everyone was referring to Si'ad as Ted's horse. Soon they all recognized the special bond between the two and, regardless of what his papers said, Si'ad would always belong to Ted.

Still, as happy as he seemed, living there over the past several weeks, Ann couldn't help feeling Ted was holding back something. She did not doubt his friendship, nor would she question his loyalty, yet Ted never talked about his past before working for the Arabian breeders in Arizona—other than to mention initially that he was an orphan. She knew he was her age—sixteen—and by quick calculation she figured he couldn't have been more than fifteen when he took that job, so he'd probably lied about his age in order to drop out of school and go to work so young. She could bet it was not by choice, since he'd been so grateful for the opportunity to return to school with her to finish his education. At the rate he was making up the work he'd missed, she felt he'd easily be eligible to graduate with her next year. Ted had already proven himself a quick student. Knowing him as she did, she couldn't help but wonder what had happened in his past that he didn't want known. But until he was willing to share it with her, she would just have to wait. She believed in his basic honesty. It was the rock upon which their friendship was founded.

Her thoughts were interrupted when Ted suddenly burst to his feet. "Let's ride over and pick up Jock. He and Scotty should be done by the time we get there." He whistled to Si'ad and vaulted into the saddle.

"Good idea." Ann followed suit, leaping aboard Banshee with ease. They headed for the trail that took them down Flat Top to the north, circling along the back of their property, through the woods, and eventually coming out by the boundary to the Garrison place.

Known as "Garwood," though no one ever called it anything but "The Garrison Place," this farm was bigger than Stormy Hill. Actually, at one time the Garrison farm had been part of Stormy Hill. But when Michael Collins inherited the farm, he'd also inherited its debts. In order to keep from losing everything, he was forced to sell off the portion of land now belonging to Garrison, who'd used his vast wealth to develop the nearly 1,000 acres into a gaudy, pretentious showplace. No expense had been spared. The main house was a pillared replica of a Southern plantation home, where his wife threw lavish parties attended mostly by business associates, but seldom by members of the "Bluegrass society." While Garrison could fill his barns with fine Thoroughbreds to earn him many victories, keep his own well-groomed track complete with grandstand and enclosed viewing box, and in every other way act the elite gentleman breeder, he would never achieve what he most desired—acceptance. The fact remained, the Garrisons would always be thought by the Old Guard as upstarts.

Their money had been able to buy them everything but a place in Kentucky society, the one thing they craved. Perhaps this was why Greta Garrison was so insufferable toward Ann. Like it or not, the Collins family was accepted as part of the aristocracy, despite their current financial difficulties. Stormy Hill had been in the family for five generations, and that alone was reason enough. They were Southerners to the bone, a fact that seemed to escape Greta. Fortunately for Ann, Greta, though the same age, attended private school, while Ann went to the public high school. She only had to see her on the occasions that she rode over to the farm to accompany Jock or Ted home. Sometimes she was not present. Ann hoped this was one of those times.

She and Ted rode onto the Garrison place, past the endless white four-board fencing that enclosed countless horses peacefully grazing, many with foals at their side. A small lake extended off to the left, several large white swans gliding slowly in the warm sun. Beyond it sprawled the mile-long track, where a number of horses were being worked.

"Just like Garrison to be sprinting horses in the heat of the day," she commented disgustedly to Ted.

"Probably impressing a business client," Ted remarked sourly. He, too, thought little of the way Garrison was always meddling in his trainers' concerns.

They rode closer, spotting Scotty holding a horse beside the outer rail. Jock could be seen cantering a horse slowly down the backside of the track. There was no sign of Greta. Perhaps they could just grab Jock and head for home.

Ted trotted Si'ad up to where Scotty was standing, conversing with Mr. Garrison about his colt's progress. Scotty was a wiry, tough little Scotsman ten years Michael's senior, though his weathered face and thick, dark wavy hair, showing only a smattering of gray, belied his age. He was regarded as a superb trainer, having learned from the master—Angus McDougal, his father. Angus had developed most of the past great Stormy Hill champions, passing his vast knowledge onto his son. Scotty needed only another great horse to guarantee his own reputation. Despite his often-gruff exterior, the three youngest members of Stormy Hill idolized and respected Scotty because experience had taught them to always trust his judgment.

Scotty finished his conversation and turned to the patiently waiting Ted. "Guess you two are here to collect Jock," he said, handing the horse he was holding over to a groom standing by. "He should be just about done. Ann," he said as she rode up, "ride over and tell Jock to bring me that horse he's on. I'll take care of him so you three can go ahead."

"Thanks, Scotty. I'll tell him." She pointed Banshee out onto the track, where she spotted Jock riding a chestnut with four white socks and a broad blaze. She waved and he spotted her. Waving back, he trotted over.

"Scotty says he'll take over your mount so you can ride home with us."

"Great," Jock replied, riding the chestnut over to the men and jumping down. Jock was a younger version of his father—same wavy thick hair and brown eyes. His rugged, regular features suggested that Scotty must have been good looking as a younger man, for looking at Jock now was like seeing Scotty some thirty plus years ago. The major difference between them was Jock's taller frame. A late growth spurt had added inches to his height and pounds to his weight. Unfortunately, the latter prevented him from continuing his career as a jockey, but Jock seemed to have put that behind him in favor of being a trainer like his father. At the moment he, like Ted, worked exercising horses for Garrison.

Jock handed his father the reins and thanked him as he swung up behind Ann. "See you later, Dad," he called as Ann and Ted started their horses forward, also waving. They were just rounding the track when they heard a familiar voice.

"Oh, Jock, can't you stay a little longer?" It was Greta. She appeared from the direction of the house, catching up with them as soon as they were out of earshot of Scotty and her father. She was a pretty girl in an artificial way, with immaculately groomed blond hair, lots of makeup, and a fashionably expensive outfit over her trim figure. The sight made Ann grimace self-conscientiously as she mentally compared her own careless appearance, though she loathed herself for doing so.

Behind her, Jock stiffened. He groaned, though so low that only Ann could hear it. Jock did not like Greta, and that made Ann smile. "Sorry, Greta, I'm afraid the boys can't play today," she said, smiling sweetly. "They're needed at home now."

"That's too bad," Greta returned just as sweetly. "Here I was hoping you boys would like a dip in our pool. It's such a warm day." She added a melodramatic sigh.

Ann almost laughed but caught herself. After all, these "boys" needed their jobs. No sense in riling Greta unduly. "Another time maybe," she said, urging Banshee into a canter. "Ta ta." Before the girl had a chance to respond, they were out of earshot, Ted letting Si'ad into an easy canter ahead of her.

They moved out across the field, taking the most direct route home. None of them looked back to see if Greta remained standing there, and only when they crossed onto Stormy Hill land did they slow to a walk.

All of a sudden the three friends began to laugh.

"Oh, Jock, come for a swim," Ted teased in a high pitched voice, keeping Si'ad well away from Banshee so Jock could not retaliate.

"Shut your mouth!" Jock retorted angrily, taking an ineffectual swing at him anyway, nearly unseating himself in the process.

"Hey, watch it!" Ann screeched at him. "You'll dump us both."

"Sorry, Ann, but you were priceless back there. 'The boys can't play today.'" Ted mimicked.

"Pure inspiration," she chuckled.

"Poor Greta," Ted smirked. "When is she going to figure out that none of us can stand her?"

"'Poor' nothing," Ann scoffed. "That's her problem. She's spoiled rotten. Can have anything she wants, so she thinks she can buy friendship."

"Well, she has no business treating you the way she does," Jock stated emphatically. "Where does she get off anyway?"

"I think she's just jealous, that's what," teased Ted.

"Of what?" Ann snorted at him. "What do I have to be jealous of anyway?"

"Oh, I can name a lot of things," Jock said loyally.

"Name one. She's rich. She's pretty. She has a great wardrobe—"

"But she's not nearly as much fun to be with as you—" Ted added, cutting into her tirade.

"Most definitely," Jock agreed.

Ann pretended not to hear them. "Blond hair—" she went on.

"Bleached—obviously bleached. Wouldn't you say, Jock?"

"Absolutely."

"Daddy buys her anything she wants—"

"So what," Jock countered. "You've got Lightning, and Stormy Hill, and…and us, your two best friends! What more could you want?" he pinched her to make light of his serious words.

"Ouch! You're right, of course. No reason I should be jealous of her! Come on. Let's go home. It's my turn to ride Lightning this time.

Remember, Ted, you promised." Greta forgotten, they urged their horses forward, laughing with glee.

As they passed by their own training track, Ann refused to compare its shabby neglected appearance with that of Garrison's well-kept one. At least they had one, she figured. One day, she thought, they would be successful and finally rich enough to buy back the Garrison land, making it Stormy Hill property once more. *We'll see how Greta feels then.* After all, with Lightning back, anything was possible.

2

SURPRISE

At the familiar whistle, the great black colt lifted his head from the lush green grass. For a moment he stood, neck arched, gazing off down the hill at the small figure climbing the fence. Recognizing her, he abruptly came to life, shook his head, and sent his long, heavy mane and forelock flying out behind him. His thick black tail rose up nearly over his back as he thundered down the hill toward her. Fearlessly, Ann stepped out to greet him, laughing as he slid to a stop before her, thrusting his nose trustingly against her hand. She affectionately rubbed the funny, jagged blaze on his forehead that had earned him the name "Lightning."

"Hey, fella," she murmured lovingly. "Wanna go for a ride?" As she spoke, she eased the bridle she held in her other hand over his head. Then opening the gate of his pasture, she vaulted on bareback and went to find the boys.

"Let's go," she called out when she saw them. Ted had already put Si'ad away and was astride Banshee, waiting for her. Jock was not far behind on his brown gelding, Tag-along, an ex-racehorse he'd piloted to several victories before he was retired.

The boys swung out behind her as she headed up the lane, letting Lightning jump the gate as casually as his sire, Si'ad. Both Ted and Jock were content to follow while she set the pace, admiring anew the beautiful picture they made, Ann clinging to the stallion with perfect balance, nearly swallowed up by his large size and long mane.

Though Jock had seen Lightning grow up on the farm, had an intricate role in raising the orphan, and had often helped Ann work with him, he was totally unprepared for the metamorphosis that had become the new Lightning since his return. He had left them a yearling colt and come back a full, half-wild stallion.

Despite the fact that he was still only two, whatever had happened to him during his disappearance had forever changed him. No more the gentle, docile pet, circumstances had replaced trust with fear and hatred toward all men. At this point only Ann could handle him. He had not forgotten her, the beloved mistress for whom he would do anything. What an incongruous picture they made, the slight slip of a girl and the towering, powerful black horse. Even now, as she let him out into a ground-eating canter, she was nearly engulfed by the heavy thickness of his mane. Actually the only control she did have was his desire to please her.

But though Jock could admire the pair as an exquisite example of human oneness with a horse, it was really Ted who understood the bond between the two and why Lightning responded so readily to Ann's requests. It was the same one he shared with his own Si'ad. Just as everyone referred to Si'ad as Ted's, because no one had the uniqueness of spirit as he had with the horse, likewise Ann's union with Lightning was cut from the same mold. Scotty had a favorite saying for it. "They're two of a kind," he would say by way of explanation. And that settled it.

As they rode into the first open field, Ann, unable to restrain herself any longer, called back, "This time it's my turn. You guys up for a race?"

"Sure, why not?" they chorused, their masculine pride somewhat aroused, though neither doubted the outcome. Laughing and whooping to their horses, they took off in her wake.

Ann on Lightning was unbeatable. They all knew it. Still, they flew across the field, running for the love of running, the sight of the coal-black stallion-colt in full flight before them a breathtaking experience—even if they were forced to eat his dust to witness it.

There was much shouting as they tore in and out of the woods, back across the field, and over some downed logs. Finally they came out across from the big field currently being used to pasture the geldings. The meadow ran along the back side of the house, where it sloped downward to a large pond fed by a slow-moving stream that wound its way out across the drive and into fields on the other side before leaving their property. In reality, many years ago a previous

Collins had seen the advantage to damming up the stream at this spot to form a wonderful swimming area for generations to come.

They slowed to a stop, Ann's face flushed with excitement as she turned to look back, the undisputed victor. "I know," she called out, glancing longingly at the pond. "Tomorrow let's all take a dip."

"Can't," Jock groaned. "I've gotta work again."

"Bummer," Ted sympathized. "We'll miss you. We'll have to take a couple of extra dunks just for you."

"That's it. Rub it in, creep," Jock grumbled back at him, though he did not seem unduly upset by Ted's teasing. The boys had become fast friends in the past month, and joined forces to annoy Ann about as often as they went at each other, Ted providing the usual catalyst that got them all harassing one another.

Then Ted spoke up, saying something that was on all their minds. "Hey, Ann, with speed like he's got, isn't it time we start niggling your dad and Scotty about racing him?"

Ann grinned, patting Lightning's neck affectionately. "I should think so. In fact, with summer here, we need to get serious about pushing for it. Jock, can you tell how Scotty feels? Has he mentioned racing him?"

"You know Dad," Jock replied. "Always close mouthed. He hasn't said anything, but he's been watching Lightning closely. It's my bet the thought has crossed his mind."

"I hope so. As far as Dad goes, I think we can sway him. I know he'd love another winner around here. It's been a long time since Tag."

Jock stroked his horse's neck, a distant smile crossing his face. "Those were the days, huh, fella?" he sighed.

"Ever wish you were still racing?" Ted asked softly.

"On him, yes, once or twice. But as a jockey, riding all different horses? No. What I did with Tag was special. I don't think it would be the same if I were to do it full-time. Maybe it's just as well I can't make the weight anymore." He was referring to his late growth spurt that prevented him from continuing as a jockey after Tag was retired.

"Well, if Lightning gets to race, he'll need a jockey," Ted pondered out loud. "Too bad girls can't race. Ann, you'd be perfect for him."

It was her turn to sigh. "I know. Boy, don't I wish. It doesn't seem fair. He responds better for me than anyone. But if I can't, then the only one I'd want to race him is you."

"Me?"

"Sure, why not, Ted? You're an excellent rider. Look how you handle Si'ad. Besides, the way you sit a horse, you look like a jockey already."

"Well, I should, I learned..." He stopped, not wanting to reveal any more.

But Ann caught the hesitation in his voice. "Who taught you to ride like that?" she asked eagerly, hoping he'd divulge some of his past.

"Oh, just a horse trainer I knew," he hedged.

"Where, at Desert Sun?" Ann pressed.

"No, at...at this Thoroughbred place where I worked before I went to Desert Sun." When he didn't elaborate, Ann would have pressed him further had he not appeared to close down, shutting her out of any more discussion on the matter. She'd have to be content with that until he felt comfortable enough to talk to her about his past.

They crossed upstream of the pond on a path that worked its way out along the edge of the hayfields, eventually taking them beyond Stormy Hill's boundaries to cut over to the land on the other side of their road. As they rode, they laughed and joked, anticipating the endless summer ahead, reluctantly returning to the barn only because it was time for the night feeding. They all feared Scotty's wrath should they be late. The horses were dry and breathing regularly when they rode into the courtyard.

"Good ride," Jock commented as they brushed down their mounts.

"Um, yes, but for one thing," Ann protested.

"What's that?" Ted asked.

"Sure wish we had a horse around here that could keep up with our boys," she said, voicing their old complaint. "Banshee's nice, but he's no racehorse. We need something fast." Ted nodded in agreement.

"Well, I'm satisfied with old Tag here," Jock stated, giving the plain brown horse an affectionate pat. "He's all the horse I need."

"That's because he was a racehorse once," Ann smiled, knowing how Jock felt about his horse. "That's not the same. Banshee's hardly in the class of Lightning or Si'ad."

They would have gone on debating the subject had it not been for Scotty calling out from the feed room to remind them of their evening chores. Swiftly they all finished cleaning off their horses, then turned them out in their respective fields before joining him to help with the feeding. By the time they were done, Jessica was calling everyone in for dinner.

All the members of Stormy Hill's family tried to make it a practice to spend the evening meal together. It was the one time of the day set aside to share the day's happenings and discuss future plans. Decisions concerning the farm were always a joint effort, as they inevitably included or concerned all of them. That night was no exception.

The first couple of weeks of summer vacation passed quickly. One warm evening late in June, they were once again gathered around the kitchen table for dinner. When everyone had had their fill, Jessica suggested they adjourn to the den for coffee. "I made a special desert," she told them brightly, shooing them out of the kitchen, "so go on and get comfortable. I'll be along shortly."

As they all descended on the big, comfortable den down the hall, Ted and Jock jokingly jostled Ann out of the way in an attempt to beat her into the room. As a result, she was the last to enter.

"Surprise!" they all shouted at once. She stopped, stunned. There in the middle of the floor was a good-sized pile of presents.

"Happy birthday!" everybody cried as Jessica entered right behind her, carrying a huge decorated cake.

Suddenly everyone was talking at once. "Did we surprise you?" Jock wanted to know.

"You bet—especially since my real birthday isn't for a couple more days," she replied.

"That's why we planned it for now," her mother said, smiling. "Then you wouldn't suspect."

"And you're right," Ann returned. Then turning to the boys she said, "Did you two know about this? How did you keep it a secret?"

Ted grinned. "It was tough. You're so nosy, Jock and I were sure you'd overheard us talking about it a few times."

"Me, nosy? Look who's talking! Ted Winters, you have some nerve." She made as if to hit him, but her father intercepted her.

"Wouldn't you rather open your presents first?" he suggested before things escalated into one of their now-famous tussles.

Ann redirected her attention to the pile of presents before her. "I'll settle with you later," she shot at him, sticking her tongue out as she began to open the first present.

"How old are you? Seventeen going on seven?" Ted shot back. Ann chose to ignore him.

Soon she was concentrating on her presents as she opened each one, exclaiming over them as Jessica passed around coffee and cake. Most were little things she either needed or had wanted, but when she got to the huge box from Jock and Scotty, she was overwhelmed. In it was a beautiful racing saddle of well-oiled, soft leather. While it was not new, this was better, because she did not have to break it in. Ann held it up, her eyes huge with excitement. "Oh, my gosh," was all she could say, over and over, as she stroked the fine leather lovingly. Suddenly she jumped up and hugged each of them in turn. "Thank you, oh, thank you. I can't believe this. I really need this. My other one is so…so…"

"Old?" Jock filled in, trying to make light of her appreciation to hide his embarrassment.

She started to answer but Ted chimed in with, "Don't know why she needs a saddle when she usually rides Lightning bareback."

Scotty interrupted before Ann could answer. "Try it out. See if it fits." So she did just that, placing it across the back of the couch and sliding up on it, nodding affirmatively.

"Not there," her dad smiled. "Why not on a horse?"

"Why not?" she said, picking up the saddle and starting for the door before Ted stopped her.

"Wait. Let me give you my gift first," he said mysteriously. "I'll be right back." As he left the room, she sat back down, suddenly realizing all of them knew what she did not.

"Uh-oh," she said, looking about, "you all know about this one, huh? What's Ted done to me this time?" But everyone just grinned without saying a word.

Apprehensively, Ann watched for Ted to reenter the room. Suddenly from around the corner came a black-and-tan blur that burst into the room and headed straight for her lap. Ted followed at a slower pace, a big, silly grin on his face. Stopping the ball of energy long enough to see what it was, she exclaimed, "A puppy! For me? How wonderful!"

"Not just any puppy," Ted told her, pleased by her response. "You've always said how you'd like a dog that could keep up with you on horseback. Well, this one just might."

She held the puppy slightly away from her so that she could get a good look at him. He had longish, silky ears and a fuzzy whip-like tail. His body was lanky and greyhound-like, with the longest set of legs she'd ever seen on a baby puppy. "What is he?" she asked.

"He's a rare breed from the desert. A Saluki, bred to hunt by sight. Very fast. Their background is the same as the Arabian horse."

She whistled, impressed. "Where'd you find him?"

"Pure luck. Someone who sent a mare to Si'ad had one. She had a litter. I was intrigued and asked to see one. Soon as I saw them I thought of you."

"What an adorable little beggar you are," she said, stroking the wiggly baby who responded by licking her face. "I just love him. Thank you so much. How did you ever hide him from me?"

"Not easily," he laughed, remembering. "We were all in on it. Your mom went to pick him up this afternoon and hid him in Jock and Scotty's apartment. But he was homesick, I guess, 'cause he put up an awful racket. We were sure you'd ask what was going on."

"What an adorable little beggar you are."

"Poor little guy. Of course you didn't want to be by yourself." She scratched the puppy's neck and back as he wriggled with glee.

"There goes Ann spoiling another animal," Jock teased.

"Of course. What else are puppies for?" Ann countered. "Does he have a name?"

"They called him Barak, which means 'lightning.' I thought it was a good omen, so I chose him."

"Perfect! Barak it is." She hugged the squirming puppy that licked her face in return. She would have been content to sit with the puppy for the rest of the night, but her father spoke up.

"Aren't you going to try on that saddle?"

"I suppose," she replied, clearly reluctant to leave her new pup. She rose, still holding Barak, and after again hugging him appreciatively, passed him over to Ted. Then she retrieved her saddle and started for the kitchen door. The rest of them trailed behind her, making her the first outside. She was brought up short by the sight that greeted her.

Standing tied to the fence beside the driveway was a beautiful grey Thoroughbred mare. Her exquisite ears perked up as she spotted Ann, the finely chiseled head bespeaking quality. As Ann moved toward her, she realized this was no ordinary horse. From her dainty muzzle to her delicate, impossibly long legs, she showed superb breeding. "Who's this?" she asked. "Where'd she come from?"

"Her name is Velvet Vair. She's a direct descendant of Stormy Hill—and as of today, she belongs to you," her father replied.

"What? She's gorgeous, but—" Ann was awestruck.

Michael hastened to explain. "You and Ted are always arguing about not having a horse good enough to ride with either of your boys. So when Velvet was made available to me, I saw a chance to end this bickering," he grinned knowingly, "and get ourselves a valuable broodmare in the bargain."

"But, Dad—she must have cost a fortune!" Ann was still running her hands over the mare's wonderful lines, now joined by Ted, who'd not seen her before either.

"She would have, if she hadn't been spooked by the crowds the first time she was raced. She's got plenty of speed, though, and since the people who owned her had no use for a broodmare, they were willing to let her go for a fraction of what she's worth. When I saw her pedigree, I knew we had to have her for Stormy Hill. So your mom and I decided to get her and give her to you for your birthday."

"Wow—and what a birthday it is! Thanks so much," she cried, hugging first her father, then her mother in turn. Then she turned to Ted.

"Did you know about this?" He shook his head, trying to pat Velvet and hold the restless puppy at the same time. Finally he gave up and put Barak down. The curious puppy scampered about them, eagerly sniffing everything.

"Afraid not," Scotty jumped in. "We wanted to surprise him, too."

Ted grinned. "You sneaks. Thought I'd spill the beans?"

"Possibly," Jock said. "You think keeping the puppy a secret was hard? Imagine hiding a horse!"

"How did you do it?" Ann asked.

"She's been in the yearling barn since she arrived this afternoon. Scotty slipped out while you were fussing over the puppy and got her. As soon as he came back, I suggested trying on your new saddle." Michael was obviously pleased with the success of his plan.

"Ah, yes—the real reason we all came out here." She looked down at the saddle she still held. Deftly she fitted it to the mare and immediately vaulted up, taking the lead rope in one hand. "Perfect fit," she commented, walking Velvet around the courtyard. Then she eased her into a light trot, Velvet responding readily to her leg aids. When Ann attempted a gentle canter, the mare reacted as if she were fully bridled. She rode back to them, slid to the ground, and removed the saddle. "Perfect—both the saddle and the horse. I can't thank all of you enough." She reached down and chucked the puppy under the chin as he clambered for her attention. "And Barak, too, of course," she added with a grin for Ted.

"Does this mean we'll all get a little more peace around here if you two aren't bickering about which horse to ride?" her father taunted, clearly pleased by her reaction to all her gifts.

"Oh, I doubt that," Jock smirked. "Those two will just find something else to fight about."

"I'd be inclined to challenge that remark, Jock, if it weren't so late," Ann told him. "Instead, first thing tomorrow we'll go riding and see just how fast Velvet is. I might even let you ride her."

Jock started to retort, but Scotty interrupted. "This is where I bow out and call it a night. Thanks for a lovely meal, Jessica. Michael," he said, nodding to his friend as he headed for his apartment over the broodmare barn.

Ann's parents soon followed suit, leaving the three to continue their discussion as they took Velvet back to the barn, Barak trailing behind. However, as soon as the mare was put up, all three, tired from the day's exertions, left each other's company with promises to take an early ride the next day.

Ann might have overslept the next morning had it not been for the whimpering Barak, who, thanks to an early nature call, was no longer content to lie quietly beside her. Rising sleepily, she yawned and reached out to pet the puppy that leaped off the bed and romped about her eagerly.

"Need to go out?" she asked him. "I'll bet you do." She pattered barefoot through the kitchen and opened the screen door. Barak immediately scampered out to the lawn where he hastily relieved himself before returning to her.

"Bet that felt good, huh, fella? You're such a good boy." Giving him another pat, she returned to her room to dress and take care of her own needs, before heading out to see her horse—horses, she corrected herself, remembering the beautiful grey mare, Velvet.

But when she tried to shut Barak in the kitchen so he could not follow, he set up a terrific howl at being left behind. "Not this time, Honey," she told him. "You're too small yet. You'll only be in the way. Mom will be down soon to keep you company." Barak was not to be appeased, however, and continued to fuss until she gave in and let him come with her.

When she arrived at the tack room, Ted and Jock were already there, horses saddled and ready.

"Oversleep, lazybones?" Ted teased.

"Hardly, not with your dog to wake me," she countered.

"Not mine—yours," he corrected her.

"Whatever. Anyway, Barak wouldn't stay in the kitchen without waking the whole county, so I finally had to bring him with me."

"So that's the awful sound we heard," Jock said with a laugh.

"Spoiled already?" Ted reached out to pat the black-and-tan puppy. "His breeder warned me about letting that happen," he chided her.

"Well, I couldn't let him wake up Mom and Dad, could I?" Ann defended her position. "Perhaps we can leave him in one of the stalls for now."

"Sure, but hurry," Jock said. "Let's get riding."

Ann took Barak and put him in the nearest empty stall, turning a deaf ear to his howls. Then she went to mount Velvet, who was ready for her, thanks to the boys. Actually, she thought, Ted was probably responsible, so he'd be sure to ride Si'ad this morning. She let it pass this time, since she really wanted to try out her new mare anyway.

She was not disappointed. Velvet moved forward with smooth, fluid lines, so light it was as if she was floating somewhere just above the ground. As she sent her into a trot and then a canter, she was rewarded with even transitions. It was quite different from Lightning, whose forward propulsion was so powerful that she swore she could feel the earth move beneath her as he thundered along.

"Saddle sure is comfortable," she commented to Jock as they rode. "Can't thank you enough, you and your dad."

"Good, I'm glad you enjoy it. We thought it was time you had a really nice one of your own, instead of hand-me-downs."

"Okay, enough talk," Ted interrupted, grinning. "Let's do some real riding. Let's see what that mare's got." Before either of them could reply, he urged Si'ad forward into a gallop. Laughing, his two friends took off after him. The mock race was just long enough for them to realize Velvet was no Banshee. She had plenty of speed. Though Si'ad still came out ahead, the grey mare was more than up to the challenge. Ted and Ann were delighted.

As Ann pulled up beside Ted, she hopped down and handed him the reins. "Okay, your turn," she said, taking Si'ad's bridle. Ted did not hesitate. He leaped into the saddle and tried her out. He came back feeling as thrilled as Ann.

Then he passed the reins over to Jock. "You're next," he said. So Jock also took her for a spin, and when he came back to them, he too was smiling.

"Nice, huh?" Ted commented.

"Very," Jock agreed, remounting Tag. "Almost as nice as this guy." Ted and Ann passed a look between them and shrugged. Jock would never admit that another horse—any horse—was better than his Tag.

After their chores were done and the sun was high in the sky, Ted and Ann chose to take a dip in the pond across from the house. The day's promise of heat had been fulfilled to the point where both genuinely felt sorry for Jock having to work on such a day. But that didn't stop them from enjoying their swim.

Next to the pond grew a huge live oak with wide-spreading branches. Hanging from one was a thick rope with a large knot on the end. They took turns swinging out from the bank, and as the rope took them out to the middle of the pond, they'd let go and land with a tremendous splash. One of their favorite games, it vied with one involving riding their horses out into the water and diving off their backs. Velvet and Lightning were commandeered for duty this time. The new mare caught on quickly and seemed to like it—or at least she tolerated it. All the while, Barak ran back and forth along the bank, barking incessantly—until he too jumped in and joined the fracas.

Finally, tiring of their games, they retired to their towels for a rest. Barak came over and after a quick shake, sending them into cries of dismay, he flopped down beside them. The horses, relieved of their obligations as diving boards, went off grazing.

Ann gazed idly at the grey mare. "She's a wonderful ride," she finally commented. "Just perfect to use with our boys, don't you think?"

Ted nodded in agreement. "You're lucky to have her."

"*We're* lucky," she added, emphasis on the "*we.*"

Ted caught her tone, but all he said was, "I guess."

"Really, Ted," she said, growing slightly annoyed. "Don't you realize by now that you're as much a part of our family as the rest of us? You stand to benefit from Velvet as much as I will."

"I suppose you're right."

"Of course I am. Why would you think otherwise?"

"I guess I'm still surprised when people are kind enough to include me, as you folks are. Sometimes all this seems like a dream—you know, living here, being with Si'ad, getting to ride him."

"Why should that surprise you?" She turned over on her side to face him, but Ted continued to stare at the sky, arms behind his head. She went on. "Why wouldn't we want to include you in what goes on around here? You're a part of us, too."

Ted finally turned and looked at her. "Am I really?" he asked softly.

"Of course you are. You're a very important part of all that goes on here. If you don't know that by now…" She stopped, catching a look she could only read as disbelief. "Why would you doubt it?" She hesitated, then blurted out the question that had been on her mind since he first came. "Ted, what happened in the past to make you so—I don't know—so distrusting?"

As soon as she said it, she was sorry. She immediately felt him withdraw. Wishing she could take it back, she added contritely, "I'm sorry. I shouldn't have asked that. It's none of my business. Please forget I said anything."

Ted was quiet for so long, she thought maybe she really had offended him. Just when she began to wonder what to say next to smooth things over, he finally spoke. "No, you have nothing to be sorry about. You have every right to know. Maybe it's time I told you about myself."

"Please, don't—not if you don't want to."

"Actually I've wanted to tell you for a long time. There never seemed the right moment. Promise though, that you'll hear the whole story before you pass judgment?"

"Why should I do otherwise? You know me better than that," she flared.

"I know. I guess I just..."

"No, Ted Winters," she scoffed. "Nothing you could possibly tell me about yourself is going to change my opinion of you, so there."

He smiled, because all at once she'd put a light tone on what, to him, was a very serious subject. "Well, I'll tell you, then we'll see."

Ann sat back, waiting patiently for him to begin, feeling instinctively that they had come to another turning point in their friendship. Whatever Ted had to say about his past, she was sure it would not color how she felt toward him.

3

REVELATIONS

Ted began his story hesitantly, very aware that Ann was listening intently. At first, conscious of her and her reaction to his words, he sort of forgot her presence, as he was drawn back into the past—a past so painful at times that he'd tried to shut it out of his mind forever.

He had no recollection of his parents. They'd died when he was very young, his only memory a vague vision of a beautiful, warm, loving woman, the mother who was gone all too soon.

An only child, he'd been sent to live with his aunt and uncle, who were childless. From his earliest memories, he sensed their deep resentment for having him dumped on them. They themselves were far from a happy couple, living in shabby apartment squalor in a less-than-desirable neighborhood of Arcadia, California. Theirs was a dull, colorless life that neither of them had the education nor energy to rise above. His aunt worked as a waitress, when she worked, at one or another of the greasy diners that flourished in the district. His uncle worked at whatever odd job he could get, but his poor attitude kept him from staying at anything for very long. Their only pleasures seemed to be drinking and fighting with each other.

Long before Ted could put a name to it, he understood what living with an alcoholic was like. He recognized the pattern early in life. If his aunt was home during the day, she usually began drinking early, so that by the time his uncle got home, she neither felt nor cared about his abuse. Often whole evenings, even weekends, were wasted as they chain-smoked and drank beer, getting more abusive toward each other as time wore on. They forgot his presence as they wallowed in their sorrows, each blaming the other, until one or both passed out in a drunken stupor.

Neighbors in the adjoining apartments heard the noise caused by their arguments, but of course any complaints went unheeded. Actually in this area, behavior such as theirs was not uncommon. The squalidness of poverty left its residents angry and frustrated. No one really paid attention.

Ted learned at an early age to be invisible, a shadow in his own home. School became his escape, his sanctuary in his early years. He never missed a day. Because he didn't wish to bring attention to himself, and thus let anyone find out about his home life (something for which he was profoundly ashamed), he became a model student, getting good grades and staying out of trouble. If his aunt failed to show up for required conferences, his teachers were not disturbed. Not all parents came—and besides, he was such a good boy, they tended to overlook him for more pressing needs. Thus Ted's home life went ignored in an overcrowded school system.

At home he learned to stay out of his aunt's way and to avoid his uncle altogether. They, on the other hand, seldom acknowledged him. He took to fending for himself, eating whatever he could find in the kitchen—which was often very little, unless his aunt brought home leftovers from her work. Then Ted would get to eat somewhat decent food. The rest of the time it was catch-as-catch can. One thing was sure. The refrigerator always had a six-pack or two chilling.

Because he was ashamed of his home, he avoided attempts to make friends and remained a loner, often spending hours in his bedroom with his books, listening to his aunt and uncle's endless fights, and wishing he were anywhere but there. By the time he was nine, he had taken to wandering the streets to avoid going home. If his aunt was conscious of his long absences, she never asked questions. His uncle ignored him completely.

Who knows where he might have ended up if not for one very important discovery? One afternoon his wandering brought him to the entrance of Santa Anita Racetrack, only blocks from his home. Drawn by something exciting he felt just out of sight, he tried to enter the gate, only to be turned away by the guard.

"Get away, Kid—you're not allowed in here," he yelled at the startled youngster. Ted bolted, terrified of the forbidding stranger. However, he didn't run far. Intrigued now that he'd been repelled, he knew he had to see for himself what was behind those tall fences. Having learned in his short life how to be both devious and practically invisible, Ted set out to find another way in.

Not far along the outside fence, he discovered a spot where a split in the chain link had only been partially repaired. By pushing on it a little, he had no trouble squeezing his slight body through. A shiver of excitement passed through him. He felt as if he'd entered another world. Indeed he had, one that was to have a profound influence on the rest of his life.

Having entered at the point where the shed rows were located, he stepped around the corner, awed by the scene before him. Lots of activity was taking place, for it was early in the morning, at a time when the backside of the track was at its busiest. Horses seemed to be everywhere, some being walked, others being groomed or saddled, and still others being bathed, steam rising from their bodies. To Ted, who had only seen horses in pictures, the sight of these beautiful, proud creatures, with muscles rippling beneath their glistening coats, was awesome indeed. Instantly infatuated, he knew this was what he'd waited for his whole young life.

Things might have been different that day had he not been fortunate enough to be spotted by one weather-beaten, stooped old man. Noticing Ted's wide-eyed interest, he'd called him over and befriended him on the spot.

Old Ben, a minor trainer at the track, treated the boy as an equal, a fellow horse lover, right from the beginning. If he wondered why such a young child should be there unsupervised, he never let on, nor asked uncomfortable questions. Ted would be forever indebted to the old man who inadvertently played such an important part in his life. It was only much later that Old Ben would glean from him the various pieces of his "other" life. But by then, they were fast friends, and Ben sought only to render trust. Old Ben was the first real friend Ted had ever known.

In the years to follow, Ted was to become a familiar figure along the backside of the track. He would spend every free waking moment practically living at the barns, learning all he could about racing as he tagged along behind trainers, exercise boys, grooms—anyone who made horses their life's calling. For the first time, he actually resented his time spent in school, for it kept him from the track. Still, he continued to keep his grades up, for now more than ever he wanted to protect his privacy and maintain the status quo. What his aunt thought of his frequent absences from home, he had no idea. She never asked, nor did he divulge any information. Usually she was too busy wallowing in her own misery to notice.

Ted proved to be a natural with horses. He knew instinctively how to handle them, recognizing that these beautiful beasts were often high-strung and flighty. He absorbed knowledge like a sponge and made himself welcome with everyone because he never shirked work of any kind. He became a familiar figure at the track, cleaning stalls, bathing horses, walking hots, cleaning tack—in short, doing all the menial tasks with a cheerfulness that endeared him to all. He eagerly learned to wrap legs, change dressings, and apply ice packs. Eventually there wasn't anything he couldn't do, and he loved it all.

But the best part was when the racing season began. Then, in the afternoons, he took to slipping over to the backstretch rail and watching the colorful Thoroughbreds pounding around the track, the crowds cheering across the way. It mattered not who won; the excitement was what mattered. It was there he dreamed, in his most secret thoughts, that someday he too would be a jockey.

Then Old Ben, having seen the longing in the boy's eyes, lent credence to his desires by offering to teach him to ride in exchange for all the work he did for him. His eyes grew huge with anticipation. Could anything be better than to sit on one of these glorious creatures, he thought?

The first horses he rode were only the gentle exercise ponies, used to escort the often-volatile, finely tuned Thoroughbreds to the track. These horses were safe and good-natured—and later, after he knew how to ride, often boring, as they offered no challenge at all. But they were a start, and they taught him patience.

With all the work he picked up around the barns, Ted was beginning to earn a little pocket change for himself, giving him a sense of independence he had hitherto not known. He could afford an occasional pair of jeans or something to eat when he was hungry. By the time he turned twelve, he no longer felt dependent on his aunt and uncle. He'd begun to feel better about himself.

Then Ben, seeing Ted's unusual ability with the horses, his soft hands and gentle voice, decided to train him as an exercise boy. Ted was elated. His dreams were coming true.

For the next two years, he studied the art of working horses—conditioning, training, and listening to trainers who expected him to follow their instructions to the letter. He developed a time clock in his head so he could let a horse out just so fast, clipping off a furlong pole in exactly the time the trainer asked for, learning how to hold a horse back, rate him, let him out a notch or blow him out, whatever was desired.

When the trainers recognized Ted's ability to get results, he became a popular choice as an exercise boy. Most mornings he had to rise quite early to get out to the track to work a string of horses before leaving for school. Yet, though he was known by nearly everyone there, only Old Ben really understood what motivated the boy.

At this point, Ted was almost happy for the first time in his life. Then something happened that shattered his near-perfect world.

It was June. School had just gotten out, and Ted looked forward to spending long days at the track. He would be fifteen soon, and his expressed interest in becoming a jockey was finally reaching fruition. Old Ben promised to help him achieve this goal by looking into an apprenticeship.

His mind heavy with such thoughts, he did not at first take notice of the police car parked in front in his apartment building. After all, it was hardly a phenomenon in his neighborhood. But when he reached his apartment, he found the door wide open and two policemen standing in the hallway, talking to the woman from the apartment next door.

"That's him," she stated, shaking her head hard enough to send curlers bobbing in all directions as she gathered her filthy bathrobe around her.

Ted felt trapped. What had he done? He could remember nothing in his immediate past that might warrant a visit from the police. He hesitated. The officers, sensing his fear, quickly reassured him, then brought him inside and shut the door on the nosy neighbor.

"You've done nothing wrong," one told him. "We're here because we have some rather unpleasant news for you. Please sit." Ted perched nervously on the edge of the sofa, horribly aware of the filth and clutter all around him. Shame crossed his face as he painfully surveyed the empty beer cans, overflowing ashtrays on every surface, a broken chair propped up against the wall where an uneven hole showed plaster coming through.

Then the officer finally got his attention. His aunt and uncle were dead, killed when their car, speeding out of control, went down an embankment. Fortunately no other car had been involved.

Ted was numb, unable to feel anything. He realized that, to him, they'd been dead a long time. He sat perfectly still, registering nothing. The cops, thinking he was in shock, grew concerned.

When he finally spoke, there was no emotion in his voice, and the two officers, having seen so much of life's seedier side, understood that here was a child who had long ago stopped caring about the people who raised him. How sad to have lived such a life that at his age he could no longer feel empathy.

"What's to become of me?" he finally asked.

"We'll need to get in touch with your closest relatives. Can you provide any addresses?"

Ted shook his head. "Not really. My aunt talked about a brother, but I don't know where he lives."

"We'll try to locate him."

"And if you can't?"

"We have foster homes until arrangements can be made." When he saw the alarm on the boy's face, he hastened to add, "But I'm sure it won't come to that. We're pretty good at finding people."

Soon after that the officers left, but not before Ted assured them that he'd be fine staying there for the night. The next-door neighbor promised them she'd look out for him, although as soon as they were gone, she returned to watching television and forgot all about him.

That was what Ted had counted on. Once alone, he sighed with relief. Try as he might, he could find no grief for his aunt or uncle. Any affection he'd had for them had died long ago, killed by years of selfish neglect. To them, he'd never been more than a nuisance. Understanding that now, he could feel nothing but emptiness and a curious sense of freedom, as though a heavy weight had been lifted from his life.

Standing in the middle of the living room, staring at the remnants of their shabby, dead-end life, he suddenly recognized that for him it was over. Never again would he have to tiptoe into his own apartment, wondering what condition he'd find his aunt or uncle. Would they be fighting? What phase of their drinking would they be in? Would they notice him? And if so, would he become the butt of their self-pity? No—at last, that was over. He was free!

Then it hit him. He was not free—yet. Still underage, he could be taken and placed into foster care, for he knew there was no relative. He'd made that up to stall the officers from taking him then and there. What fate awaited him as a ward of the state, he could only surmise. Whatever the case, he would not like it.

He had a better idea. Already a plan had begun to form in his head. He'd leave, run away, now, before the funeral, while he had the chance. No one would expect that. Quickly he began dashing about the apartment, grabbing up anything he wished to take with him. It wasn't much. Everything of value would fit in an old army duffel bag he found in a closet. When he was done, he slipped the strap through his arm and hoisted it onto his shoulder. Lastly, he reached under his mattress and stuffed the little bit of money he'd saved into his jeans pocket.

Years of practice made it easy for him to slip past the open door of the apartment across the hall. Sure enough—the television was on, and she never heard him leave. Ted fled down the stairs, never looking back.

Once outside, he took a deep breath. No one seemed to be around. Still, he was cautious as he ducked into the nearest alley and melted into the shadows. There was no doubt as to where he would go. The track was the only real home he had. There he had friends who would hide him until a plan could be formed. There he'd be safe. And better still, there he could find work to sustain him when the little money he had ran out.

He was right about his track friends. Without question, they all took him in as one of their own. By now most of them, having learned of his background from Old Ben, felt sympathy for his plight and were willing to shelter him. Without a doubt his disappearance would be discovered soon, and the authorities would be looking for him.

In the meantime, Ted stayed with Old Ben, sleeping in the tack room and eating his meals at the track. He was much in demand as an exercise boy, and the money he made more than paid for his simple needs. For the first time in his young life, he could say that he was completely happy.

His contentment was soon shattered when, barely three weeks later, one of the grooms came to warn him that a policeman had been by asking questions about a runaway. While the groom said he'd denied knowing him, the description fit Ted, and he was now sure he was still being sought. He went to Ben for advice.

"Well, I suppose we could wait it out. Perhaps it's just a random inquiry," the old trainer said.

"Do you think so?" Ted asked hopefully.

"Can't rightly say. What if they catch you?"

"Then I'm sure to be sent to a home. I'd just die in one of those."

"I know, Son. You're one of us. Horses, it's our life. In our blood, you might say. Nothin' else for folks like us."

"Then what'll I do?" he wailed. "I can't let them find me."

"Look, you lay low. Keep riding your mounts, of course, but keep out of sight. We'll all cover for you if anyone else comes around asking questions. Mayhap, it's just this once."

Unfortunately for Ted, Ben was wrong. There was another query the next day. Though the stable boys all pretended to know nothing about a missing boy, it was now apparent it was too risky for Ted to stay at the track. Sooner or later he'd be found out. He'd have to leave.

One of the other trainers presented Ben and Ted with the perfect solution. Several Thoroughbreds were being shipped to a track in Arizona. Ted could go with them as a groom. Horses were hauled in and out of state all the time, and no one would be the least bit suspicious of a groom traveling with a load of horses headed for another track. Best of all, they were leaving that night. Ted was both relieved and saddened. This had been the only real home he'd known, and now he had to leave it behind, along with the only true friends he'd ever had.

For a boy who'd never been out of the town where he grew up, the idea of traveling to Arizona overwhelmed him. Even though everyone assured him that, with his experience, he'd have no trouble finding work around the track, he was still worried about the outcome. His goodbyes were too hasty, and he couldn't help wondering if he'd ever see these dear faces again. Old Ben, who had been like a father to him, was the hardest to leave. The old man, who'd come to mean so much to him, personified the only happiness he'd ever known.

Ben had been right about several things. For one, he was able to travel with the shipment of horses without hint of suspicion. No one made association between him and a runaway being sought in that area. And upon arriving in Arizona, he found that Ben was right again. He had no trouble picking up work around the track, and pretty soon he fit right in, just as he had back in California. If anyone suspected he'd lied about his age, it went unquestioned because of his expertise around horses.

Before long he had more than enough mounts offered him as an exercise boy. He still longed to be a jockey, but opportunities along those lines seemed to elude him. Then a chance encounter with a horse owner of a different sort changed his future again.

This owner's interests lay in racing another breed of horse—Arabians. Upon seeing Ted handling the often temperamental Thoroughbreds and liking his touch, he immediately offered him a job working his string. Since the opportunity also included the strong incentive of jockeying, the boy eagerly accepted. In doing so, he entered a world quite unlike the one he had known.

From the start, Ted enjoyed working with the Arabians. He was awestruck by their delicate beauty, so much more refined than the rangier, leggier Thoroughbreds. While he loved and appreciated both breeds, he developed a real weakness for the Arabs.

Things began to work well for him, and he at last seemed to find his niche. Then once again disaster struck, when the owner died suddenly and his wife, having no interest in the horses, decided to sell out and move to a smaller place. All the horses were sold, and once again Ted seemed to have lost his home.

But luck was with him. One of the local Arabian breeders bought several of the horses and hired Ted to accompany them. The ranch was a large operation with wonderful facilities. One glimpse and Ted immediately asked for a job. With the additional horses they had just purchased, there was indeed an opening. Thus he came to work for Desert Sun Arabians and subsequently met the beautiful stallion on lease from the east—Si'ad.

4

IN TRAINING

Ted sat back after he finished his story, his eyes on Ann. At first she said nothing as she digested everything he'd just told her. Finally he said lamely, "There…that's all of it."

Clearly, he was waiting for a response, some hint of her feelings after what he'd just revealed. But Ann was so overwhelmed by his story that she wasn't sure how to reply. She would have to pick her words carefully. As Ted was telling his story, she'd felt various emotions. First there was anger toward the people who'd been so callous toward him, an innocent child. Then she felt sorry for him, growing up in such an environment. Meanwhile, she was grateful for the kindness shown him by the people at the track. And finally she admired his courage, for making something of his life in spite of the adversities he'd suffered. Now, looking at him, waiting expectantly for her to say something, she struggled to bring all these emotions under control and tell him what he needed to hear. She instinctively knew he didn't want her pity.

She let out a pent-up breath. "Whew. That took a lot of courage for you to do what you did," she finally said.

He was taken back. "Courage?" he asked, puzzled. "Why courage?"

"Well, just look at what you went through to get here. You lost your parents, then your aunt and uncle, then you had to leave your friends at the track. None of that could have been easy. Yet in spite of it all, you managed to develop the skills you needed to get jobs and keep going. All that takes courage, lots of it."

"Wait a minute," he said, incredulous. "You think what I did was brave? Jeez—most of the time I was scared stiff!"

"Of course you were. After all, you were just a child."

"Then you don't think less of me? I mean, knowing all this…"

"Why should I?" she asked, surprised. "What for?"

"Well, for one thing, look at what I came from. I grew up in the slums; my aunt and uncle were heavy drinkers, alcoholics. It was far cry from a normal life."

"But that's not your fault. You had nothing to do with what they were."

"I used to think so. Oh, when I was small, I used to think, if only I weren't there, maybe they wouldn't fight so much. I tried to be as invisible as possible, tried to make them forget I was around. Sometimes it would even work. But then, those other times…" he stopped, a bleak expression coming over his face as he resurrected memories long buried. Ann's heart broke just seeing him.

"Look, Ted, what they were had nothing to do with you. You were just a victim. If you hadn't been there, they'd have been the same. They were two very unhappy people using alcohol as a crutch to forget their misery. The real crime was that their suffering had to involve an innocent child. That's what's not fair. But I guess lots of things in life aren't fair."

Ted looked at her as if in a new light. "You know, when you put it that way, I can almost believe it."

"I hope so, because it's all in the past. You have nothing to worry about."

"Still," he said, "I did run away. They could still be looking for me."

"I doubt it, after all this time. I can't imagine one lone runaway would cause a nationwide search," she said, grinning, "especially since you have no relatives pushing it. I guess you belong to us now."

"Your folks will still want me?"

"Why wouldn't they? I just told you—you're not responsible for your past."

Relief flooded across Ted's face. Then, to cover the surge of emotion he felt, he glanced away, calling softly to Barak. The puppy had been stretched out, dozing while they talked. He jumped up and raced to Ted, licking him incessantly. Amused, the boy added lightly, "You're pretty wise, you know—for a girl."

She laughed, not at all offended. "Not really. At least not if you ask Dad. But then we've not had it easy around here either. Not like you, of course. Still, through all our setbacks, we've had each other." Then realizing how her words sounded, she hastened to add, "And now you have us. We're your family now."

"And what do you get out of this deal?" He smiled, beginning to relax as he continued to stroke the puppy.

"Why, someone to handle Si'ad, of course—especially his breedings. Anyway, I can't imagine ever splitting you two up. For some crazy reason, that horse is nuts about you," she added mischievously. "Oh, yes, there's one more reason."

"And what's that?" His eyes lit up with their old fire.

"Jock and I need you around here. You make us laugh."

Ted felt unexpectedly humbled by that statement. "That's good," he said seriously, "because you two are the best friends I've ever known."

"You weren't thinking of leaving here, were you?" she asked softly, with sudden insight.

"Not now. The thought did cross my mind. I was afraid of how you'd react to my past. But now I feel relieved that you know. It's like a big weight has been taken off me."

Ann nodded. "No more secrets?" she asked, smiling.

"No more secrets," he replied. Then a thought struck him. "I guess I'd better tell your dad, too. He might feel differently."

"Dad? Never! Anyway, leave that to me. It'll be fine. You'll see. 'Sides, you're one of us now. One thing here at Stormy Hill, we all stick together. Life is tough enough. We need each other."

Ted smiled gratefully. "Thanks," was all he could say. His throat was too choked up to say more. But Ann understood. She squeezed his hand.

"Well, if that's solved, it's time to get to our chores." She rose and made a big display of gathering her towel and things, turning her back slightly so he would not see the quick rush of tears forming in her eyes. Hastily she blinked them away, trying to get her emotions under control. "Perhaps there'll be time for another quick ride," she murmured.

As they left the pond, Barak scampering ahead of them, they walked in easy silence. Neither voiced it, but both felt their friendship had turned another corner now that there was an element of trust to bond them, beyond their mutual love of their horses.

§ § § § § §

"Get your horses put up and come on over to the tack room," Jock called out to Ann and Ted as they came in from riding the next evening. "Dad's got something he wants to discuss with us, and it sounds pretty important."

"What's up?" Ann begged, growing excited. By the expression on Jock's face, she could tell it was something big.

"Don't know. He wouldn't even tell me, so you'd better hurry." Jock pitched in and helped them, but the three kept getting in each other's way in their haste to hear what Scotty had to say. By the time they got there, tack in hand, they were all laughing as they nudged each other to be first through the door. Upon entering the tack room, they suddenly stopped, seeing both Michael and Scotty. Something serious was in the wind, if the looks on their faces were any indication. Hastily they all found seats on various pieces of furniture and waited expectantly.

Scotty didn't keep them in suspense long. "Since Lightning returned, I've been watching him quite closely. Obviously he's not the same colt he was when he was stolen. He's matured, of course. Whatever adventures he had while gone from us seem to have given him more muscle, more breadth of chest, and greater size than I'd have expected he'd get. In essence, he left a colt and returned a stallion. Of course you've all seen this, too. The point is, Michael and I have been talking about his potential as a racehorse—"

Simultaneously, the three let out shrieks. "You mean it?" they all cried excitedly, each talking over the other in their enthusiasm.

"I knew it!" Jock yelled. "I knew he'd make a racehorse."

"And what a racehorse!" Ted chimed in.

"Kentucky Derby, here we come!" Ann hollered.

"Hold on, kids," Scotty said, smiling. "Don't go jumping to conclusions. We have no idea what we're facing yet."

But he was cut off. "I do! I've ridden him. He's fast!"

"Speed alone doesn't make a racehorse, as you well know," Scotty reminded them. "Yes, I agree he's fast, but there's a lot more we need to know before we can put him on a track. Wait, Ann," he held up his hand. "Before you disagree—and, yes, I know you've done a wonderful job with his training so far—but think about this. He's developed several strong quirks, shall we say, while he was gone. For instance, his fear of men."

"But he's better around all of you now," Ann argued. "He even lets you get close to him."

"But what about strangers? Anyway, we can work on that, but until we begin his training, we can't be sure what fears he has developed that we will have to retrain."

"So, what Scotty's trying to say, in his round-about way," Michael interrupted, "is that we think it's worth a try. After all, with school out, what else do you kids have to do anyway?"

They laughed together excitedly, each talking over the other again.

"Hold on." For the first time, Scotty grinned at their enthusiasm. "Tomorrow I want to put Lightning on the track and blow him out for a half-mile. I want to see just how fast he really is. And for the moment, Michael and I feel, Ann, that you should ride him." He stopped, waiting as Ann let out a scream, before continuing. "Since he's used to you. If all goes well, later we'll need to train him to a male rider, and that's where you'll come in, Ted." Again he waited for the second shriek. The two looked at each other, huge smiles on their faces.

"Seems like the kids are in agreement," Michael commented.

"Well then, it's settled," Scotty said in closing "All of you be at the track at dawn tomorrow. Ted, you ride Velvet. And Jock, saddle up Banshee. Since Lightning's used to him, we'll start using him as a lead pony."

The next morning, as the first streaks of light were barely crossing the sky, Ted, Jock, and Ann mounted their horses and rode out of the courtyard. Ted's mare sensed the excitement in the air and danced along with the equally eager colt. Scampering before them, young Barak dashed back and forth, enthusiastically looking for something to chase in the tall grass. Only Banshee, seasoned mount that he was, remained untouched by the commotion.

"Just wait till Scotty gets a glimpse of how fast Lightning can really run," Ann remarked to Ted. "He'll have no doubt about his racing potential."

"You bet," he called back as Velvet shied at a dark spot on the ground, Ted easily holding her in check.

Together they rode past the paddocks used for the yearlings or as turnouts for visiting mares. From there the path led out alongside the training track before continuing on to the hay fields. They turned to the right and pulled up beside the rickety old stand that marked the track's finish line. Laid out on the only really level spot on Stormy Hill, it was hardly more than a half-mile strip of sandy loam forming an oval. The inner edge was marked by a low rail, falling down in some places, overgrown weeds nearly burying it in others. The outer edge was defined by a once-white fence, now badly peeling and in need of repair. At one end was a straight strip, used as a run up, where a rusting old starting gate, with three slots for horses, stood. Ann wondered, as she rode past, if it would even still function, it looked so old. Actually, the whole track required a make over. If Lightning were to go into training this summer, they would need to fix it up so it resembled something closer to the real thing.

Her thoughts were broken by Scotty's voice. "I see you three wasted no time getting out here this morning," he said, coming from behind the stand. His eyes caught sight of the wildly exuberant puppy bouncing about at Lightning's heels. He called the pup over to him and caught hold of his collar. "Sorry, fella, but you'll be sitting this one out," he told the eager pup.

Ann smiled. "Did you really think we'd be late on the morning you call for breezing Lightning?"

"Hardly. I never saw such eager kids. Okay, take them all out and warm them up. Jock, Banshee won't need much. Just keep him near Lightning, as you would any outrider. Ted, I want you to pretend you're training Velvet. Work her around the track a couple of times, like a morning workout, but don't breeze her. Lightning isn't ready for that yet. Still, I want him to begin to get used to distractions, just like he'll have on a real track. Might as well use what we've got here." As the two boys rode out onto the track, Scotty added to Ann, "Watch for my signal, then turn him loose. But only a half mile, though. Understand?" She nodded, suddenly all business as she guided Lightning out onto the track. This is it, she thought—the beginning.

The strapping black two-year-old belied his young age. He moved out with the confidence and pride of a much older horse. Prancing with impatience, the colt tossed his thick black mane, all but obscuring Ann from view. She looked too small to have any control over the powerfully built horse. And indeed, if she were to rely on strength alone, she would have *no* control. In reality it was the strange bond between the two that kept the stallion-colt under control far more than any riding skill Ann may have had—not that she wasn't a superb horsewoman, having ridden all her life. Yet she recognized how tenuous her command over this colt could be, were it not for his love for her and his desire to please her.

Now, as they began to circle the track, she could feel the power barely held in check. Already a sheen had broken out across his neck and flanks as he anticipated a good run.

"Easy, boy," she whispered. "I don't know how you can possibly know why you're out here, but you do, don't you. Guess you've just got racing in your blood, huh, fella?" Softly she crooned to him. It mattered little what she said, as long as he continued to hear her voice. She watched his ears as they flicked back and forth, listening to her. It was important that he remained tuned in to her. Later, when he faced distracting crowds and other horses, he had to be able to focus only on her. Conveniently, she chose to forget that ultimately she wouldn't be riding him in a race, for in her fantasies she was always the one aboard him in the winner's circle.

When she had traversed the track several times in the wrong direction, first walking, then trotting, she saw Scotty signal a light canter. Lightning maintained the required gait, only the angry twitching of his long, high tail showing how impatient he was to be off. Just when Ann thought she could hold him back no longer, Scotty waved her in.

"Reverse him and pick up a light canter. As you pass by the stand, let him go. Blow him out once only. Pull up as you pass us the second time. I'm setting the stopwatch on you. Got it?"

She nodded, noticing her father had joined Scotty in the stand. She smiled at him before heading down the backstretch. Jock and Ted brought their horses in and stopped them beside the two men.

"This is it, Lightning," she murmured, taking him down the track before turning him the right way around. She let him out a notch, and he eased into a canter. As they neared the starting post opposite the stand, she whispered, "Okay, boy, show 'em what you've got," and gave him his head. With unleashed fury, Lightning burst forth, reaching incredible speed within seconds. He charged down the track, a black blur, his ground-eating strides swallowing the distance with deceptive ease.

Ann, who'd ridden him at what she'd thought was his top speed, was stunned. Never had she gone *this* fast on him. She didn't even think of taking back the reins, for she knew he'd never hear her now. He was running for the love of running, and nothing would stop him until he ran out of steam. Actually, it was all she could do to stay on.

Too late Ann remembered Scotty's instructions to pull him up at the half-mile pole. Too soon the stand flashed past them, a mere blur on the edge of her vision. Belatedly she eased back on the reins, but Lightning was still fresh and ignored her efforts to slow him down. He ran on, heedless of any restraint Ann wished to impose upon him.

He'd completed another turn of the track before he slowed noticeably in response to Ann's urging. Yet they were better than halfway around again before she regained control over him. Even as he slowed to an easy canter, he seemed still fresh and eager to run. Ann, her face

He charged down the track, a black blur, strides swallowing the distance with deceiving ease.

red from exertion, yet grinning from ear to ear, rode him back to them, her limbs trembling with exhaustion. A warm glow overtook her as she remembered the ride she'd just experienced. Even she was unaware he possessed such speed, overwhelmed by the power driving him. Most amazing of all was that by the time they reached Scotty and the others, he was hardly blowing, he was so fit.

By the looks on their faces, she could see that she was not the only one to be amazed by his speed. Even Scotty just shook his head and stared at his stopwatch in disbelief. "Well, let's get him cooled out, then we'll talk," was all he said.

While Michael and Scotty stayed behind to discuss the colt's workout, Ann, Ted, and Jock rode on ahead, the puppy, now released, bouncing along with them. Eagerly the two boys descended on Ann for her reaction to her ride.

"What was it like, sitting on that powder keg?" Jock wanted to know.

"Fantastic!" she replied breathlessly. "I've never gone so fast, even on him!"

"Can't wait to hear the time," Ted remarked. "The way Scotty and Michael kept looking at their stopwatches, it must have been impressive."

Jock nodded. "You know, few things excite Dad, but this time he was speechless."

"I'm afraid I wasn't able to keep him down to the half mile Scotty requested."

"How did you finally slow him anyway?" Ted wanted to know.

"Dunno. I was too busy trying to stay on," she said, laughing. "Anyway, he finally stopped on his own. It sure was a thrilling ride!"

"I'll bet," they chorused.

After the horses were cooled out and put away, they all gathered once again in the tack room. Scotty didn't keep them waiting. "No doubt about it, that colt certainly has speed," he began. "Even if I didn't believe what I saw with my own eyes, the stopwatch is concrete proof. Both Michael and I clocked the same thing." He showed the time around, and everyone was suitably awed. "It's incredible, the time he turned in today. He could have set records at some tracks, and he wasn't even pushed!"

"I knew it! I knew he'd be a racehorse!" Ann exclaimed.

"Hold on, Lass," Scotty admonished. "I know he has potential, but he's a long way from winning with it. Now it's up to us to channel that speed so he gives it when we want it, not just let him do what he wants. Wait. Before you argue with me, I saw what happened out there. He got way from you, am I right?" She nodded miserably. "Nothing to be ashamed of. He's a powerful horse, and quite headstrong."

"But he will listen to me. I know he will," she pleaded. "I'm sorry, I guess I just got caught up in his speed and forgot to bring him back until it was too late and he was already out of control. I'll try…"

"I know you will. Control is the first thing we'll need to work on. We know now he has the speed. No more blowouts until he can be held in check. He had manners once. Let's see if he can get them back."

"Then he's going to be a racehorse?" At Scotty's nod, she screeched, then sobered. "I am still riding him, aren't I?"

Scotty smiled. "For now. And, Ted, I want to see you working Velvet so we can use her when it comes time for his sprints. Jock, it wouldn't hurt to see what old Tag has still got. We could use him also." After the boys eagerly agreed, he continued. "Now let's map out a training program."

5

RIDERS UP!

Now that Scotty had officially declared Lightning in training, the days that followed were busy ones for Ann. Usually Ted and Jock accompanied her as she fell into her new daily routine of working the black colt. Needless to say, Ted was thrilled to be an important part of Lightning's training, and he took his role seriously. Now that he'd finally told Ann the full story about his past, and she'd accepted it without passing judgment as he feared, he felt more at home than ever at Stormy Hill. Whatever she'd told her father and the rest, no one had said anything. Though the scars of his childhood would always be there, he'd begun to feel less ashamed and more able to put the past where it rightfully belonged—in the past. Knowing he had Ann to thank for this and for his acceptance at Stormy Hill only strengthened the bond between them that had begun to form the day they met.

Each morning the three youngest members of the Stormy Hill team would rise before dawn, hurry through their chores, saddle their horses, and head out to the track. They'd leave a very unhappy Barak behind to sulk rather vocally in Lightning's stall because they didn't want to risk the puppy getting in the way and possibly getting himself or someone else hurt.

As the sun climbed over the distant line of trees, they began their morning workouts under Scotty's intense tutelage. The boys were just as serious about their work, for each knew that, when the time came, both their horses would be needed to push Lightning as in an actual race. Among the colt's lessons, he'd need to learn to be rated, to run from anywhere in the field—and especially to conserve his strength for the stretch drive. None of these goals could be achieved without competition. Even though neither horse was his equal in terms of speed, they would help the colt get used to running with other horses. Therefore, Tag and Velvet had to be in fit condition in order to serve as the kind of competition Lightning would meet on the track.

For Ann, these idyllic days of summer, spending time with her beloved horse as his training as a racehorse unfolded, were the best days of her young life. She had always found dawn her favorite time of day, when the earth was just waking, the air crisp and clean and everything new. Sometimes a mist hung in the air, enveloping them in a strange, silent world as it floated about them. Then she felt as though she and Lightning were alone, adrift on a white sea in a sur-real land. Sometimes the other two horses would appear as phantoms, drifting past, then gone as the silent pale screen descended upon them again. Ah, those were the mornings she loved the most!

Ann did not kid herself into believing it would last forever. She knew, because so far no girl had been granted a jockey's license, that eventually she would have to be replaced by a male jockey who would actually race Lightning. She hoped that person would be Ted. He was the only person to whom she felt she could relinquish her colt. At least he was family. Still, in her most private dreams, she alone always rode him to victory.

After Lightning's initial show of speed, Scotty did not ask Ann to breeze him again. "We know he's got it," he told her when she impa-tiently questioned him. "That's not a problem. Right now we've got to build his stamina and work on other things, like getting used to all the new and strange things he'll see when he gets to the track. In other words, track manners."

The first important thing that required attention only involved Lightning indirectly. The dilapidated condition of the track would never pass muster. It required a complete overhaul. Thus they all joined in to give the ancient track a facelift.

First the track itself was dragged to smooth out the surface and get rid of the countless weeds that had taken up residence. In too many places the fencing, both the inside and the outside rail, was falling down or non-existent. Together Ann, Ted, and Jock organized their time, donating a couple of hours each day to renovate the old rails to look like new. With the help of Michael, who supplied the lumber, pipe, and white paint, the track began to take on a whole new image. It took most of the summer, but the outcome made it a worthwhile effort. Stormy Hill's training track finally displayed a resemblance to those of its more affluent neighbors.

"Now we need a better viewing stand," said Ann, after surveying the fruits of their handiwork.

The two boys groaned.

"What?" Jock moaned. "You mean we aren't done yet?"

"Not quite," she said. "Look at that broken-down old stand. It's hardly safe to stand on. We need someplace for folks to stand and watch his workouts."

"Sounds good to me, since I'm the one doing the standing and watching," Scotty agreed, affably.

"Oh, no," Ted sighed. "Here we go again, Jock. More back-breaking labor."

"Oh, hush, you two," she said, laughing tolerantly. "You both know you want it as much as Scotty and I do. It all helps our image."

"What image?" Ted countered.

"Well, the one we'll need to promote when Lightning starts winning races, of course. We'll need to look prosperous to our fans," she said.

"Dream on," he told her.

"Can't we just wait until we're famous?" Jock suggested. "Maybe then we'll be rich enough to hire someone to build it for us. Meanwhile, Dad can just use a ladder if he wants to see better."

Ann was about to launch a rebuttal, but Scotty stopped her. "I think not, Son." He threw him a look that brooked no argument. Then he added lightly, "Enough, all of you. You're bickering isn't getting it done. Besides, we're a long way from winning races. Lightning needs a lot more training before we can even think about the track. Speaking of which, tomorrow I'd like to start him against competition. It's time to work on rating him in a pack." As he saw three pairs of eyes light up in anticipation, he clarified. "We'll start with short bursts of speed, using Tag and Velvet to teach Lightning how to handle running with other horses. I think he's ready for it now."

Simultaneously the three friends let out a holler. "Now we're a real racing team," Ann voiced for all of them.

"Then show it by getting to work on the viewing stand," Scotty suggested, smiling at their glee.

"Oh, why not?" Jock grinned back.

"We were only kidding," Ted grunted, pretending to sulk. "After all, a new stand would look nice."

"It'll be the finishing touch to the old track," Ann added. "We'll hardly recognize the place."

That night, just before bed, Ann slipped out to Lightning's pasture to be with her colt. Barak, now a gawky, half-grown puppy, tagged along. Since it was a warm summer night, all the horses had been turned out. As soon as they reached the black colt's pasture, the Saluki dashed off looking for field mice to chase. Meanwhile, she climbed the fence and sat on the top rail to admire her colt as he grazed bathed in moonlight. How fortunate she was to have him back, she thought for perhaps the millionth time since he'd miraculously returned to her. While she'd never know all the details of his adventures during the time they were separated, she would be forever grateful to the winds of chance that brought him back to her.

Too soon her thoughts were interrupted as he caught her scent and immediately trotted over to her. Thrusting his head out to be scratched, he nearly knocked her from her fragile perch. Sliding to the ground, she laughed at him, complying with his request by rubbing him in all his favorite spots. Softly she crooned to him, "Tomorrow you get to run against competition, fella. This is your first big test toward proving to everyone else that you're a racehorse. We know how fast you are. Show 'em what you can really do, huh, Lightning?" She continued to stroke his neck, enjoying the moment.

She knew the road ahead of them would not be easy, but she had complete faith in her horse. Lightning had the strength, the power— and, most important, the speed. The unknown factor was whether they could channel all those assets into a champion. Would his untamed spirit win out? Well, tomorrow's test would be the first of many obstacles they would need to overcome before he could step out onto a track and prove his mettle.

The following morning, Jock, Ted, and Ann arrived at the track early, eager to test Lightning's speed in an actual race. As they warmed up their horses, a slight mist rose from the ground, enveloping them in a dreamlike world as they passed in and out of the swirling fog. Ann wondered if Scotty might cancel their workout until the mist burned off, but he called them in as usual and gave his instructions.

"Ann, today's not about whether your horse can run. We all know he can. We need to see if he can be rated against other horses. See if he'll respond to you as his rider. Got it?" When she gave him an affirmative nod, he continued. "I want the three of you to break at the start line when I give you the signal. Just like a real race. Once around. That's it. Ann, try to hold him with the pack until you get to the homestretch. Then let him go. Let's see if you can do it, okay?"

"I'll try," she replied. "If he gets away, then what?"

Scotty shrugged. "Try to reach into that thick head of his and slow him down. I know I'm asking a lot, but if you can't rate him, we don't have a racehorse."

The three took their horses over to the starting line and waited for Scotty's signal. Ann tried to hold Lightning back a bit so the other two would get a head start, but as soon as they took off, he bolted forward with such speed that he caught up to them in a couple of strides. From then on Ann fought him to stay with Velvet and Tag, but he wanted no part of her wishes. The best she could do was keep him within a length or so ahead as they circled the track. As they approached the head of the homestretch, she gratefully gave him his head. Lightning left them behind as though they were standing still. Ann was halfway back around the track before she was able to slow his speed to a reasonable gallop. She returned to Scotty, a glum look on her face.

"That certainly wasn't what you had in mind," she stated when she was within hearing distance. "I tried, though."

Scotty shook his head. "No, but it wasn't as bad as I was expecting from him actually. Guess this one won't be trained the conventional way. Okay, go cool them out and then we'll talk."

Later, Scotty gathered everyone in the tack room. "Don't blame yourself," he said to Ann, who still looked pretty disgusted with herself. "I don't think anyone will be able to hold him back if he wants to run. That desire is going to make him a champion, but it'll also hurt his chances, too. We've only just begun his training. Somehow we'll find a way to channel his energy."

"So you're not giving up on him?" Ann asked fearfully.

"Are you kidding?" He smiled. "He's got all the potential in the world. We'd be foolish not to at least try. Besides, it's not like we've got a lot of horses in training around here. What else do we have to do with our time, anyway?" he added lightly.

"That's for sure, Dad," Jock agreed.

"And we have plenty of time till the Derby," Ted added.

"Whoa. Wait a minute, kids," Scotty cautioned. "That's an awful big goal to set. You know how many three-year-olds actually make it to the starting gate?"

"Are you saying you don't think Lightning could be one of them?" Ann asked anxiously. "What about his speed? You said he was fast."

"Takes more than speed. I don't have to tell you youngsters that. We've got some big barriers to overcome here. We have to find out if he'll run with other colts, whether he'll accept the starting gate, the crowds. And none the least of which, he'll need to accept Ted as his rider. It's a long road yet before we commit him to the Derby."

"But you are considering it?" Ann asked hopefully.

"Of course. If we can channel his speed, this could be the colt of the year. But before you kids get too excited, that's a big 'if.'"

As summer wound down and the start of school loomed, Scotty continued his training program for the black colt. While Lightning showed continued disdain for being rated, preferring to outrun his competition from the start, Ann did see some progress. He was getting better at allowing her to control his speed—enough so Scotty was pleased with her progress. He'd be racing against the fastest three-year-olds of the season. There'd be no way he could run wire to wire at top speed and still have enough left at the end to win.

Meanwhile, they were kept busy in other areas. Favorable weather meant it was time to bring in the next cutting of hay. A hot and tiresome task, haying took several days to accomplish. It wasn't just for their own horses that they put up hay. Michael also sold hay at the store in town. The income was necessary for the upkeep of the farm.

Work on the training facilities also continued. The finishing touches were put on the track itself, and they all pitched in to take down the old observation box and replace it with a newer, bigger one. This pavilion had room for several observers and would offer some shade as well. Even though the boys had initially groaned over the work involved, they were pleased with the results of their labors, exclaiming that now they had a training track worthy of a Derby contender.

One day they all showed up for their usual training session when Scotty waved them over to the old starting gate. It, too, had received a makeover. Besides giving it a new coat of white paint, they'd all helped oil the hinges so each gate opened freely and silently.

"Ann, I want you to have Lightning watch the first time," he instructed. "Tag and Velvet are experienced, so I want them to do it first and show your colt how it is done. Got that?"

She nodded, then took Lightning for a walk around the starting gate to stand at its side. The black colt had walked past it many times, even stepped in and out of the gates, so he showed no concern with the contraption. However, when the other two horses were loaded in and the gates were shut, he began to show interest. He sensed this was not the usual scenario.

"Hold him close," Scotty called out. "I'm going to release them." Ann took her reins in a notch as the gates clanged open and the two horses sprang out. Lightning spooked to the side, trying to follow his companions as they raced down the track. Fortunately for Ann, they did not go far before Jock and Ted pulled them up. Unable to hold him back, she was forced to let him canter after them as she tried to pull him into a circle back toward the starting gate. Only when he saw Velvet and Tag returning did he finally obey Ann's wishes.

"Not too bad," Scotty commented as they all drew up to him, "for him," he added as Ted, Jock, and Ann laughed.

"Boy, that's an understatement," Ann said, grinning. "All he wants to do is run."

"Which is why I've come to the realization there'll be no training him the conventional way." Scotty walked up to the pair. Taking his bridle, he said, "Let's just go ahead and load him and see what happens. Jock, give your horse to Ted and lend a hand here, okay?"

Jock jumped off Tag and threw the reins to Ted. He went to the front gate and closed it before climbing up on the side as Scotty led the colt up to the gate from the back. Ann urged him to walk in, which he did without a fuss, even though this time the gate was shut in front of him. It wasn't until Scotty had closed the rear door that he began to paw and shake his head uncomfortably. Scotty didn't give him a chance to panic, releasing the gate immediately. Lightning hesitated for only a second before bursting out, hitting top speed almost instantly. He was halfway around the track before Ann could slow him down.

"Smart horse," was Scotty's comment. "He's already figured out what the starting gate is for. This time we try it with all three horses. Put him in the middle so he feels more secure. Jock, before you mount up, help me shut the front gates."

Jock eased the three front gates shut, then remounted Tag. The three of them gathered around Scotty behind the gates. "I want you two to go in first. Then I'll load Lightning. Be ready. As soon as he's in, I'm going to release you."

Velvet and Tag calmly walked in and stood patiently while Scotty shut the gates behind them. Lightning, knowing the routine this time, was more excitable and proved a handful for Ann. Each time he was almost in, he'd bolt backwards before Scotty could shut the door, one time almost running over the trainer. Finally he settled for a split second, long enough for Scotty to push the button to release them. Lightning broke fast, no pause this time, and cleared the other two in two jumps. Once again he was halfway around the track before Ann could pull him up. She dropped him to a canter and rode on in.

By the time she got back to Scotty, Jock and Ted were already there, slowly circling their horses to cool them out. There was an apologetic look on her face.

"That's it for today," Scotty signaled. Seeing the expression on her face, he added, "Ann, don't worry too much about it. He'll get better. This was his first time, after all. Look on the bright side. At least he breaks fast."

"Dad, if that's an attempt at humor, I think it fell flat," Jock chuckled, trying to lift Ann's spirits.

"I still wish he'd be easier to rate. All he wants to do is run."

"That's why I think it's time we give him some real competition. I think it's time to run him against Si'ad."

Ann's face lit up. "Scotty, you mean it?" She glanced over at Ted, who was grinning from ear to ear. There was no question how he felt about the news.

"Sure do."

"But won't they try to fight?" Ted asked.

"I expect they'll try. Your job will be to prevent it. Make them run instead."

"Sounds complicated," Ted said.

"Probably, but Lightning will be running against other colts. He's got to learn to run, not fight. By training him with his sire, he'll get the idea. I'm betting his desire to run will win out in the end. Now let's get these horses cooled out."

The three friends rode off to the barn, chattering excitedly among themselves. Finally they were going to get a chance to race Lightning and Si'ad. This was the moment they'd all been waiting for.

6

FIGHTING STALLIONS

Scotty's plan for racing Lightning and Si'ad was actually quite simple. Ann would take Lightning out for his regular work early in the morning. Jock would accompany them on Tag, letting the colt think it was business as usual. Then Ted would appear on Si'ad, just as Ann was ready to breeze her colt for a fast half mile. Until Lightning got used to being released from the starting gate, he preferred not to complicate things the first time the two met. No one was sure exactly what they would do, as they had not been together since that fateful day back in May. They all hoped that the two rivals would choose to run instead of fight.

Ann rode Lightning out onto the track, Jock beside her on Tag. All the while she spoke to him in soft tones, knowing what a calming influence her voice had on him. Their bond was so special; it was as if they could read each other's thoughts. While she sensed the restlessness in her mount, she also attributed it to his desire to run once again. Understanding him as she did, she also felt the same. There was nothing quite as exhilarating as running for the sheer love of it. In that, they were one. She reveled in the moments when Scotty signaled her to breeze him, whether it be just the two of them or with others. However, Si'ad would present the first real challenge for Lightning in terms of speed. He alone of any of their horses could push the big black to his maximum potential. She knew Ted was as excited about the confrontation as she was. When they got Si'ad and Lightning to run against each other, it would be the thrill of a lifetime.

She and Jock warmed their horses by taking them the wrong way around the track first. After making the complete circle at a walk, they eased them into a light canter, still moving clockwise. By now, Lightning was accepting Ann's control over him, aware that he was not to run unless he was turned in the opposite direction. Even so, he was like a coiled spring beneath her as he anticipated the release that would send him flying down the track.

Ann was nearly even with the stand where Scotty was standing when, out of the corner of her eye, she saw Ted enter the course on Si'ad. Lightning caught sight of the stallion immediately and tensed under her. Every fiber alert, he pranced forward, ready to do battle. Si'ad likewise set his eyes on the rival stallion and immediately issued a challenging scream, in spite of Ted's attempts to control him by turning him away. Scotty signaled for Ann and Jock to release their horses. Tag immediately obeyed, surging forward to eat up the empty track ahead of him, but Lightning hung back, reluctant to leave the obvious challenge the grey stallion had flung at him. Si'ad drew ever closer, and for a brief second it appeared that the two stallions would come together in spite of the best efforts of their riders. Then Ted finally redirected Si'ad's attention to the rapidly retreating Tag, urging him to take up the chase. Calling on every skill he possessed, he tried to get the stallion to focus on the brown gelding. Just when he thought all was for naught, Si'ad suddenly broke after the rapidly disappearing Tag, leaving Lightning standing in the middle of the track.

But not for long. The black colt saw his adversary leaving him and responded by leaping forward in pursuit. The desire to run had outweighed the wish to fight.

The two, black and grey, raced after the gelding, who was already into the first turn. Swiftly they gained on him. Si'ad drew even with Tag coming out of the turn and, with a mighty leap, blew past him as if he were standing still. In a matter of seconds, Lightning had caught and passed him as well, leaving him falling rapidly behind, enveloped in a cloud of dust. From then on it was a two-horse race. His job now done, Jock pulled his horse up and returned to his dad at the stand.

Si'ad had had nearly a two-furlong lead on Lightning before he joined the chase, but the young colt pounded relentlessly down the track, determined to catch his sire. His huge strides ate up the distance between them as he gained steadily with each step. He forged on, Ann merely a passenger now. Still she continued to communicate with him in her low voice, encouraged by the occasional ear flick that told her he was listening. Fearful of what might happen when they drew even with Si'ad, for she had no doubt he would eventually catch his sire, she struggled to regain her tenuous hold on his will. She knew that up ahead Ted was also trying to communicate with his horse. They must not fight.

The track lay clear and open ahead of them, inviting their race. The two, father and son, flung themselves around it, Lightning only a couple of lengths behind the grey. Si'ad now realized the threat and increased his speed. In spite of his determination, he was unable to open the gap between them. Instead, Lightning continued to close on his sire, his longer legs an advantage against the smaller stallion. As they passed the finish pole the first time, Si'ad was only a half a length in front.

Scotty waved his arms frantically to pull them up, but there was no stopping the frenzied horses. As Lightning drew even with Si'ad, he acknowledged the other horse, but the desire to fight had been replaced by the instinct to win—an instinct born of generations of racing blood. Si'ad was up to the challenge. The second lap around the track they stayed nose to nose, neither giving an inch. Si'ad called upon the endurance of his desert ancestors as he continued to match his son stride for stride. As they passed the finish pole for the second time, his nose was a scant hair's breath ahead. Ann glanced over quickly to see a triumphant grin on Ted's face before he returned his attention to his riding. *He's actually enjoying this,* she thought—*and so am I,* she realized with sudden insight. After all, they'd speculated for months about whose horse was faster. Unfortunately, since they couldn't ride the stallions together, they hadn't been able to find out. Now, out here on the track, they were finally given their chance. Ann was sure she'd never ridden her horse at such speed. *Was he only coasting before?* she wondered. The challenge of Si'ad racing beside him brought out previously untapped speed that none of them realized he had. She felt like she was flying. She did not have to glance at Ted to know that he was experiencing the same reaction.

But even as they continued to fly down the track, both Ted and Ann knew they needed to slow their horses. Running until they were both exhausted could only mean injury to one or both. As they rounded the far corner, Ann began to coax Lightning to slow down. At first he showed no sign that he heard her. Like Si'ad next to him, he was out of control, running for the sheer love of it. She began to panic a little bit. Would he run until he finally dropped from exhaustion? The poles flashed by her on the left, and still he ran, showing no signs of responding. Another lap. Then ever so gradually, she felt his speed begin to decrease. Still, it was one more complete lap of the track before she felt him give to her hand and drop back. Meanwhile, Ted was asking the same thing of Si'ad, who was finally beginning to respond as well. By the time they ultimately eased back to a canter, the horses had gone over two miles, most of it flat out. Both were blowing heavily by the time Ann and Ted got them to come in to the stand where Scotty was waiting. But one thing was certain—each had lost the desire to fight the other.

"Get them cooled out," Scotty ordered, "then meet me in the tack room." He did not look pleased with what had just transpired.

Sheepishly, they both jumped down from their horses and loosened their girths. Though they knew Scotty would not blame them, they felt equally guilty that they had been unable to control their horses' speed. Running a horse until it was exhausted was inexcusable, and that was very close to what had occurred back there.

"Okay, let's all analyze what happened so we can avoid any repeats the next time," Scotty began after Ted, Ann, and Jock had cooled out their horses and put them away. They had all gathered in the tack room to discuss the morning's events.

"Well, at least we avoided a fight," Ted began.

"True, but it was luck more than skill," Scotty countered. Then, seeing their faces, he added more softly, "I'm not saying I wasn't expecting it. Unfortunately, when Lightning was returned to us, he was no longer the sweet, tractable colt he used to be. He's gained some issues I'd rather he'd not developed. Somewhere he's learned to challenge other stallions. While we've known this all along, now we'll just have to deal with it—if we're going to turn him into a racehorse, that is."

"Maybe using Si'ad isn't such a good idea," Ted suggested.

"If you mean because he's apt to fight back, perhaps not. However, right now he's all we've got. On the other hand, we do need his speed." They both looked surprised until Scotty explained. "Ann, I know you felt the difference."

She nodded. "Did I ever! For all I've ridden him, I had no idea he had speed like that. It was as if he went into overdrive or something."

"That's because he was pushed."

"I'll say. It was exhilarating!"

Ted grinned. "We did our best," he replied.

"Your colt has never been paced before. Si'ad brought that out of him."

"So, you want to continue using Si'ad?" Ted asked hopefully.

"Of course. As long as we can keep them from fighting each other, that boy of yours will teach Lightning to use his speed. He'll have to if he wants to stay within range of him. He won't be able to loaf against him." Seeing Ted's snug look, Scotty continued. "But you've got to do your part, too. Keep him under control."

"I was trying," Ted replied. "He's a lot of horse when he wants to be."

"I'm aware of that. But you need to convince him to run whenever he sees his son, not fight. Same goes for you, Ann," he added, lest she get too cocky.

"Lightning will listen to me. This was only the first time," she argued.

"Lass, I know you were trying your best. Both of you." He acknowledged Ted, too. "And I'm not criticizing, though I guess you two think I am. Only stating facts, that's all."

"But, Scotty, how *are* we going to solve this?" Ann asked

"That's what I'm asking you two. You know your horses better than anyone. Lightning needs to think that every time he goes out on that track he's there for one thing—to run. He cannot be distracted by anything else. He'll be pitted against the best three-year-olds in the nation. He'll need all the speed he's got. Got any ideas?"

Ted spoke up. "What if the next time you let Lightning break from the gate?"

"Thought of that," Ann replied. "Once he's trained to the gate, he should know what it's for, in spite of Si'ad's presence."

"Trouble is, Si'ad's never been in a gate," Scotty pointed out.

"So I can train him," Ted offered.

Ann looked skeptical. "You really think you can make a racehorse out of him?" she teased.

"And why not? He's got the speed," he defended.

"Ted, he's a semi-wild stallion who's never been on a track," she argued. "He can't be trained to break from a gate. He'd fight it first."

"Possibly, but he can learn, oh ye of little faith," he argued, getting defensive over any criticism of his favorite.

Scotty jumped in before he had to pull them apart. "Okay, you two. End it. One fight today is plenty. I don't need the two of you going at it."

"We were only kidding," Ann said, smiling as she stuck her tongue out at Ted.

"Heard that before," Scotty grumbled, settling back down in his seat. "So, Ted, go ahead if you think you can. Meantime, I want to try

this. Next time we'll break Lightning from the gate with Si'ad alongside it. See how that goes."

"It's worth a try," Ted said.

"I'm hoping they get the idea that they're out there to run instead.
But the bigger issue is how you're going to stop them. We can't let
them run until they're exhausted every time."

"Easier said than done," Ann murmured.

"I understand. Still, it's all up to you. Talk to them. They'll listen.
Ann, you've got to have complete control of that colt before I put Ted
up on him."

She stared at him. She was so caught up in the *now* that she'd completely forgotten that she'd eventually have to relinquish her colt to
Ted. A wave of jealousy went through her, followed immediately by
guilt. After all, it wasn't Ted's fault that she was a girl and couldn't
race him herself. She should be glad that Lightning would have Ted
on his back instead of a stranger. If she couldn't ride him, at least it
would her best friend.

"When?" she asked.

"Soon. One thing at a time. Right now we've got this problem to
solve. The next time they meet, I want them to go only once around
that track at top speed. Then start pulling them in. Think you can do
it?"

"We'll try." Ted replied for both of them.

"It better be a big 'try.' I know you both enjoyed your little race
today." He caught the look that passed between them. "Thought I
didn't guess your secret, huh? I'm not blind, you know. I know you
both too well. Ever since the day we got Lightning and Si'ad back,
you two have been dying to find out which one is faster." He looked at
them for confirmation and caught them grinning in spite of themselves.

"Ah, Scotty, you've got to admit it was quite a race," Ann said,
squirming a bit awkwardly. Neither of them liked getting caught by
Scotty. He would be a harsh taskmaster if the horses were compro-
mised.

"Fine, but it will not happen again. At least not deliberately. Got
that?"

They both nodded uncomfortably. "We're sorry," Ted said. "We'll
really make every effort to follow your directions. We don't want
them hurt either."

"I know you don't. That's why I've got to be sure you understand
what's at stake here. If Lightning's ever going to see a real track,

much less the Derby or any other big race, he's got to be trained. All the speed in the world is useless if you can't control it."

Scotty started to rise, signaling he was done with his little lecture, when he remembered something. "One more thing. Ted, start handling Lightning more so he gets to accept you better. Let him get good and used to you, especially in his stall. Wouldn't hurt also for you to see if he'll let you get up on him in Ann's presence. Like in his stall and such."

"Sure," Ann agreed. "We can do that."

"Good. It'll be easier when we switch riders. Now go tackle your chores." He waved them off.

Ted and Ann scurried off, eager to escape so they could discuss the race that morning. With the help of the exuberant Barak, they found Jock, who was cleaning stalls after turning all the horses out in their pastures. He, too, was eager to discuss the morning's events. Grabbing pitchforks, they each picked a stall and began conversing excitedly.

"Hey, Jock, did you see them run?" Ann called out, trying ineffectually to shoo Barak, who was darting around her feet. Thinking it was a game, the puppy only played harder.

Jock smiled. "Of course," he said. "Pretty impressive. You guys sure left Tag and me in the dust. But then he's not as young as he used to be. Back in the old days, he'd have given them a better run for their money." Ever loyal to his favorite horse, Jock refused to put him down.

Not wanting to hurt his friend's feelings, Ted sympathized. "I'm sure he would."

Making another unsuccessful pass at the puppy, Ann agreed with him. "I don't think I've ever gone as fast on Lightning as I did this morning. It was fantastic!"

"Neither have I on Si'ad—at least not since the first time I rode him back in Arizona, in the Superstitions. Did Scotty clock their time?"

"No, unfortunately," Jock said, throwing a forkful of manure in the cart in front of his stall. "After you two outran us, I just pulled Tag up and went back to the stand where Dad was. He was bemoaning that fact when I got there."

"Just what did he say about it?" Ann asked, despairing of controlling Barak and choosing instead to lean against the stall Jock was cleaning. "He can't be very pleased with us."

"Same as what he told you in the tack room, pretty much. You're right he wasn't thrilled to see Lightning and Si'ad try to run each other into the ground. But he wasn't surprised either. Kind of expected that's what they'd do when they met on a track. At least he was glad you kept them from fighting."

"This time," Ted grimaced, joining them, pitchfork in hand. "I'm not sure we'll be able to do that every time." He reached down to pet Barak, who wiggled all over with glee.

"We have to, Ted. You heard Scotty. He's no good on the track if he wants to fight other colts."

"Do you think he will? Or just Si'ad?"

"What do you mean?"

"We have no trouble with him running against Tag or Velvet."

"But they aren't colts," Ann argued, unconsciously watching Ted and the puppy interact.

"And colts aren't stallions either, yet."

When she looked confused, Jock chimed in. "I think I know what Ted's getting at here. Si'ad is already a proven stallion. Besides, he's still semi-wild. Lightning was away from us a long time. No doubt in his wanderings, he must have met a mature stallion or two. He knows the difference."

"And he's more stallion than colt himself now," Ann added, understanding. "So what you're saying is he's not your average two-year-old thoroughbred colt being trained for the track."

"Exactly," Ted finished as he watched Barak dash off after a barn cat. "He may feel threatened by Si'ad, but he won't necessarily feel the same toward other colts he meets in a race."

"Let's hope not. Should we tell Scotty our theory?" She was ready to find him immediately.

"Not yet," Jock cautioned. "Besides, I think he's already figured that out anyway. Let's think this through first. I like Dad's idea about breaking Lightning from the gate with Si'ad alongside."

"So do I. He should be focused on the gate, and he might not even be aware of Ted coming up alongside with Si'ad."

"If that works for the start, how do we go about slowing them down? They're both so fit they aren't going to tire easily."

"I know, Ted. That's what I'm thinking, too."

"In the past those two have always listened to you," Jock said. "Why not now?"

"They both like to run," Ted replied. "Which is good, of course."

"But Scotty's right," Ann added. "They need to be controlled. One thing for sure. If we can get Lightning to rate himself against Si'ad, he'll do it out on the track against other horses."

"Well, starting tomorrow, I'm going to begin training Si'ad to the starting gate," Ted said. "And I'm also going to start asking him to slow his speed before he's ready to quit. I'm afraid I've been too soft on him lately. He thinks he's in control just 'cause I like to let him run."

"You've got a point, Ted. I'm just as guilty. I love to run Lightning, too. And you've got to admit—today was fun. Guess we won't be doing that again though."

"Not if Scotty has anything to say about it," Ted agreed. "Still, Si'ad had him by a nose when they passed the finish pole the first time," he teased her.

She bridled, as he knew she would. "Oh, yeah? Only because Lightning broke way behind him. We had lots of ground to make up, you know."

"Not that much. Come on, Ann, you caught up with us by the far turn."

"So if we'd broken together, Lightning would have been way out in front." She turned and lifted her pitchfork, which contained a particularly rich chunk of dirty bedding.

He countered with a mock threat of his own. "I doubt that."

"Oops," laughed Jock, ducking out. "I know where this is going. I think it's time for me to go drag the track."

"Coward!" they both yelled after him, laughing as Jock ran for the barn door.

7

THE JOCKEY

It was nearly a week before Scotty tried Si'ad against Lightning again. Ted used the time wisely, working with Si'ad every day. Usually Ann and Jock came out to ride with him on Velvet and Tag. Together they tried to teach Si'ad to break from the gate. The stallion, however, proved to be a challenge to their training skills. He wanted nothing to do with the confining enclosure of the starting gate. Time and again he rushed through, popping the gate before they had time to spring it. For safety's sake, they'd set the front gate so that if a horse pushed against it, it would release automatically, thus avoiding possible injury should the horse get claustrophobic and begin to struggle. They all nearly despaired of accomplishing their goal before the week was out. It began to look like the desert-bred stallion was too strong-willed to stand quietly in the gate until released.

"Well, at least I can get him to break from alongside the gate," Ted sighed after a particularly trying practice that had left them all winded from their struggles. Again and again Si'ad had stymied their efforts, as each time they got him to enter the gate, he'd just burst out the other side in spite of Ted's attempts to hold him still.

"At least you're making progress in getting him to slow his speed," Ann said, brushing ineffectually at the strands of hair that had come loose from her ponytail. They were all feeling the oppressive heat on

65

this particularly hot day, though none of them complained. School would be starting next week, marking the end of summer. Neither of them looked forward to it.

"And so are you with Lightning. Now if we can do the same when we race them together..." He left the thought hanging in the air.

They got their chance the final morning before school started. Scotty ordered Ann to take Lightning into the starting gate and brought Si'ad up alongside. While the black colt was instantly aware of his rival's presence, by now he'd been started from the gate enough to know why he was there. Ann was thrilled to feel him tremble with anticipation to run, more or less ignoring the other stallion. This time they broke together, Lightning reaching his top speed within seconds. Instead of fighting, Si'ad was forced to go with him. Following Scotty's instructions, Ted and Ann let their horses run without restraint for the first lap of the track. As they passed the finish pole for the first time, they were dead even. Then came the challenge. Would they slow on command?

Pretending this was an actual race, Ann stood in her stirrups and gathered her reins, signaling to him that the race was over. Ted did the same with Si'ad. Even so, it took another lap around the track before either of them slowed significantly. This time Ann immediately pulled Lightning across the track, away from Si'ad. Realizing she still had a lot of horse under her, she was not taking the chance that he'd go after the stallion, or vice versa. As she cooled him down, she stayed on the far side of the track until Ted had ridden his horse out of sight. Only then did she return to Scotty for further instructions.

He immediately commented on her wise decision. "Good thinking, Ann. Today they were better than I was expecting. Not to say we won't have setbacks, but I do think there's a good chance we can over-come this problem. Now go cool him out."

Ann was eager to relay Scotty's words to Ted. Scotty could be a hard taskmaster, so it was not often they gained his praise. Too often his approval consisted of a grunt or nod that they had grown to accept as sanction for a job well done. Even so, all three of them respected Scotty highly because his methods got results.

As the weeks went by, there were more matches between the two. Ted stubbornly persisted in trying to get Si'ad to accept the gate, but he remained too erratic to count on breaking with Lightning, so he continued to break from alongside. Each confrontation between them showed some slight improvement, enough that Scotty was pleased with their progress. By mid-fall, he began talking about putting Ted in the irons.

With senior year in full swing for Ted and Ann, they each carried a heavy load for the first semester. They planned on a lighter final semester, when they felt they'd be more involved with racing preparations. This resulted in a busy schedule of farm chores, working their horses, and their studies. Fortunately they were enrolled in most of the same classes, and they could tackle their homework together.

The day Scotty chose to put Ted up on Lightning dawned warm and sunny. Kentucky was in the midst of several days of Indian summer. He decided to take advantage of the weather before winter settled upon them. So on a Saturday toward the end of October, he called the three over to him after one of their workouts. Si'ad had not been used that day, nor had Ann been asked to breeze Lightning.

"Okay, Ted, you're up," he said bluntly, surprising them all.

"You mean it?" Ted was all smiles. He'd been waiting impatiently for this day, even as he knew Ann was not.

"Change your mind?"

"No, Sir." Ted scampered down from Velvet, flinging her reins to Jock. Ann slipped from Lightning's back and stood holding him as Ted adjusted the stirrups. The last couple of months he'd spent more time with the black colt, handling him from the ground and sitting on him in his stall. Ann was always right there, and though he was not easy about having Ted on his back, he did not resist as Ann reassured him, urging him to accept the new rider. She'd even led him with Ted on his back around the small paddock next to the stallion barn. But this would be different. The track was wide open. He'd be riding Lightning away from Ann. None of them knew for sure what to expect.As soon as Ted had the stirrups adjusted, he took a leg up from Scotty and eased into the saddle. Trained to stand quietly, Lightning stood waiting for a command.

"Just walk him about at first. Let him get used to you," Scotty directed.

Ted clucked him forward at a walk, planning to circle him first before taking him a little way down the track. Lightning walked forward as obediently as he'd been taught. *This is going to be a breeze,* Ted thought. "Nothing to it," he called out, relaxing.

That was his first mistake. Suddenly Lightning became aware of the change of riders. There was his beloved mistress standing on the ground. Someone else was on him. Recall flashed in his brain of the last man to sit on his back. With it came the recollection of the pain he'd endured as that man had tried to cowboy him into submission, confusing and terrifying him into surrender. The experience had ended badly when the girth of the heavy western saddle had broken, freeing him and causing him to flee into the surrounding wild mountainous country. Ann and her family only knew the sketchy details involving Lightning's ordeal, but to the colt they were embedded forever in his memory, causing him to fear all men who attempted to ride him.

There on the open track he unexpectedly came alive. Down went the head. Before Ted realized what was happening, Lightning let out a vicious buck, leaping across the track. As good a rider as Ted was, he was unprepared for this sudden turn of events. Unseated, he struggled to get the colt's head up. He did not last the second buck. Instead he was thrown wide, landing in the deep loam. Sheepishly he rose from the ground as Ann quickly caught her disobedient colt, chastising him as she did.

"You hurt?" Scotty asked, concerned.

Ted brushed himself off. "Only my pride," he replied ruefully. "Should not have let my guard down," he grumbled.

"Where did that come from?" Jock said. "He looked like he was going to be fine about another rider."

Ann reminded them of his past. "We know he's afraid of men. But Ted's worked with him so much on the ground I thought he'd be okay with it."

"Let's try again, okay?" Ted said, walking up to the big colt. "This time I'll be more prepared."

Once again Scotty gave him a leg up. This time he immediately sat deep in the saddle, ready for the next explosion. It came almost immediately. Ted only stayed into the third buck before he was unseated. Unhurt, he grimly picked himself up and returned to try again.

"You sure?" Scotty asked, somewhat skeptical.

"I'll ride him," Ted grumbled, leaping quickly into the saddle again. He caught up Lightning's head before he could get it down, but the colt only crow-hopped across the track, refusing to obey Ted's directions while still attempting to unseat his rider. When that didn't work, he reared and jumped sideways at the same time. As good a rider as Ted was, he again lost his balance and once more tasted dirt.

Over and over he tried to stay on the colt, but each time Lightning managed to unseat him. Even Jock tried, with the same results.

Down went the head. Before Ted realized what was happening, Lightning let out a vicious buck, leaping across the track.

Finally, in desperation Ann mounted Velvet and tried to ride alongside Lightning, hoping he would see her and forget about his rider.

"Pretend it's a race," she called out to Ted, taking Velvet into a canter and willing her colt to follow. Lightning saw the mare take off in front of him and accepted the challenge. Exhilarated by speed, the black colt forgot his rider and immediately took off after Velvet. Ted could do nothing but sit tight and hang on.

Wildly out of control, Lightning sped down the track after the mare. He caught and passed her before the next pole, but showed no signs of stopping. Breezing by her, he continued his headlong flight around the track. Ted was merely a passenger, if the colt was indeed even aware that he had a rider. He ran on, Ted clinging to him like a burr. At this speed, he had no intention of coming off. He completed one more lap around the track before he finally came to a stop in front of Ann, where he shook Ted off like some annoying fly, depositing him almost at her feet. Then he walked over to her to stand docilely, head down in submission. He didn't even seem contrite. If it wasn't so serious, Ann might have laughed at his expression.

Instead she groaned, "Oh, Lightning, why must you behave so badly? Don't you know what this means to us?"

Once more Ted pulled himself up off the ground. This time he was slower as he checked over his various body parts. Nothing seemed hurt, but he sure wasn't feeling fit after hitting the ground so many times. The falls were taking their toll on his body, young as it was. He started to return to Lightning to try again, but Scotty stopped him.

"Enough," he said, putting his hand on his arm. "He's not going to give in and accept you on his back." When he saw Ted's determination, he continued: "Nothing can be accomplished by getting you hurt."

"But—"

"No, Ted, it's over. He's made it clear he'll only let Ann ride him, and that's that."

"But, Scotty," Ann wailed, fighting her emotions. She was both disappointed that Lightning wouldn't allow Ted on his back and secretly pleased that she was his only rider. Angry with herself, she struggled with her conscience. If he wouldn't let Ted ride him, his racing career was over. "What are we going to do now? He has to accept a male rider to race."

"Nothing we can do for the moment. I'm going to have to think hard about how to solve this problem." He patted the black colt's wet neck affectionately. "All that speed, big guy, but what must we do to get it channeled properly?" Then he waved his hand toward the barn. "Now you three better get these horses cooled out. We're done for today." With that, he sent them off.

Ann led Lightning despondently back to the barns. Ted walked beside her silently. He was favoring his left ankle slightly, but he remained mute about it, trying hard not to let it show. He didn't need their sympathy. He already felt like a failure.

But Ann sensed his pain and asked him about it as they were bathing their horses. She couldn't help but notice his unusual silence. She'd seen him wince inadvertently when he put weight on his left foot too quickly. "Hey, Ted, you hurt your ankle out there?" It was more of statement than a question.

"Naw, just stepped wrong, that's all," he replied, ducking back behind Velvet, trying to avoid calling attention to himself.

"For crying out loud, Ted," she sighed, exasperated. "The number of times you took a fall, it's a wonder you didn't break something. If all you did was twist your ankle, you're lucky. Let's see." She dropped her sponge and started toward him.

"Forget it. It'll be fine. We'd better get these horses finished." He sounded annoyed.

Sensitive to his feelings as always, she stopped. "Hey, what's bothering you? And I don't mean the ankle."

He shrugged. "I feel I let you guys down, that's all."

"Why? Because he wouldn't let you ride him?" When he nodded, downcast, she continued, "That's nothing. He wouldn't let Jock either."

Jock, who was working on Tag, agreed. "And he didn't even give me the thrill of running away with me either. Just dumped me flat. Rather embarrassing, too."

"But I should have been able to stick better than I did."

"Stop beating yourself up over it, Ted," Ann said. "This has nothing to do with your riding ability. You're a great rider. Better than me. Look, if it makes you feel better, if he didn't want me on his back, I'd be on the ground, too. I only ride him 'cause he lets me." She'd finished scraping the excess water off Lightning and began to walk him out. The big horse followed docilely, as if he were an overgrown dog. He hardly looked like the wild savage he'd been only moments before. The complete turnabout in personality was disarming to say the least.

Ted set his scraper down and joined her, bringing the mare alongside. He struggled not to limp noticeably as he walked. "So where does that leave us? If you can't race him and he won't let me…"

"Correction, Ted. It has nothing to do with you personally. He's afraid of *all* men. Whatever that guy who stole him did, he's now fearful of anything male, even though he's learned to accept you, or Jock, handling him from the ground. Even sitting on him a time or two. It's not the same as riding."

Jock, who'd joined them, added. "Especially racing. Looks like he'll only race and give his best for Ann."

"So what'll we do now?" Ted's question hung in the air.

"You willing to keep trying?" Ann asked him. "I mean, after your ankle feels better, that is."

"Of course. I'll try anything that works."

"So we'll keep at it. Maybe we can convince him you mean no harm." She stroked her horse's neck. Talking to him, she murmured, "Why do you have to be so stubborn, Lightning, huh?"

"It's not his fault," Jock said in his defense. "What he's been through had to have been pretty traumatic for it to leave its mark like this."

A thought suddenly hit Ann. "Jock," she said, "You think Scotty will give up after this? If we have no rider, I mean, what's the point?" She didn't want to think about the possibility that Scotty would decide that, for all his speed, Lightning couldn't be trained for the track.

"Dad? All he talks about is that colt's potential. With the incredible times he's clocked on him, I doubt he's thinking about giving up just yet. It'll take a lot more than today's performance to shake his faith in Lightning."

"I hope you're right," Ann said. "So, Ted, you still in?"

"You bet. I've got to admit that when he ran away with me, it sure was a thrilling ride. Now I know what you feel when you're on him, Ann. I wouldn't mind experiencing some more of that speed down the road."

"Pretty awesome, huh?" She smiled with pride for her beloved horse, even as she fretted inside for a solution to this latest roadblock. Still, as much as she wanted him to take his place beside other racing greats, as she knew he could, she took a certain pleasure that this magnificent horse truly belonged only to her.

8

A Solution?

Until a solution to the jockey issue could be found, Scotty went ahead with the training schedule as planned. Lightning began his sprints, and Ann had to admit to herself that she was pleased to be getting the opportunity to continue riding him. Even so, she and Ted continued to try to get Lightning to accept Ted as his rider. So far it was having no affect on the belligerent colt. He would accept Ted sitting on him in the stall, or even for short periods in the small paddock, but in no way would he carry him out on the track. Scotty, fearing Ted would eventually get hurt, finally told them to stop trying.

As the year wound down, they all got caught up in the approaching holidays. With school halted for Christmas vacation, Ann and Ted had more time to devote to projects around the farm. With Jock's help, they finally put the finishing touches on the track. Both the inner and outer rails now gleamed with another coat of white paint. In addition, the viewing stand was completed, sporting a new roof to replace the old leaky one. There were new rails all the way around, and the rickety old steps had also been replaced with new boards. The last thing they did was to add a couple of coats of white paint to them as well.

"Now we look like a profitable racing operation, don't you think?" Ann said with satisfaction as she stood back and admired her work, a paintbrush in one hand and a can of paint in the other.

"Yeah, now all we need is the horse," Ted teased, ducking as she threw the paintbrush at him. It narrowly missed Jock, standing beside him.

"Hey, you two. Leave me out of this," Jock yelped as the wet brush sailed past.

"Seems to me I heard a lot of complaining from your end too, Jock," Ann countered. "Now aren't you glad we got it done? Maybe we should keep going and tackle the tack room next," she suggested.

"And what's wrong with that?" Ted queried innocently.

"Well, the tack room could sure use an overhaul. You know—more saddle racks and hooks to hang things. A sink would be nice. And get rid of those awful cabinets and make some new ones. Let's see. Blanket racks would be good. And a place for boots, helmets, coats, other clothing. Yeah, I could think of a lot we could do to improve it." Ted and Jock looked at each other.

"Is she kidding?" Ted asked, incredulous.

"Ann, aren't you carrying this 'showplace' thing a bit too far?" Jock asked.

"Heck, no. When Lightning becomes famous and we get visitors here, you'll thank me."

"We will?" they asked together.

"Sure, and then we could fix up the stable yard. Put in some plants, paint the barns. Maybe a rock garden. And a fountain."

"She's gone over the edge," Jock sighed.

Ted had other plans. "Let's get her," he screeched, chasing after her.

Laughing, she ran off and called over her shoulder. "You guys have no sense of style."

Ann got some help with her half-serious suggestions from an unexpected source. When Scotty saw the completed viewing stand and gleaming track, he was very impressed. So impressed, in fact, that he suggested they put their talents to work sprucing up the old van prior to using it to take Lightning to the track.

"What's wrong with it the way it is?" Ted asked.

"You need ask? Just look at that old bucket. If we use that to haul Lightning, we'll be laughed off the track. No one will take us seriously." It was true. The old van wasn't very attractive, to say the least. Its paint was peeling badly, its seams showed rust, and it hiccupped when it was fired up, threatening to backfire at every bend in the road.

"Perhaps we could retire it and give it the funeral it deserves," Jock said, laughing.

"Sure, and what would we use in its place? Last I looked, none of us were flush enough to buy a new one," Scotty grumbled. "Sorry, kids. That—" he pointed to the van standing mournfully next to the tack room "—is our next project."

In the past, the duty of fixing up equipment and keeping it running had always fallen to Scotty. He had a particular knack for all things mechanical—unlike Michael, who'd never been especially talented in that area. Scotty had saved the farm considerable money over the years with his skill with machinery. Once again it was time to put that skill to work.

With the help of his son, Jock, whose assistance could be best described as reluctant, he tuned up the old engine, changed the fluids, replaced cracked hoses and belts, and generally got it purring again. Meanwhile, Ted and Ann got to work stripping and repainting the body, replacing the floorboards, washing the rubber floor matting, and hanging the hay nets. Then they dragged out an old trunk for their equipment they found in the storeroom, and placed it in the front corner. A few hooks were installed to hang various brooms and pitchforks. When they were all done, the old van was hardly recognizable. They were all pleased with the result.

"Just in time for a trial run to Keeneland," Scotty announced.

"What? Why Keeneland?" Ann asked as they stood there admiring the van.

"I think it's time to introduce Lightning to an actual track, don't you?"

"Oh, yes," Ann replied excitedly, chills running through her. *Scotty thinks we're good enough to run Lightning on a real track,* she thought. *How great is that?*

"We'll take Velvet and Tag along to pace him. Since the van holds four, I'm going to take Banshee, too. I want to use him as a pony horse for Lightning, so he might as well start now so Lightning gets used to him."

"Oh, wow," was all Ann could say. It was really happening. Lightning was going to be a racehorse. She conveniently forgot about the ongoing dilemma of a rider for him.

Scotty chose the first Saturday of the new year to take Lightning to Keeneland. Three very excited kids joined him in the van. It was only a short drive over to the historic track, and as they passed beneath the lovely old oak trees along the entrance, Ann felt a shiver of anticipation. Turning to the boys, she saw the same expressions reflected on their faces. Words were not necessary to express how they felt at this moment.

As they prepared their horses, Scotty went to talk to the person in charge. He returned with two men at his side. They were all talking animatedly, as if they were old friends. Though Ann had never seen them before, she recognized a certain familiarity in their mannerisms and dress, from the slouch caps on their heads to the worn, scuffed boots on their feet. She knew right away they must be trainers. Sure enough, Scotty introduced them as two old trainer pals, Bud and Marty.

"Fellas, this here is our new hopeful, Stormy Lightning. Brought him out to acclimate to the track." The two old trainers recognized and appreciated the black colt's good looks and responded accordingly.

"Scotty, good to see you back with something to run," Bud said. "It's been awhile since you've had something competitive out."

"Last one I remember was that handicap horse, wasn't it?" Marty asked, gesturing in the direction of Tag.

"This one?" Jock asked, bursting with pride for his horse, standing quietly beside the van, tacked up and ready to go.

"Sure is," Marty exclaimed. "And you've got to be Jock. My, but you've grown up. Last time I saw you, you were just a skinny little kid sitting on that horse." Ted and Ann couldn't help giggling at Jock's expense, earning a dirty look from him in return.

"Yep, this is my boy all right," Scotty returned proudly. "And he has grown, hasn't he? Too big to make jockey weight now."

"Dad, stop," Jock begged, turning beet-red from embarrassment. To draw attention away from himself, he swung up on Tag. "Can we go out onto the track now?"

Scotty shrugged, "Sure." A look passed between him and his two friends that said volumes about father-and-son relationships. The two old men just grinned. Fortunately, Jock had already turned away and was heading out onto the track, not waiting for Ted and Ann who would, no doubt, rib him some more if they got within range.

Ted swung up on Velvet and followed Jock, but when Ann started to do the same with Lightning, Scotty stopped her. "Wait, I want to lead him out onto the track, just as we would do in an actual race. If Banshee is to be his lead pony, he needs to know that from the beginning. Let him get used to the restraint of the post parade."

"Okay." Tucking her long braid under her cap, she mounted Lightning and waited while Scotty got Banshee ready, uncomfortably aware of the look of surprise on the two trainers' faces when they saw her in the saddle.

Finally Bud had to ask, "What's with the girl? Thought you'd be putting one of those boys up." He'd assumed Ann was out of range of his voice, but unfortunately she caught his comment. Now it was her turn to be embarrassed. *What did he mean by that?* she wondered? *Girls can ride just as well as boys—at least this girl can.*

"At the moment, she's the only one who can handle this colt. It's a long story," Scotty replied. "Tell you later. Right now we've got work to do." He rode over to her side and snapped a lead rope on Lightning's bit to lead him out onto the track. The two trainers followed at a distance, eager to see this handsome colt run. The novelty of a girl rider fascinated them. They sensed a good story here, one that would make great backside gossip among track regulars. Bud fingered the ever-present stopwatch in his pocket, hoping he'd get a chance to use it. Scotty, aboard Banshee, led Lightning across the track and clockwise down the backstretch to let him know they were just warming up and to let him get the kinks out. He jigged beside them, head up and eager, interested in his surroundings but not overly nervous. Ann was able to keep him in check with a light rein. At first he was confused by Banshee's close presence and shook his head to rid himself of the extra restraint, but after few minutes he settled into it without a fuss. Other horses went by in the same direction, none of them moving faster than a canter.

"Just another track," she told him, speaking softly to him. The soothing voice had a calming affect on him. Scotty picked up a trot, and he eased into a collected canter, still under control. They were moving along the backstretch when Scotty reached down and unsnapped the lead rope. "Seems quiet enough. Why don't you go ahead and warm him up like normal. Keep him well away from strange horses. Just let him get used to them. If anyone breezes today, make sure you are well to the outside when they go by."

"He'll want to follow, you know."

"I expect he will. But, Ann, you've got to keep him under wraps. Whatever happens, don't let him get loose from you. This is no place for a wild, out-of-control stallion. You understand?"

She nodded, gritting her teeth. "I'll do my best."

"I know you will," he softened. "A lot is at stake today. We need to know that he can be controlled—"

"Or no racehorse," she finished. "I understand." She took him on down the track clockwise at a light canter, keeping him off to the outside, well away from other horses also working on the track. Seeing Ted and Jock up ahead, she let him out a little so he could catch up.

As soon as he joined his two stable mates, two horses raced by, running counter-clockwise, breezing. Lightning tried to turn to go with them, but Ann held him in check with difficulty. Ted and Jock crowded him with their horses, trying to prevent him from getting away from her. He settled restlessly, showing his dissatisfaction with the arrangement.

"Your turn will come soon," she told him, continuing to sandwich him between Tag and Velvet. He was nearly responsive again when the next group of horses went by in the opposite direction, also breezing. Lightning jumped forward, fighting Ann's tenuous control. She had all she could do to hold him back. Ted and Jock forced their horses in beside him again to prevent him from getting away, though they all knew if he really wanted to run, nothing could hold him. Finally he came back to Ann's hand and slowed down to a light canter. By the time they completed the second turn around the track, Lightning was again listening to his mistress. The next couple of horses to breeze by only piqued his interest for a moment before he returned his attention to her.

As they passed the entrance to the track, they saw Scotty standing there, holding Banshee's reins. He signaled them in. They also noticed his two trainer friends were still beside him.

"Not bad," he told them. "Now I want you to go back out and breeze them for a half-mile. Take them the wrong way down the track till you get to that quarter pole, then turn them and let them go. Try to start together with Lightning a bit behind the others. Just like you've done at home dozens of times. Got it?" They all nodded.

"Scotty, what if Lightning gets away from me?"

"Don't let him."

She laughed. "Easier said than done."

"I know. But Ann, try not to let him reach top speed and get too far ahead of the others. I realize I'm asking a lot of you, but he needs to learn to be rated. And there are others out there to consider."

"I'll give it my best shot," she said, frowning. Taking him in hand, she rode with Ted and Jock back out onto the track as they all trotted to the far pole where Scotty had pointed. Once there, Ann took Lightning a little beyond it.

"Ready?" Ted called out. They turned their horses, and the race was on. Despite breaking behind the other two, Lightning caught and passed them almost immediately. Ann struggled to gain control of his speed as he ate up the track in front of him. At first he failed to heed her, eager to stretch his legs in an all-out run. She persisted in trying to communicate her wishes to him until he finally began to respond. He was now way ahead of Tag and Velvet. He ran nearly three-quarters of a mile before he slowed to a canter and allowed her to return to

Scotty. Ted and Jock were already there. The two trainers were talking excitedly as she came up.

"Well?" she asked, eager to know what Scotty thought about her first attempt with Lightning on a real track.

"Could have been worse," was all he said.

"Come on, Dad. At least she didn't run over anyone out there," Jock kidded.

"I hope not. Guess it's okay for his first time." The attempt at a joke had gone right over Scotty's head.

Bud was holding his stopwatch for Marty to see. Marty whistled. He turned to Ann, "Lass, was that his top speed out there?" he wanted to know.

"At first he got away from me, but then I was able to rate him a little," she replied. "I'm sorry he ran a quarter mile more than you wanted, Scotty. He loves to run." She patted his sweaty neck. The colt shook out his long mane and stomped his hoof. "See, even now he wants to do it again."

Scotty shook his head. "That's all for today. We need to get these horses cooled out, then head for home." He signaled the three to go on ahead and begin working on the horses so they wouldn't tie up.

But Marty wanted to know more. "Scotty, you've been holding out on us," he said, walking beside him as he and Bud followed them back to the van. "He's a three-year-old, you say? Seems you've got a stakes racer here, if this time has anything to say about it." He held up Bud's stopwatch. "Look at these times." Bud had caught him at both the half-mile and the three-quarter-mile poles.

"And you say he wasn't even trying?" Bud added.

"We're a long way from an actual race," Scotty said. "We still don't have a jockey that can stay on him." Scotty had briefly told them Lightning's story while they were watching the workout.

"Too bad that little girl can't ride him. She's pretty impressive, the way she sticks that horse," Marty said.

"Yeah," Bud added. "She's every bit as good as the jockeys I've seen. Better than most." Scotty made no comment.

On the way home, Scotty remained rather quiet and thoughtful, saying little. If Jock, Ted, or Ann noticed, they said nothing about it, being too busy chattering excitedly among themselves about the day's events. Besides, they all knew he had a lot on his mind about Lightning's training.

Bud was holding his stopwatch for Marty to see.

The next couple of days, training went on as usual. If Scotty seemed preoccupied, no one noticed. Jock caught him one night poring over the Jockey Club rulebook, but again he thought nothing of it. Racing had so many rules; no one could keep them all in his head. He also had a long serious talk with Michael, but they all assumed it had to do with the farm. One day, about a week after the Keeneland trip, he dressed in a business suit and drove off. He was gone most of the afternoon, getting back just at dinnertime.

Everyone was gathered at the dinner table when Scotty came in. He was still in his best suit, not even having taken the time to change before joining them.

"Wow, Dad, I've never seen you dressed up just for dinner," Jock exclaimed.

"Had a business meeting," was all he said as he made a big pretense of helping himself to portions of the food being passed around, trying not to call attention to himself. A look passed between him and Michael, and Scotty nodded. Michael beamed but said nothing. Ann, who caught the look, glanced over at Ted. He's seen it, too. Something big was in the wind.

"What's up, Dad?" she said.

"Nothing."

"Ha. I know that look. Something's up," she surmised, grinning at Ted.

"Not now. Finish your dinner first," Scotty said. "Then we'll talk."

"I knew it," she said with a smirk.

"Ann, quit pestering your father and Scotty, and eat," Jessica interrupted. "They'll tell you soon enough. By the way, Scotty, you look very nice," she added, glancing his way. He reddened slightly, not used to getting compliments on his appearance.

As soon as dinner was over, Ann impatiently said. "Okay, spill it."

Scotty took a sip of his coffee. "I've just come from the Jockey Club," he began. "Wanted to check something about the rules for jockeys." He had everyone's attention now. "I've read over the rules and Michael and I've already talked about it, but I needed to make sure."

"About what?" Ann interrupted.

"I'm getting to that," he said smiling. "I wanted to see what the rules said about female jockeys—"

"What?" Ann exclaimed excitedly, now realizing where Scotty was going with this. She could hardly contain herself. "And?"

"Well, nothing specifically says they can't race. There just is no precedent for it, that's all. No female has ever approached them for a license."

"Does this mean—" Ann cried.

"Easy, Lass. I went today and asked if they would issue an apprentice license to a girl, to you. With your father's permission, of course." Michael nodded.

"What did they say?"

"They want to see you ride first. So I've just arranged for a committee to come out and observe you on Lightning this Saturday."

"Really? Wow!" Unable to sit still, she jumped up and whirled about the kitchen, hugging first Scotty, then her father, and finally everyone else at the table in turn. She couldn't contain herself.

"Think you are up to it? A lot rides on this. They will base their decision on whether you can race or not, on how well you can handle him."

"I'll be up to it," she assured him. "And so will Lightning. Count on it."

"If you pass this test, they may want you to repeat it over at Keeneland. We'll need to practice there some more as well."

"Done," she laughed. "Oh, do you think there's a chance I could actually race Lightning myself? That would be a dream come true!"

"We'll see. They need to know you can control him on the track. It's been a problem, but the more we work at it the better he's getting."

"Yes, he is. Whatever made you come up with this solution?" she asked happily.

"Actually, a chance comment one of my trainer friends made out at Keeneland the other day," he replied thoughtfully. He repeated the conversation out on the track. "Got me thinking. Well, why can't a girl ride? So I did some research. If it works, this'll be the answer to our rider dilemma."

"It sure will. I'll do my best to show them a girl can be just as good as the guys."

"Good. Then tomorrow we'll go back over to Keeneland and have another workout, okay? I'd love to take Si'ad, but I'm afraid he wouldn't handle it well. Sorry, Ted."

"I understand. He's got too much stallion in him. I'm not sure I could control him in that environment. It would be too much for him." He felt bad, but he knew his horse was never meant to be a racehorse.

9

TRIAL RUN

The second trip to Keeneland went much better. Used to his routine by now, Lightning accepted the order of his workout. He began to understand that when he was ridden the wrong way around the track, he was only warming up or cooling down. He was to maintain nothing faster than a slow gallop, in spite of what other horses were doing around him. While he continued to show an interest in horses being breezed past him, he did not try to follow them anymore. But when it was his turn, he was like a coiled spring. As soon as Ann rode him over to the inside rail and turned his head around, he was off. As per Scotty's instructions, Ann let him take the first furlong at his speed before she asked him to come back to her. Reluctantly he slowed down, decreasing his speed, even though he was far ahead of his companions. Scotty was satisfied, however. Progress was being made in little increments.

Ann and Ted were having their semester finals during the week prior to the visit by the Jockey Club committee. As most of their courses were the same, it was easier to study for their finals together. Each night she and Ted went over the material, quizzing each other until they felt confident they were ready for the tests. Jock also lent a hand by taking over some of their chores each day. With such a busy week, Ann was too preoccupied to think much about her upcoming trial on Saturday.

By noon Friday, exams were over. Ted and Ann had borrowed the old family station wagon to come home early, rather that wait for the school bus. Glad exams were behind them, they began to discuss the impending race as soon as they got in the car. "What do you think they'll want to see tomorrow?" Ann asked Ted.

"I expect they'll want to see if he's really fast enough to race against the top three-year-olds," Ted surmised.

"You think? But isn't it more about me? That is, if they'll consider giving me a license to race him, I mean."

"Sure, but in order to do that you'll have to prove you can ride him at speed—especially against other horses."

"I suppose you're right. Are you going to bring Si'ad out?"

"Scotty hasn't told us yet. He probably will though. He's the fastest horse we've got, the only one who can push Lightning. I'd kind of think Scotty would want to show them a match race between those two, don't you think?"

She nodded. "I just hope I'm good enough."

"Why wouldn't you be? No one else can ride him like you. Actually, you're the only one who can. Isn't this what it's all about—proving to the Jockey Club that Lightning deserves to race and you deserve to be his rider?"

"It's an unusual request, isn't it? I wonder if they've ever had one like it."

"At least they're willing to give you a chance. That means they're taking this request seriously. They didn't deny it out of hand, and they could have."

She appeared to consider his words. Then changing the subject, she said, "I'm sure glad we fixed up the old track, aren't you?"

"I am now. It was a lot of work, but it should look grand enough to the committee."

"Yeah—makes us look more prosperous than we are."

"You mean like a farm that could have bred a Derby colt?"

"Yep. I think they'll take one look at Lightning and know he's not just your average three-year-old."

"He's impressive, that's for sure. But, of course, he gets it honestly from his sire."

"Ha!" She laughed. "He had a dam, too."

They pulled into the driveway and came to a stop by the house. "But his speed comes from Si'ad," Ted argued.

She flared back. "You think?"

"Just wait until tomorrow and we'll see who's the faster."

"If Scotty gives us the chance," she countered.

"Oh, he will. I'm sure of it."

She jumped out of the car. "You're on," she challenged. "I hope you don't have to eat those words, Ted Winters." He just grinned. Now she had something else to think about besides being nervous in front of the committee.

The next morning, Jock, Ted, and Ann met Scotty and Michael out in the barn. Scotty's orders were to saddle up Lightning, Velvet, and Si'ad. Ann and Jock were to warm up their horses on the track, but Ted was to warm up Si'ad by taking him out across the field beyond the track, only bringing him back when Scotty signaled him. He did not want to take a chance of any confrontation between the two stallions beforehand.

Ann and Jock had been out on the track about twenty minutes when a car pulled up alongside the viewing stand and four men got out. Scotty and Michael came down and shook hands with them, then they all climbed the steps and took the chairs provided for them. Introductions were made as Jessica appeared with a thermos of hot coffee and passed around cups. Then Scotty signaled Ann and Jock to come in.

As Ann rode up, she couldn't help but notice the admiration in the eyes of these longtime horsemen. All of them recognized a good-looking colt when they saw one. And Ann was well aware of the impression he made as Lightning strutted his stuff before them, all power and muscle. He was keen this morning, as if sensing something important was in the wind. He crow-hopped and shied at shadows as he pranced across the track, sleek and fit, his black coat already shiny with a thin sheen of sweat. He knew what was coming. Through all his antics, Ann sat perfectly still, at ease and at one with her colt. When he tossed his head, his long black mane almost hid her from view. Yet her hands were light on the reins, holding him in with no more than a feather touch. She overheard one of them exclaim at his magnificent presence. *Just wait till you see him run,* she thought.

While Michael headed for the old starting gate, Scotty walked out onto the track. His instructions were simple. "Take them down to the starting gate and wait for Michael to release you. As soon as Ted comes alongside with Si'ad, I'll signal. Then, Ann, I want you to blow him out for the full mile and a quarter."

"That's the Derby distance," she remarked, surprised. He'd never purposely asked her for that distance at speed before.

"I know. We might as well show them he's capable of going the distance, right? That *is* what this is all about today, after all."

"You bet," she smiled, pleased. She would show them Lightning was a Derby colt, all right.

Scotty returned to the viewing stand and rejoined the committee members. Meanwhile Jock and Ann rode their horses down to the starting gate where Michael waited. By the time they got there, Ted had joined them. Lightning and Velvet were loaded quickly, with Si'ad standing just outside. Velvet was placed between the two stallions as a buffer. As soon as all three were ready, Michael pushed the button.

Lightning bolted from the gate, his long legs eating up the ground before him. Ann bent over his neck, swallowed up by the long mane, calling to her colt, asking him to give his best. "This is it," she told him. "Show 'em what you've got, Lightning. They came to see you. Make us proud."

Poor Jock and Velvet were never a threat. Before they had reached the backstretch, it was clear she was outdistanced. Rather than frustrate her, Jock pulled her in and let the other two go on without her while he walked her back to the outside rail to watch father and son battle for supremacy.

Si'ad stayed with his son for the first half-mile, pushing him to top speed. But the Arabian was no sprinter. His strength was of another caliber. Like others of his breed, he was bred more for endurance, able to cover long miles, but at a lesser speed. As they rounded the track for the second time, Lightning's blinding pace started to tell on Si'ad, and he began to give ground, still game but falling farther behind. From the mile marker down to the wire, the race belonged to Lightning.

Atop the black powerhouse, Ann did not have to do more than urge him on with her voice. She knew he was giving his all, that he was at top speed. She reveled in the power beneath her, feeling the ripple of muscles as they undulated along his body. He was running for the love of it. This was as close to flying as she'd ever get.

Too soon she saw the quarter-pole flash by, and knew it was time to pull him in. Reluctantly he came back to her, still prancing and eager to run again as she cantered him lightly the long way around the track before returning to the group now standing beside the rail. As she approached, she could see them gesturing excitedly to each other. Two were holding up shiny objects—stopwatches—staring at them as if they couldn't believe what they saw. She smiled. "I think we impressed them," she told the black horse. She was very aware that Lightning had just run one of the best races of his young life. It was as if he understood how important it was to show these people his potential. Amazingly, he was hardly blowing after his effort. As she reached them, one of the men was saying, "Look, I know what I saw—but this," he held up his stopwatch, "doesn't lie. That colt just broke the Derby record."

"If it's accurate," another said skeptically.

"I got the same thing," an older, gray-haired man responded, holding up his stopwatch for all to see. "I doubt they'd both be wrong." There was some more mumbling as they all compared the times on the stopwatches. Finally the first man, obviously the spokesman of the group, turned to Scotty.

"Okay, we have to admit he's fast, but the purpose of this visit was to see whether this girl here should race him. That's the issue."

"She looked pretty good to me," Gray-hair remarked. "She looks like she could get the job done."

"Sure she can ride him, all right, but why can't he be ridden by a male jockey?" the spokesman wanted to know.

Scotty signaled Ted over. Michael had already taken Velvet back to the barns to walk her out, leaving Jock free to take Si'ad from Ted. He did so then, leading the stallion off to the side, well away from Lightning.

"This is Ted," he introduced the boy to the committee. "He rode the pace horse, the stallion, which incidentally is this boy's sire. We've tried putting him up, but well, you'll see what happens."

Ann slipped off Lightning and stood at his head as Scotty gave Ted a leg up. Ann released her hold on the reins and Ted attempted to take the black colt out onto the track. As soon as Lightning realized she was no longer beside him, he turned into a different horse, letting loose a series of bucks that would do a rodeo horse proud. Ted stayed with him as long as he could, but eventually he was unseated and ignominiously tossed in the air. He'd been ready for his sudden dismount and rolled himself in a tight ball, coming up unhurt. He stood up, dusting himself off.

"Again?" he questioned Scotty.

But one of the men waved him off. "Not necessary. Does he do that for others, too?"

"Everyone but Ann," Scotty replied. "I can bring my son, Jock, out and have him try, but it will be the same result. She's the only one he'll allow on his back. Those he knows can handle him on the ground, but that's it."

The man shook his head. "So that's why you made such an unusual request. Well, fellas, what do you think?"

"I'd like to see what he'll do on a real track." It was the fourth man, who hitherto had remained silent, finally speaking up. "I want to see if she can handle him in a real situation before I'd even consider this request."

"Sure," Scotty replied. "We've been taking him over to Keeneland to work him. Would that do?"

They agreed that before a ruling was given they would like to see another demonstration, this time at Keeneland. The date was set for the following Saturday. As soon as the committee left, everyone began talking excitedly.

"Scotty, were they impressed? They seemed to be," Ann said.

"How could they not be? They said he set a record for the Derby distance," Ted put in.

"Yes, I think that was an eye opener for them. Now they know we've got something worth looking at with this colt," Scotty agreed. "I don't think any of them questioned his place on the track. Thing is, that's not why they're here, as you know. They have to be convinced that he'll only run for Ann and—this is the important part—that she can control him out there on the track in an actual race."

"Well, as far as him being ridden only by Ann, I think I proved that," Ted said.

"You were pretty convincing," Jock said, laughing. "You took one heck of a fall."

"Yes, ouch. I was kind of glad they didn't ask for a repeat."

"Thanks for the heroic effort," Ann said.

"Any time," he said, grinning.

"At least they were satisfied enough by your attempt not to include me," Jock said.

"So now they want to see him work out at Keeneland?" Ann said. "That must mean they're still considering our request to let me ride, don't you think?" She looked hopefully at Scotty.

"Definitely. If not, the answer would have been a flat 'no' today, and that would be it. So since they want to see more, I take it as a good sign."

"Did they say what they wanted to see? Besides whether I can manage him, I mean?"

"Not exactly. But, no, you won't be asked to go the full Derby distance again."

"Darn! That was really fun."

"I'm sure it was. Now that we know he can do it though, it's back to his conditioning program. I still want him brought along slowly. It's endurance I'm after. Building him up to peak in May, not now. He's a great colt, but we can't lose sight of the fact that he'll be up against the best three-year-olds in the country. He'll have to be in top form then."

"I know." She sighed. "It's just that he's so fast. That feeling— there's nothing like it in the world."

"There'll be other chances, Ann. If you get to race him, that is."

"Oh, they've got to say 'yes,'" she groaned. "I'll do whatever I need to Saturday to convince them."

"I know you will. The rest is up to him." Scotty glanced meaningfully at Lightning.

The following Saturday dawned crystal clear and a bit chilly. Scotty chose to arrive at Keeneland midmorning when most of the horses would be finished their early workouts. This way less attention would be drawn to them. At least they hoped so. Both Tag and Velvet were brought along to pace Lightning, as Scotty wanted Ann to hold his speed down. Today was all about control. The committee knew the colt was fast. Now Ann had to convince them that she could sit him as well as any male jockey.

Lightning was full of himself. Ann felt it the minute he stepped out onto the track. She had to use all her powers of communication with him to get his attention. If ever he needed to be tractable, it was now. So much was riding on this demonstration. How she would have loved to let him go, as she had the previous Saturday, and feel that power and speed once again. But she had to remain calm, keeping him focused on her. He could not get away from her. It would be so easy for that to happen.

By the time Scotty gave the signal to turn the three horses and breeze them around the track, Ann had Lightning listening to her. She only let the reins out a notch, but he immediately sprang forward, eager to put distance between him and his stable mates. She spoke to him through the wind whistling past and was encouraged as she saw his ears flicker back toward her. For once he did as she requested, as if he knew what was at stake. Keeping his full speed in check, he completed the half mile Scotty had called for and slowed obediently when she pulled back on the reins. This time he was willing to be rated. Ann returned to Scotty, an elated grin on her face. She was rewarded by seeing his face light up with pleasure as well. The committee members were nowhere in sight.

"What did they say? Were they even here?" she wanted to know.

"Been here and left," he replied. "Unfortunately nothing was said, other than they're going to discuss our request and get back to us."

"When?"

"Soon, I hope," Ted cut in.

"Hopefully by the end of next month."

"They'd keep us in suspense that long? Why is that?"

"They only meet once a month for things like this, and they just had their meeting, so we have to wait till next month."

"Bummer," they both agreed.

"I know, but if it's any consolation, you handled him perfectly today, Lass. What happened?"

She laughed. "Can you believe how obedient he was? Honestly, I had a long talk with him about how important it was that he is good today, and I think he listened." She patted his sleek neck.

"Or maybe the training on track manners is finally beginning to pay off?" Scotty returned, a bit more pragmatic. "Whatever the reason, I'm glad you were able to make a good impression when it counted."

"So am I."

10

ONE TO GET READY

As February stretched out without an answer from the committee, life at Stormy Hill continued as usual. In spite of the uncertainty of the outcome, preparations moved along. Scotty kept to his training schedule for Lightning, building on the colt's strengths as he added muscle to the already powerful colt. Every so often he hauled the horses over to Keeneland for a workout. Though he didn't say much, Scotty was pleased with the colt's progress. If given the chance, he would be ready for the Derby.

One minor change that slowly evolved was the growing friendship between Lightning and his young mascot. Barak had now abandoned Ann's bedroom for the relative comfort of the big colt's stall. Otherwise inseparable from the black colt, he fussed bitterly when he was forced to remain behind each time Ann took Lightning for his workouts on the track. But all felt it was safer to have the rambunctious puppy locked away from the activity. Upon returning to the barn, however, he was given his freedom once again and tore madly around Lightning as Ann tried to bathe him, often getting in the way and having a bath himself.

As winter drifted toward spring, there was little time to ponder the reasons for the committee's delay in responding. Life suddenly became very busy at Stormy Hill. Foaling season began with the arrival of the first foals. The birth of each filly raised speculation as to whether this one might be worth keeping as a future addition to their small but grow-ing herd of broodmares. Such was the case of Bit O' Ginger's foal, a chestnut filly. Named Ginger Peachy, both Michael and Scotty considered her nice enough to keep as a potential broodmare.

It was during this time that Velvet came in heat. Scotty and Michael decided to use Lightning on her. Putting her to a stud worthy of her fine breeding would cost more money than they had, especially with Lightning's racing career potentially looming in the future. Her pedigree complimented his, making this a wise choice. Everyone involved looked forward to an exciting foal from this combination.

Foaling season coincided with breeding season. This would be the first full year Si'ad was standing at stud. Ted grew excited as the first mares booked for his horse began to arrive. Back in Arizona, he'd gained experience working with the stud manager at Desert Sun. Now he was solely responsible for Si'ad's breeding program.

The extra stalls in the yearling barn were turned over to the visiting mares, the first ones beginning to arrive in early March. Several had foals at their sides, since they would be bred on their foal heats. This added to Ted's workload, so Ann and Jock offered to help whenever they could.

Each mare was turned out in her own paddock every day. The paddocks used were laid out between the barns and the racetrack, several on each side of the lane that connected the barns with the track. As some hadn't been used in quite awhile, Jock, Ann, and Ted stayed busy repairing and maintaining the fences.

There was an added bonus to all this work for Ted. For his efforts, he would receive half of Si'ad's stud fees. The money would be set aside to enable him to attend the university with Ann next fall.

One morning toward the end of March, Ann was out on the track working Lightning when she noticed a stranger standing next to Scotty, observing their workout. She had just breezed him, using Ted on Si'ad as the pace horse. Velvet had been pronounced in foal to Lightning, leaving Scotty no choice but to rely on Si'ad to push Lightning on the days he asked for a breeze. Although the stallion was still considered too unpredictable to trust on a real track, he bowed to Ted's control on his home turf. He had even begun to tolerate the starting gate, a fact that Ted never failed to point out to the others any chance he got. He proved to be an excellent challenger for the black colt, pushing him to his top speed and making him use himself in order to best his sire. More and more Ann and Ted were able to limit these breezes to the required distance Scotty requested as the two horses learned to listen to their riders.

This particular day had been a good one, with both horses responding quickly when Ann and Ted asked for slower speeds. They had pleased smiles on their faces as they turned their horses at the far end of the track and cantered back to Scotty. As they neared the viewing stand though, the stranger took his leave of the trainer and walked off toward his parked car.

"Walk them out," was all Scotty would tell them, leaving them to wonder what that was all about. Dying of curiosity, they did as they were told, knowing no amount of coaxing would get an explanation out of Scotty until the horses were cooled out. Normally they did not mind this important part of the process. But today it seemed to take much too long as they waited impatiently to hear the reason for the stranger's visit. Ann was sure it had to do with their request to the Jockey Club. Why else would he be interested in watching her early morning workout?

Ted had just turned Si'ad out in his pasture when Jock appeared. "Dad wants to see you and Ann. He and Michael are in the kitchen. Is she done with Lightning yet?"

"I think so. She should be putting him away now."

They met her coming from the colt's pasture. "Come on to the house," Ted called. "Scotty wants to see us."

Eagerly she ran to catch up. "Did he say anything?" she asked Jock.

"Not yet."

They all burst through the backdoor together, all talking at once when they saw Scotty and Michael sitting down to breakfast. "What did he want?" Ted asked.

"Can I race?" Ann exclaimed.

"Is the answer 'yes'?" Jock added.

"Hold on a second," Michael said, laughing. "First, all three of you sit down and have some of this delicious food Jessica's spent all morning cooking. Then we'll talk." They slid into their seats, but while Ted and Jock began to pass plates around, helping themselves to big portions of eggs and bacon, Ann was too excited to eat yet.

"He was from the Jockey Club, wasn't he?" she asked, looking at her dad.

He nodded. "Yes. I'll let Scotty fill you in, though."

Scotty put down his fork and smiled at Ann. "He was from the Jockey Club. He was on the committee, but wasn't able to come out here before this. Seems he wanted to see you and Lightning for himself before he made any decision."

"And was he impressed?" she asked hopefully. "That was a great workout for him to see this morning. Both of the boys were very well behaved, right, Ted?"

Ted nodded in agreement. "Yep. Si'ad was a complete gentleman today. He did everything I asked of him, even pulling up after we passed the quarter-mile post. I think he's beginning to understand why he's out there."

"I agree. You two couldn't have choreographed a better example of a mock race then you did this morning," he smiled. "And, yes, I think he was quite impressed with your performance. Unfortunately, all he said was 'Thank you. We'll be in touch soon.'"

"What? That's it?" Ann sighed. "Still nothing definite? What are they waiting for?"

"I know, Honey," Michael said soothingly. "This waiting is so hard—on all of us. But that's the way they do things. Can't make a decision without a vote."

"How soon is 'soon'?" Ted wanted to know.

"I got the impression they're meeting within the week," Scotty said lamely. "Wish I had more complete news than that. But these things take time. After all, we're setting a precedent here. Jockeying has always been a male sport. If they allow you, others will want to follow suit."

"And, Honey," her father added, "It's not like we're asking if you can ride in some minor races like maiden or claiming races. You'll be racing in a very prominent race. Nothing gets more publicity than the Kentucky Derby. They have to be completely sure you can handle him out there on that track."

"But I can—I mean, I *will*. *I* know Lightning better than anyone. He'll listen to me."

"We know that," her father agreed. "But they don't. We have to convince them you can do as well as a male jockey."

"Better," she corrected emphatically. Then, noticing Ted's face, she added, "At least where Lightning is concerned. No one can get more out of him than I can."

"I know. Because he won't let anyone else ride him but you, Honey," Michael said, completing her thoughts. "Well, we'll just have to hope the Jockey Club agrees with us and lets you ride."

"In the meantime, Ann," her mother interrupted, "would you please eat some of this good food I fixed, before it gets cold?"

"Sure, Mom, sorry," Ann said, taking up the plate of eggs and scooping some onto her plate.

Several nights later, they were all at the dinner table when the call finally came through. Jessica was passing around a plate heaped with fried pork chops when the phone rang. Michael put down his napkin and went to answer it. When they heard the tone in Michael's voice, they all stopped eating. While the one-sided conversation was made up of mostly grunts and one-word answers, they could see by the big grin on his face that it was good news.

"Thank you very much, Sir," he said into the phone as he ended the call. "You've made some people at this end very happy—especially one young girl."

As he set the phone back into its cradle, he was immediately stormed by five very eager people. "Well?" they all wanted to know.

"Ann can ride Lightning in a pre—"

He was cut off by loud whoops of glee as big grins lit up their faces, and Ann, Ted, and Jock began to hug one another while jumping up and down.

"Wait," Michael said, "I'm not finished—there's more." They stopped and looked at him expectantly. "They want you to ride him in a preliminary race first. There's a maiden race at Churchill Downs, the Monday before the Derby. If he acquits himself well there, then it's a go for the Derby."

"Oh, poo, that's easy," Ann scoffed. "We'll show them he's Derby material."

"You're probably right," her mom said supportively. "If he's as fast as you say, he'll win easily."

"I don't think it's that simple," Scotty said reflectively. When they all looked at him, he explained. "I mean, I think what they want to know is not so much if he can win, but rather if Ann can control him in an actual race. Winning is the least of it."

"Then we'll just have to prove to them how good we are," Ann stated. "And then they'll have to say 'yes' to the Derby, right?" She looked around expectantly.

"My bet's with you and that horse of yours," Scotty said, smiling. "What's the length of this race they want us to enter, Michael?"

"It's only a six-furlong maiden."

"That's good. We can use it as a stepping stone for the Derby."

"What do you mean, Scotty?"

"Well, Ann, we'd need to blow him out anyway several days before the race, so this way we'll use this maiden as our practice run. It will also give Lightning a chance to feel out the track, get used to the crowds, et cetera. If we need to change anything, we'll know that too. I think it's a very good idea, actually."

When they heard the tone in Michael's voice, they all stopped eating.

Ann beamed. "We're going to the Derby!" she said as the news hit her full force. "Jock, Ted—we're going to the Derby! Whoopee!" Again she was hugging them and punching the air at the same time.

"Guess I'd better make an entry for this maiden then," Michael said. "And get the final payment in on the Derby. Scotty, you with me? We don't have a whole lot of time." He and Scotty headed to the office to fill out the paper work. Meanwhile, the three younger members of Stormy Hill's family headed out to the barn to tell Lightning the good news. If Ann noticed that Ted seemed somewhat subdued, she thought little of it, as excited as she was at that moment.

11

TWO FOR THE SHOW

The Kentucky Derby was only a little over a month away. As the realization struck them that they were actually going, everyone at Stormy Hill was thrown into a whirlwind of preparations. So much to do.

Jessica set to work making Ann a set of jockey silks to wear. The farm colors were blue and gray, had been ever since the first horse raced for the farm back four generations of Collinses ago. That was even before the farm had taken the name "Stormy Hill," after the name of her most famous winner. The blue and gray colors were chosen in remembrance of the days of the Civil War, when the family had been split in their loyalties—father against son, brother against brother. By the end of the war, only Michael's great-grandfather remained to carry on the farm. It was he who chose the colors to serve as a memory of the farm's darkest moment, as he strove to pull the farm up from the ashes of that hideous war. Sadly, he did not live to see her finest hour. Instead his son carried on the tradition, culminating in the great Stormy Hill, whose record made their farm a force with which to be reckoned. His only loss was the famed Kentucky Derby. Would Lightning be able to avenge that loss?

Meanwhile, Ann needed to get permission from her teachers to take her exams early if she was to take time off to be at the track preparing for the big race. Seniors took their exams before the rest of the school, giving them time to enjoy a week of activities leading up to their graduation. Unfortunately for Ann, exam week coincided with Derby Week.

Several days after the Jockey Club's pronouncement, Ann and her parents met with the school administration. At first her teachers were a bit skeptical, for her request was quite unusual. After her father explained the events leading up to the Jockey Club's decision, though, one by one they began to take her side. Ann was known as a quiet, agreeable student who tried her best to achieve good grades, who turned her work in on time, and who was not one to ask for favors. Fortunately she carried a light load this semester, making it easier to prepare for exams ahead of time.

Her biology teacher, however, rather than give her a separate test, chose another method to test her knowledge. Since his was an honors university course being taught at the high school, he suggested she write a paper based on the theory that her Lightning's ancestry would produce a winner. Ann was thrilled. Of course she would like nothing better than put together a paper on that very subject. That would be far from work for her. She agreed to turn it in right after Easter.

That night at the dinner table, the discussion centered around their plans for the upcoming trip to Churchill Downs. Scotty opened with his thoughts. "If your last exam in scheduled for Friday morning," he said to Ann, "then I think we should try to leave that afternoon, so we can get settled in by evening. Will that be a problem?"

"No," she replied, "not as long as I'm all packed."

"We'll see to that," her mother said. "That shouldn't be difficult."

"You can count on us to help," Jock added.

"Thanks—I know I can," she smiled gratefully.

"I'll be taking Banshee along as lead pony. Lightning should feel comfortable with him there. Therefore we'll need two of everything," Scotty continued, thinking out loud as he compiled his lists in his head. "We'll need to make sure the van is ready."

"Good thing we gave it that paint job," Jock said.

"We?" Ted jumped in, grinning. "What's this 'we'? I don't seem to remember a paint brush in your hand."

"Because Dad and I were working on the motor, as I recall," Jock countered.

Michael jumped in before Ted could retaliate. "Well, at least it's done."

"Then we can start putting things in as we think of them and not wait till the last minute. Jock, you remember where we stowed those cots and bed rolls? It's been a long time since we had a horse running." Scotty always chose to sleep in the tack stall beside whatever horses he had at the track. That way he could keep his eye on them at all times. In the past, when Jock had gone with him to ride Tagalong, he'd stayed there, too.

"They should be in the storeroom next to Ted's room," Jock replied to his father.

"Well, then, let's get them out and air them—if they're still usable. Who knows what condition they're in now. Fortunately, I'll only need one for me," he added, thinking out loud.

"What about me?" Ann asked.

"Ann," her father said. "One of my clients at the store has a sister who runs a boarding house right across from the track. I've already made arrangements for you to stay there for the week. She's looking forward to having you."

"Oh, good. Will we need to pack our own food?"

"You might not, since meals are included at the boarding house. Scotty, why don't you take a hot plate so you can heat up coffee or soup out at the barn. You'll probably take most of your meals from the track kitchen, though, right?"

"Yeah, most likely. It'll be nice to get to eat with the boys again. I suppose there'll still be trainers there that I know from the past."

"Come on, Dad, it hasn't been that long. 'Sides, everyone knows you."

"Thanks, Son. Guess I'll find out soon enough."

"I've gone ahead and reserved two horse stalls and a tack stall," Michael added. "Not sure which barn they've assigned us yet, but we should soon get a letter with permits and such."

"Ann, Honey, what about your clothes?" her mother wanted to know.

"What clothes?" she replied. "All I'll need are some T-shirts, a sweatshirt or two, and a couple of pairs of jeans."

"Then maybe we should make a trip to the store and get some decent ones," her mother said with a sigh, "ones that fit you, not hand-me-downs from the boys."

"But they're so much more comfortable after they've been lived in," Ann insisted.

"Our point exactly," Ted said. "Right, Jock?"

"Yeah. On the other hand, maybe you could just buy us new ones and we'll give our old, stained and torn ones to Ann. How about that?" Jock said with a grin.

"Sounds like a good deal to me," Ted agreed. "Especially since Ann hates to go shopping anyway."

Ann gave them both dirty looks. "Who says I hate shopping?"

"When was the last time you went shopping for clothes?" Ted asked.

Seeing where this conversation was heading, Jessica interrupted. "It's settled. Ann, you and I will go pick up what you need this Saturday. And I'll also pick out a couple of new shirts for you boys. Will that do?" They nodded happily.

"Let's see how long we get to keep them before they end up in Ann's room," Ted teased, determined to have the last word.

Before Ann could retaliate, Jessica jumped in. "I think we should also add a dress or two."

"Whatever for? I'll be with horses all week."

"Not completely," her mother corrected. "This is Derby week, after all. There'll be all sorts of parties."

"I wouldn't be going to them, would I?" Ann looked aghast. The idea of being in a room full of strangers did not appeal to her. In fact, it scared her to death. She hadn't thought at all about the possibility of being a part of the Derby festivities. In her dreams, she only saw herself as being with Lightning the whole time.

"Of course, Hon," her father said soothingly, not unsympathetic to her reaction. His daughter's self-confidence did not extend beyond their immediate family and the world of horses. In big crowds she was especially shy. "If we're running a colt in the Derby, we'll get all kinds of invitations. This is the biggest social week of the year."

"Do I have to go? Can't you and Mom just go in my place?"

"We won't take in all of them. But some are a must. Don't worry. You won't be alone. We'll all be with you."

"That's good. If I have to go…" she said.

"So you see why you'll need a couple of party dresses," her mother continued.

"Ann in a dress. Now there's a picture." Jock grinned at Ted.

"You two are insufferable." She slapped at Ted before he had a chance to open his mouth in response. She could tell by the twinkle in his eye what he was thinking. "I'd like to see either of you in a suit and tie. Hmm?"

"Not me." Jock shuddered at the thought. "You'd have to drag me kicking and screaming to get me into clothes like that."

"That could be arranged." She rose from her chair.

"Hey, Ted—don't we have chores to do?" Jock said, making his exit.

"You bet." Ted was right on his heels, with Ann in hot pursuit. The screen door banged in their wake.

"Well, that's that," Michael said with a sigh. "Life as usual."

"Yes, isn't it grand?" Jessica laughed, enjoying the banter that went with having three teenagers around.

By the time Ann caught up to the boys, she forgot her anger when Jock suggested they had just enough time to take a ride before it got dark. In no time at all they were saddled up and heading down the lane behind the house. For once there was no argument over which horse to ride. With Lightning so close to his first race, Ann chose Velvet, leaving Ted the pleasure of his Si'ad. While he should have been delighted, especially since she didn't put up a fight, instead he seemed somewhat subdued as they rode along. Ann couldn't help but notice his behavior. Finally she voiced her concern.

"Ted, you're so quiet. Is something wrong?"

He looked surprised by her question. "No…I—I guess I just wish—oh, never mind," he said lamely.

"What?" Ann persisted, wanting to get to the bottom of his obvious melancholy. She hated it when either of her best friends was depressed.

"Oh, nothing," he said again.

"I think I know," she said with sudden intuition. "You were the one who was supposed to ride Lightning all along. Of course. How could I have been so dense? Oh, Ted, I'm sorry. I can imagine how you must feel, being left out like this."

"Wait, Ann—it's nothing like that," he hastened to assure her, slowing Si'ad to ride up alongside Velvet. "At first I felt bad about it. More because I felt I let you down when I couldn't stay on him."

"That wasn't your fault," she replied. "No one can ride him if he doesn't want to be ridden. You know that. It had nothing to do with you. Even Jock got thrown."

Jock nodded, rubbing an imaginary sore hip. "Boy, that's the truth."

"I know that now. And I'm okay with it. Believe me. That horse has only one rider—you. He'll run his heart out for you when the time comes."

"Ted," Jock told him, "I had my turn with Tag. Now Ann has Lightning. But you'll get to ride *all* our horses in the future."

"Jock's right, Ted. *You* are our future. If Lightning is as good as we think he is, there'll be many horses for us to race in the coming years."

"I guess I know that," Ted agreed.

"Then what's the problem?" she asked gently.

"Nothing really. Forget it. I'm really needed here anyway." Before they could argue further, Ted kicked Si'ad into a gallop and ran on ahead of them, thus preventing any more discussion as they hastened to catch up. By the time they got back to the barn, the conversation seemed to have been forgotten. Though Ann noticed a rather pensive look on Jock's face, her thoughts were already on the studying awaiting her, so she failed to quiz him about it.

Time was flying by quickly, and soon it was Easter. Ann had worked hard on her paper for her biology class, spending a tremendous amount of time on it to make sure it was as accurate as possible. In researching Lightning's background, she'd utilized farm records and quizzed Scotty and her father often for details that had not been written down anywhere. She made both of them read her final copy for anything she might have left out. The end result was as much an impressive look into Thoroughbred pedigrees as it was a precise account of Si'ad's breeding and the reason for his being incorporated into the breeding coefficient. Her theory that Lightning was bred to win would soon be put to the test.

Her teacher was impressed enough to give her an A for her efforts, telling her that he planned to be in the stands, cheering for her colt.

Now if all *my finals can go that smoothly,* she thought as she left the classroom.

12

THREE FOR THE MONEY

"Hey, Dad, can I talk to you about something?" Jock asked when they returned to their apartment above the broodmare barn after dinner that night.

"Sure, Son. Let me just grab a cup of coffee—then we'll talk."

Jock had thought a lot about Ted's dilemma before he finally approached his father. In fact, it had been on his mind since the evening the three of them had gone riding together. While Ted had not expressed exactly what was bothering him, Jock, knowing his friend as well as he did, could pretty much figure out what it was. Ted wanted to go to the track with Ann and Scotty. But he also knew Ted would never say anything about it. He felt too much of an obligation to the family, knowing that he was needed here on the farm.

Sometimes it was hard for Jock to remember that Ted had only entered their lives a scant year ago. For him it was as though he had always been there, a vibrant part of everything involving the farm. He was Jock's best friend, had been almost from the first day. In friendship they were like brothers, in all but blood. Their loyalty to each other was never in doubt.

But it went deeper than that. Ted brought out a side of Jock he didn't know existed. Always the prankster, Ted involved Jock in all sorts of mischief, often directed toward Ann. In the past, Jock had been too serious, quiet, and sometimes withdrawn. Growing up, he and Ann had lived through some tough times as the farm struggled to keep its head above water. They'd learned to do without as their parents worked hard to hold on to their way of life. If they often seemed more intense than other children their age, this was the reason.

Ted, too, had come with considerable baggage, of which Jock was aware. Yet he managed to shake off the more serious side of their lives by bringing out the child in all of them. More often than not he coaxed Jock—and Ann—into tomfoolery that got them in trouble. Frequently Ann was the target of his humor as he coerced Jock into some sort of retaliation. But he himself was just as regularly the victim when their games were aimed back at him. Either way, he held no grudges, picking up where he'd left off, ready to go at it again.

The other side of Ted was just as significant to Jock. In him he saw a hard-working young man who never shirked his duties around the farm, who was always there to lend a hand—and, often as not, did more than his share for the smooth operation of Stormy Hill. It was perhaps because Jock was so well aware of the workload Ted shouldered that he felt obligated to speak with his father about his friend's desires.

"So what's on your mind?" Scotty asked as he settled into his favorite chair.

"It's about Ted," Jock began, quickly coming to the point. "He really wants to go with you and Ann to the Derby."

"Oh, he does, does he? Did he tell you that?" Scotty asked.

"Ted? Oh, heavens no. He would never say anything."

"Then how do you know?"

"He's dying to go. I can just tell by the way he's been reacting to all our preparations. After all, he was the one who was originally supposed to be riding Lightning."

"Well it didn't work out. Too bad. The kid's a heck of a rider. Of course he'll get plenty of chances to ride for us in the future if Lightning does as well as I expect he will."

"I know, and so does Ted. But he really wants to be a part of things now."

Scotty sipped his coffee, as if in thought. "Tell me, Son. Why aren't you pleading for yourself? Don't you want to go, too?"

"Me? Not really. I've had my racing days, back when Tag and I went to the track. That's all I ever wanted, so now I'm fine with staying back here at the farm. It's Ted's turn to experience it all."

"I see. Very unselfish of you, Son. However, that would pose a problem. As it is, we'll be short-handed around here with both Ann and me gone for more than a week. I'm not sure we could spare anyone else."

"I know. I've already thought about it. I could take up the slack—"

"Of three people? I doubt that even if you worked 'round the clock you could do that. There's too much to do, and unfortunately we can't afford to hire anyone to help."

"No, seriously, Dad, I could take care of things here. Hear me out. The weather is nice this time of year. The broodmares and foals will be out on pasture anyway while you're gone. That eliminates those stalls, right?"

Scotty smiled. "Yes, I suppose so. They'll be fine on pasture. But—"

"Wait. Si'ad has only one mare booked for that week. I could handle one breeding. It's not like I haven't any experience with breeding mares."

"Okay," Scotty hedged.

"And Si'ad himself can stay out in his pasture also. That's one less stall to clean. You'll have Lightning and Banshee with you. We can put Tag, Cedar, and Velvet in the gelding pasture by the house, and there—look at the work all that cuts out." Jock was on a roll now. "Then if we turn the yearlings out also, I won't need to clean their stalls either. Isn't that why we built run-in sheds for most of the pastures? Think of it. The only stall I really have to be concerned with is the one for the visiting mare. Besides, I'll be here to keep an eye on everything."

Scotty seemed amused. "I see you've given a lot of thought to this."

"Yes, Sir," Jock replied. "Besides, if we're feeding the horses out in the pastures, it will take less time. I'll use the cart and take the feed around to them. If we check for repairs ahead of time and take care of that, there shouldn't be much to fix while you're gone. No one's getting any special medication right now. Hopefully they won't need any either. And no one's going to be in training since you'll have Lightning. We won't be ready for haying yet." He suddenly ran out of steam. "Hmm, what have I left out?"

"Not much, but I'm sure I can think of something." A smile played across Scotty's face. "My, you do seem determined to convince me you can handle everything."

"I am." Jock's voice showed his sincerity. "Really, Dad, I know I can handle things here. Will you think about taking Ted, too?" he pleaded.

"Why is it so important?"

"Because. Come on, Dad. Ted deserves to go, don't you think? He works hard around here, never complains." When Scotty raised his eyes, Jock hastily added, "No more than Ann or I do. Really, you know we all just do it to rile you. We don't really mean it."

"Okay, I'll admit that Ted pulls his weight around here," his father grunted.

"Well, he does. Honestly, between you and me, I think he's just grateful to have a place to live so he can be near Si'ad. Of course, that's only my observation. I'd never say anything about it to him. It's kind of like atonement for his background—you know, all the things he finally broke down and told Ann last summer. I don't know why, but it's like he's ashamed of his past or something." Jock shook his head.

"Like he has any reason to be. From what he told Ann, he was more a victim of his childhood than anything. I thought by now he'd put it all behind him." Scotty had long ago accepted Ted as his own, as much a son to him as Jock, his own flesh and blood.

"He never talks about it. Maybe he has. I just get the feeling that's why he works so hard around here. And why he deserves to go with you. Besides, he'll be a lot of help to you. It's always easier to have a third hand, you know."

"I suppose," said Scotty.

"So you'll take him?"

"So I'll think about it," Scotty said. Then seeing Jock's crestfallen face, he added, "If you're sure you can take care of things here at home…"

Jock's face lit up. "Absolutely."

"Then I guess I could use his help," Scotty said, wavering.

Jock swallowed him up in a bear hug. "Oh, thank you, thank you, Dad. You won't be sorry."

"Did I say yes?" Scotty grinned, pleased by his son's reaction.

"I take that as a 'yes,'" his son replied excitedly. "Can I tell him now?" He was halfway out the door when Scotty stopped him.

"Wait. I'll tell him myself. Tomorrow. It's late now."

"But—"

"Oh, okay," he sighed. "Come on. We'll go down together and tell him. Otherwise I'm sure I won't get any peace."

"Just wait till Ted hears the news!" Jock cried, heading for the door.

Ted and Ann were in his room doing homework when they knocked on his door. They walked in to find math books and papers strewn all over the bed and desk. It seemed the two were in the middle of some heated argument about how to solve a math problem. Neither was very good at higher math, one of the classes they took together, so they usually tried to struggle through the homework together as they studied.

"That can't be right," Ann was arguing, shaking her head and waving a paper at him.

"Then how else do you propose we figure it out, Miss Genius?" Ted countered.

"Whew, did we come at a bad time?" Scotty said pointedly, stepping back out of the doorway.

Jock only laughed. "Must be doing math. Only thing that gets them this mad at each other."

"You're right. But we can argue about this later." Ted turned to them, pushing aside some of the papers so they could sit. "Did you come for something?"

"Nothing important," Scotty said dismissively. "We can always talk about it tomorrow."

"Talk about what?" Ann wanted to know.

"I just wondered if Ted might like to go with us when we leave for Churchill Downs next month," he said casually.

"What!" Ted shrieked, leaping up, papers and books flying everywhere. "You're kidding, right?" He couldn't believe he heard right. Ann stood there as if in shock, not responding at all.

"Now why would I kid about a thing like that?" Scotty grinned at his reaction. "Besides, I could probably use your help," he added crustily.

"Me go with you? Wow! Hear that, Ann. I'm coming, too." He grabbed her in a bear hug, then hugged Scotty and Jock each in turn. "Oh, thank you. Thank you. I can't believe it. I'm going to the Derby."

Ann came alive, screaming. "Whoopee!" She, too, hugged everyone. "Gosh, thanks for including him. I'm so thrilled for you, Ted! Oh, it's going to be such fun!"

"Fun? I'm not taking you for the *fun!* There'll be work to do, you know," Scotty stated rather gruffly, though his eyes told a different story. "This is serious business."

"We know," they agreed in unison.

"And if Lightning doesn't do well in the maiden on Monday, there won't be a Derby, so don't get your hopes up."

"I know, Scotty," Ann said. "But we'll be prepared. Lightning will do just fine. I'm sure of it."

"Then just remember it," he told her. Then, turning to Ted, he added, "This means a lot of extra work for you, Ted, if you're coming with us. You'll have to see if the school will let you take your exams early, like Ann. And get *your* stuff together. Plus, I'll want as much work done ahead of time as possible, so poor Jock—who's agreed to pick up your slack, I might add—doesn't have to do it. He'll have enough to do with three of us gone."

"Yes, Sir," Ted snapped to attention. "I won't let you down. Not when you're giving me the opportunity of a lifetime. Boy, I can't thank you enough."

"Well, guess I'll get back and turn in. Mornings come awful early these days." Scotty turned toward the door so they wouldn't see how touched he was.

"I'll be a long in a minute," Jock told his retreating back.

As soon as the door shut, Ted descended on him. "How can I ever thank you enough, Jock? And how did you get Scotty to agree to take me? I owe you big time for this, believe me."

"It wasn't me," Jock tried to deny his part in it. "Dad just decided to take you, that's all. I didn't have anything to do with it."

"I'll bet," Ann scoffed. "I know you too well. What a thoughtful gesture."

"I agree with Ann. You'll never convince me you didn't put the bug in Scotty's ear, at least." Ted clapped him on the back in gratitude. Then pensively he added, "But there's one thing I don't understand. How come you didn't want to go yourself?"

"I told you the other day," Jock reddened. He wasn't good at hiding his emotions when being praised. He hated receiving attention. "I've had my own 'Derby,' if you want to call it that. Tag and I had our day. Now it's your turn. Besides, I'll be there to help out Monday for his maiden. And Saturday, too, hopefully."

"You bet—Saturday," Ann cried. "Guys, we're going all the way! We're going to the Kentucky Derby! Nothing can stop us now!"

"Wow!" was all Ted could say as the realization hit him. For a couple of minutes all they could do was whoop with glee and jump up and down in turn.

Suddenly Ann stopped and turned to Ted. "First thing next week you've got to get your exams changed. Gosh, what if they won't let you take them early?"

"I didn't think about that." He looked glum for a minute, then shook it off. "Oh, they just have to. I can't imagine not going now, just for a couple of exams. At least I don't have to take the history one, since it's an honors class and my grades are high enough in that."

"Meanwhile, we'll all pitch in and get as much done ahead of time as we can to help you out, Jock."

"I know. I told Dad we could turn the horses out on pasture for the week to save stall cleaning."

"Good idea. Even Si'ad can go out for the week. He does have one mare coming then, but you can handle that, right, Jock?"

"I already told Dad I would."

"So tomorrow, first thing, we start packing Ted's stuff, too." She began to plan. "You still got that other cot, Jock? And the bedroll?"

"Yep, both of them were still usable. Guess you'll be sharing the tack stall with Dad," he told Ted. "Lucky you. He snores."

Ted laughed. "You're kidding, right?"

"Like a fog horn," Jock said, grinning. "But don't worry. You kind of get used to it after a while. I did."

"Gee, thanks for telling me."

With that, Jock skipped out the door.

13

FOUR TO GO

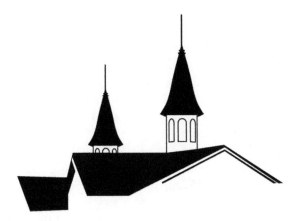

"Looks like you've got everything," Michael said as they stood in the driveway next to the van.

"Just have to load the horses," Scotty replied.

Ann came out of the stallion barn leading Lightning, with Ted right behind her, Banshee in tow. From the barn there came an awful howling.

"Whatever is that?" Scotty asked.

"Just Barak," Ann replied. "I locked him in Lightning's stall so he wouldn't get in the way. But he must know something's up. He never carries on like that."

"Sounds painful," Ted put in.

"Oh, he's just unhappy because he can't go with Lightning. They've really bonded."

"Spoiled is more like it," Scotty mumbled under his breath. Aloud he said, "Okay, let's get these horses loaded and get out of here. I'd like to be settled out at the track by dinner time."

Ann started to lead Lightning up into the van, but he held back, looking over his shoulder at the wailing sound coming from the depths of the barn. "What's this?" she asked, surprised. Lightning was always easy to load and was a good traveler. This was the first time he'd ever refused to walk on in.

"It's that confound dog," Scotty grunted. "Ted, take Banshee first." The black-bay gelding led in without a fuss. Ann attempted to follow, but still Lightning fussed.

"He's used to having Barak in the stall with him. Couldn't we just take him, too? I'll keep him tied to Lightning's stall."

"I'll see that he's out of the way," Ted chimed in.

"Oh, okay," Scotty gave in. "Go get the blasted dog so we can get this show on the road before we miss the Derby entirely."

Ted ran back to the barn and set the black and tan dog free. He bounded out into the courtyard and ran up to Lightning, who lowered his head and sniffed his friend. Then Barak leaped up the ramp and stood just inside the van. Lightning followed as calmly as if he'd never given a thought to rebelling. Ann and Ted laughed as they raised the ramp and locked it into place.

"See, that's all it took. Now he's happy."

"Wouldn't want the prince upset before the big race now, would we?" Scotty grumbled. "Well, if that's settled, can we get out of here?"

"Yep," Ted agreed. "Just let me grab some food for Barak, and his bowls and a leash."

"Anything else?" Scotty refused to be placated.

"Don't forget this," Jessica called out as she came from the house carrying a huge picnic basket. "I packed something to eat when you get there. Tuck this in the cab."

"What did you fix us, Mom?" Ann peeked into the basket. "Oh, wow! Mom made her famous fried chicken."

"Mmm, yummy," Ted cried, shoving her hand aside. "And biscuits, and potato salad, and it looks like a pie!"

"Cherry. Ann's favorite," she said, pleased. "And here's a thermos of fresh coffee for the ride. There's also some lemonade to go with your dinner." She handed the items up to Ann and Ted, who stowed them behind the seat.

"So let's get going so we can enjoy it," Scotty called out, his mood considerably improved by the sight of Jessica's cooking efforts. He started the engine. "Thanks, Jessica. Very thoughtful of you. Michael, I'll call when we get settled in. Jock, call the boarding house if you have a problem. She'll know how to reach us. Thanks, Son—I'm counting on you."

"Have no fear, Dad. Everything will be fine."

Goodbyes were said all around. Ted and Ann looked at each other as the van rolled down the driveway. "Kentucky Derby here we come!" they shouted out the window simultaneously, their excitement barely contained.

The trip to Louisville, which usually did not take long, seemed endless. Ann and Ted chattered continuously all the way, thrilled to have their exams and school behind them. Now they were focused on the adventure that lay ahead.

Finally, after what seemed like hours, Ann caught sight of the famous twin spires of Churchill Downs ahead. "There it is," she called out.

Ted strained to see where she was pointing. Having never been to the legendary track, he attempted to take everything in at once.

"We'll go check in and get the horses settled first. Then later we can get you set up at the boarding house." Scotty pulled into the gate marked "Horsemen's entrance" and stopped at the booth. He fumbled in the glove compartment for the correct papers for each horse, which he showed to the man who received him. While he was filling out the paperwork and getting their barn assignment, Ann nudged Ted, pointing out the various sights. Although it was already late afternoon, the place was alive with activity, as befitting any race day. Though this entrance was for horse personnel only, the area was still packed with people, all bent on going somewhere and in a rush to get there.

"Barn 39," Scotty told them as the man handed back his papers and he returned them to the glove compartment. He started the van forward. "I think it's off to the left." He weaved slowly in and out of the crowds. Horses were everywhere. Those who had been raced were either getting bathed or being walked out. Others were being prepared for the next race. Trainers hustled about, giving instructions, while stable boys hastened to comply. Owners stood off to the side, discussing their horses with trainers or each other. Several dogs ran in and out of the melee. All in all it was a busy area. Ann and Ted surveyed the scene, their eyes shining. This was about to be their world for the next week.

Scotty turned down the road that ran alongside the long shed rows. They counted off the numbers until they came to "Barn 39."

"What numbers are we?" Ann asked.

Scotty told her. "They should be all together in the middle, right before the aisle way." He drove the van slowly up alongside the shed row until he came to their stalls. Pulling to a stop, he watched as the two eager youngsters hopped out. "This is us," Ann cried.

"Okay," he said, getting down from the cab, a little slower than they did, but caught up in their enthusiasm just the same. "We're here," he said, smiling. "Now, the first thing is to get the straw and spread it out in their stalls. We'll use the one on the end for our tack stall. Put Lightning in the middle. I want to be able to hear every move he makes during the night. Oh, and before you do anything, check these stalls thoroughly for any sharp objects that could cut them. You never know what the previous residents could have done to them."

They hastened to comply, opening several bales and scattering straw until it thickly covered each stall floor. Then they filled two water buckets and hooked them to the stall walls. Lastly they gave each horse a flake of hay from the supply they'd brought. As soon as Scotty approved, they went to open the van door and let down the ramp, careful to catch hold of Barak as they did. Ted took him over to an empty stall, where he'd be out of the way.

Ann led Lightning out first, her heart swelling with pride. *How long I've waited for this day,* she thought. And now they were finally here. She quickly removed his leg wraps and turned him loose in the big stall, watching him walk around his unfamiliar surroundings until he settled to sip some water and munch on the hay. Once she was sure he was all right, she turned back to help unpack. By then, Ted had already repeated the process with Banshee.

Scotty had already gotten the stall curtains down from the storage area in the van. The three of them helped hang them around the stall designated as the tack stall, thus assuring privacy for its residents. Besides making Ann's silks, Jessica had also made new curtains in the farm colors. She had even embossed the front with the farm name set in gray against the dark blue background. The effect was very professional. As they stepped back to admire their work, they all felt as though they now belonged here. And to formalize the occasion, Ann announced, "There. Stormy Hill has arrived!"

"Your mom did a great job with these," Ted commented.

"Yes—we have to thank her when she comes," Scotty said. "They add the finishing touch. Now let's get the rest of the stuff unloaded so I can move this van out of the aisle before someone complains we're in the way. I'm getting hungry for that fried chicken."

Just the mention of Jessica's wonderful dinner had them hurrying to finish unpacking. When they were done, there was quite a mound of supplies piled in the tack stall to be sorted and stored. "We'll sort through this stuff after we eat," Scotty told them. "Don't let Barak near the food. And no picking at it till I get back, you hear?"

"Yes, Scotty," they both groaned. Ann took Barak's lead and tied him to Lightning's stall door, while Ted got out the chairs and arranged them in front of the stalls. Ann plopped down in one. "We're here. I can't believe it! We're finally here!"

"Neither can I. I thought the day would never come. And I can't thank you enough. I know you had a hand in getting Scotty to let me come."

"Sorry. Not me this time, Ted," she said. "I was as surprised as you when Scotty told you. It was all Jock's doing. I know he denies it, but I'm sure he's the one who put the bug in Scotty's ear."

"Then I've got to pay him back somehow. I can't believe he really didn't want to come, too."

"Actually I think he was telling the truth there. You weren't around when he raced Tag. There'll never be another thrill like that one for him. Besides, he hates being in the limelight. He hates all that fuss. After the race, he'll be the one to offer to take Lightning back to cool him off if we do well. Or even if we don't. Just you watch. I'd bet on it."

Ted changed the subject when his attention was drawn to the various horses being led past their barn. "So who do you think is here already? Of the Derby colts, I mean." The last race had gone off, and most of the crowds had left, including a lot of the owners. Things were beginning to settle back to normalcy for a Friday night as trainers and grooms finished their duties and, one by one, began to shut their barns preparatory to seeking out dinner.

"I don't know, but we'll find out. What say we take a stroll around the grounds after dinner and see who's here?"

"Sounds like good idea. Speaking of dinner, here comes Scotty now. Great. I'm starved."

He opened the picnic basket and began to hand out plates and napkins while Ann poured cups of lemonade. Soon they were all trying to balance plates heaped with pieces of chicken, potato salad, and biscuits on their laps while Barak whined from the end of his leash. Feeling sorry for him, Ann and Ted managed to chuck a piece of chicken his way every so often, much to his delight.

"There you go—spoiling that dog again," Scotty grumbled.

"Ah, Scotty, he's hungry, too."

"Then feed him his dinner," was his response to Ann's rationale.

"You think he's going to want crummy old dog food when we're eating Jessica's fried chicken?" Ted grinned, but he got up anyway and fixed the dog a bowl of his food, including some chicken scraps to entice him to eat. Barak eagerly bolted it down before going back to begging.

"Dog's too skinny anyway, if you ask me," Scotty remarked, giving in to his own rules and scraping his plate into Barak's bowl.

"He's only a year old," Ann defended him. "The breed's like that. They are running dogs and supposed to be streamlined. Right, Ted?"

He nodded. "Yep—built for speed."

"Still could use some meat on his bones," Scotty said, having the last word on the subject. "So, shall we get the rest of this stuff organized? I'll bet you two want to have a look around."

"Sure do. Scotty, do you have any idea who's here yet? And where they might be?"

"Well, Ann, I heard the two Florida colts, Roan Rambler and Time Tester, are here. I think they're over in barns 41 or 42, or maybe both. That's where all the Derby colts are. I'll know more after I catch up with the fellas." Scotty was as anxious to go off in search of some of his old cronies as they were to explore.

"How come we weren't assigned to those barns then?" Ann asked him.

"We aren't officially in the Derby yet," Scotty replied.

"Not until after Monday," Ann grinned.

"Let's hope so," the trainer agreed. "However, I'm glad we aren't stalled with the rest, for *his* sake." He nodded toward Lightning's stall where a black head poked out, watching them with interest. "Here we can avoid much of the commotion—at least until they know he's entered."

"Will it get hectic?" Ted asked.

"Ah, you've never experienced Derby Week," Scotty reminisced. "Yes, Ted, it can get downright crazy back here. This is not just the oldest sporting event, but one of the biggest. Everyone who's anyone comes to the Derby. By mid-week, there won't be a room to be had. This place will be swarming with reporters, too."

Panic crossed Ann's face. "Reporters? I forgot about them," she said.

Remembering her shyness around strangers, he hastened to add, "Don't worry, Lass. Most of them will be more interested in the other horses, not our long shot. Any reporters who come our way, let me deal with them, okay?"

She nodded gratefully. "Gladly," she said. "That's your job. I'm just here to race my horse."

It might not be that simple, Scotty thought, deciding not to express the thought out loud. If they got into the Derby, avoiding reporters

"Here we can avoid much of the commotion, at least until he's entered."

would not be an option. Let her enjoy her obscurity while she could. She'd find out soon enough.

It didn't take long to organize their equipment in some semblance of neatness. The cots were set up with bedrolls on top of them. Scotty ran a heavy-duty extension cord into the tack stall for their coffee pot, hot plate, and a light. Soon it began to look like home.

Ted chucked his duffle bag under his cot and straightened up. "My home away from home," he remarked.

"And see how nice and neat it is now?" Scotty said. "Let's see how long it stays this way."

"You won't have a problem with me," Ted responded, smiling.

"Hah!" Ann gasped. "I've seen your bedroom, remember?"

"You should talk! I've seen yours, too. It's a wonder you can navigate in it!"

"At least I'll be over at the boarding house and you won't know if I'm messy or not—because you won't see it. While on the other hand—" She held out her hands in an all-encompassing gesture. "Besides, I don't have to share with anyone," she finished smugly.

"How about you two calling a truce and taking that dog for a walk? I'm beginning to value my peace and quiet and wish I were home."

"Oh, Scotty," Ann laughed. "Sure. Come on, Ted. Let's go see who's here."

Ted grabbed Barak's leash and the grateful dog bounded ahead of them as they jogged off in the direction of barns 41 and 42, leaving Scotty to his own devices.

"According to the latest poll I read," Ted told her, "this colt from Florida, Roan Rambler, is supposed to be the favorite. Can't wait to see him."

"Yeah, He won all the big races he's been in, including the Flamingo. Guess he'll be the one to beat."

"Maybe. You never know what can happen though."

"After all, it *is* the Derby," Ann said, finishing his thoughts.

"This is sooo exciting."

"I have to pinch myself to make sure it's real. All the years we've been coming to Churchill Downs for the Derby, I always wished I were out there. Now I may finally get that wish."

"What do you mean 'may'?"

"We still don't know for sure—not until after Monday's race."

"Doubts? You have doubts? Now? You've been so confident all along."

"Oh, that's just in front of the others. I had to put on a good front for them. You're my best friend, Ted. I can tell you, now that I'm actually here, I'm…well, scared. What if something goes wrong? Or what if it goes well and they still don't let me race him?"

"Don't talk like that, Ann. Everything will be fine. You two are ready for this. Lightning responds to you. He'll run his heart out for you. You know that. I don't have to tell you. He'll be a perfect gentleman out on that track. He's not the same horse he was when he came back to you, wild and all. He's learned a lot this year. You've molded him into a racehorse. And when he runs Monday, he'll blow their doors off, and then they'll have to let you run him in the Derby. He's too good not to run."

"Thank you, Ted." Impulsively she gave him a hug. "That's what I needed to hear. I'm just getting nervous now that we're here, and the race is only three days away. I don't want to let everyone down."

"You'll never do that. You just go give it your all. That's all anyone expects."

"Look—there's barn 41. Let's see if any of them resemble either Florida colt."

They walked down the row, keeping a tight hold on Barak, lest his exuberance frighten one of the horses. The dog, never having been off the farm, was fascinated by everything around him and wanted to explore more, a wish both Ted and Ann denied him.

A small crowd had gathered near the middle of the shed row where a tall, leggy strawberry roan colt stood, his lead shank held by a thin, wiry young man. By his dress, jeans, and a faded T-shirt, they surmised he was probably the colt's groom. Those around him were talking excitedly.

Ann poked Ted eagerly. "That's him—Roan Rambler."

"The favorite? He's a good-looking colt. Big, too. Almost as tall as Lightning."

"His trainer is Neal Wyatt. That's him standing next to the woman in the white hat. She must be the owner's wife." Admonishing Barak to be good, they stayed well back from the crowd so they could observe the favorite at their leisure. The trainer, Wyatt, a short heavy-set man with bulging eyes, was extolling the roan's virtues. Ted was immediately put off by the man's surly, condescending manner. The way he was talking, it was as though his horse had already won. Yet in spite of Wyatt's superior attitude, Ted had to admit Roan Rambler looked the part of a champion. Obviously the people around him thought so too, judging by the conversation.

"Which one's the owner?" Ted asked Ann in a low voice.

"The tall guy with the thick white hair. He's got a string of car dealerships down in Florida," she explained. "Advertises a lot on TV."

"Does he know anything about racehorses?"

"He's owned them for years, but this is his first big one. I get the impression he believes pretty much what Neal Wyatt tells him."

"The guy's a jerk," Ted remarked. "Already I don't like him."

Ann smiled at that. Ted was pretty astute at sizing up people. "I agree. But he's an excellent trainer. You can't discount the number of winners in his barn. And he's got a wealthy client base. You can't knock success."

"Do any of them really know horses? Or are they the kind that just likes to dabble in racing as a hobby?"

Again she smiled. "Most likely more of the latter. Real horsemen are turned off by his manner."

"I would think so. Come on. I've seen enough here. Let's go find that other Florida colt, Time Tester."

As they walked away, Ann couldn't help but remark to Ted, "You learned a lot more than horses, all the time you spent growing up around Santa Anita, didn't you."

"I guess I did. I'd kind of forgotten. Or maybe put it out of my mind. You see plenty when you practically live at the track, and not all of it is good. I never did like that kind of trainer—one with the attitude that he's always right, that his methods are the only ones. I was lucky—the men who taught me were very humble. Maybe they didn't have a string of big winners, but they were always kind to the horses."

"Like Scotty," she interjected softly.

"Yes, like Scotty. Not the win-at-all-costs types like Neal Wyatt."

"But it's not always easy. Too often the owners dictate when they want the horse to run."

"And it's not always to the horse's benefit," he finished her thought. "Yeah, I know. That's why I admire the Scottys of the world, who stand up for what's right."

"Fortunately he only has to worry about our horses. Oh, and occasionally Garrison's, though Garrison usually defers to Scotty on important training matters." Since Scotty worked at Garrison's part-time, he was considered an assistant trainer who only worked with the horses in training at home. Garrison employed a full-time trainer who went with his horses to the track.

"That makes a difference."

"Some day I'll be a trainer," Ann said softly.

"You mean you don't want to be a jockey?"

"Sure, with Lightning. But as a regular profession? Probably not. I'd rather train horses for the track and let you ride them."

"Really? We could be a team. You train them. I'll ride them. Sounds good to me."

"Me, too." They'd arrived at barn 42, but were disappointed when they failed to see any action around any of the stalls. "Maybe we got the wrong row," Ann muttered.

A boy was yielding a rake outside one of the stalls. Ted stopped him. "Excuse me?" he asked. "Could you tell me if Time Tester is stabled around here?"

The boy looked up, a smile spreading over his youthful, freckled face. He looked to be about the same age as Ted and Ann. "Sure can," he replied, bending down to pat Barak, who wriggled up to him in a friendly greeting, his tail wagging furiously. "He's right here. He's my charge—or one of them." There was obvious pride in his voice. He led them over to the stall where a plain brown horse stood. The horse raised his head placidly before returning to his hay. After the rather impressive picture Roan Rambler made, this horse was not much to look at. But both Ted and Ann knew looks could be deceiving when evaluating speed. The boy continued to pet Barak. "What's this guy's name?" he asked.

"This is Barak," Ann replied before introducing herself and Ted.

"I go by Rusty," he laughed, "as if you can't tell." His shock of bright red hair had given him his obvious nickname. "And what is Barak? He's rather unusual, isn't he?"

"He's a Saluki." Ted went on to explain a little about the breed. "He came along to keep our horse company. They're kind of inseparable, you might say.'"

Ann clarified: "In other words, he raised such a fuss we had to bring him."

Rusty laughed at that. "I understand. Rufus here, that's his barn name, has a pet goat. That's her, lying down in the back there." They both looked in the stall again, this time catching sight of the little gray and white pigmy goat. "Her name is Rachel."

"Cute," Ann said. "Does she keep him calm?" Many racehorses had mascots for that purpose.

"Naw. He's so laid back; he's half asleep most of the time. Unless he's racing. Then he opens up. You going to be around for the big race?"

They both smiled. "We hope so," Ann replied, without elaborating. They had all decided not to say anything to anyone until they knew for sure after the race Monday.

"Then I'll see you around. Which is your barn? I assume you have horses here too."

"We're over in barn 39," Ted told him. "Come on over when you can and see our boys."

"I will. Glad to meet you."

Ann and Ted continued on past the rest of the barns until they came to the backside of the track. They stopped along the rail and stared out across the infield to the grandstand in the distance. Topped by the famous twin spires, it stood as a sentinel dominating the area. Only hours ago it had been filled with racing fans, all cheering their favorites. Now, as night set in, it was silent and empty. The only movement was that of the occasional janitor, busy sweeping up the debris left behind by disappointed losers. Tomorrow the whole process would begin again.

After a few minutes of comfortable silence, each lost is his own thoughts, Ted said quietly, a touch of awe in his voice, "The famous Churchill Downs. I've wanted to come here ever since way back when I first knew what the world of racing was all about. But back then I never dreamt my first time would be like this."

"I know what you mean. All these years we've been coming here, sitting in our box, watching the Derby, watching all the great Thoroughbreds run, and I used to dream someday it would be me, my turn. I never thought, in my wildest dreams, it could ever come true, though."

"And now it has."

"Almost."

"Think positive. Monday you and Lightning are going out on that track to make history. Once they see you two race, they'll have no choice but to let you race Saturday."

She smiled. She could always count on Ted's loyalty. "Thanks. Shall we get on with our tour?"

They walked down alongside the track until they came to the track kitchen. Ann pointed out the place where most of the track folks grabbed their meals. By the time they got back to their own stalls, Scotty was already back. He smiled as they eagerly gave him a recount of their tour. When Ted told him about coming upon Neal Wyatt and his reaction to the trainer, Scotty had to agree.

"He's a good trainer if you go by his win record but he's not very well liked by the other trainers. Too pompous. Doesn't seem to stop him from drawing the moneyed clients, though." Scotty shook his head. "Guess it takes all kinds."

Scotty glanced at his watch, then said to Ann, "Shouldn't you be heading over to the boarding house? I've already taken your things over and assured Mrs. Barton you'd be along soon."

"Gosh, Scotty, thanks," Ann said. "Yeah, I'd better get going. Got an early morning tomorrow."

"I'll walk you over," Ted offered. "Me and Barak."

"Good idea. Get a good night's sleep, Ann. Tomorrow will be a busy day. You have your pass to get back in, don't you?"

"I do." She held it up as proof. "'Night, Scotty."

The boarding house was only half a block from the gate. Ted and Ann were there in no time, and Mrs. Barton met them at the door.

"Welcome. You must be Ann." Mrs. Barton was a small, rotund woman with a round, rosy face. Her eyes twinkled when she smiled. Ann liked her on sight. "And you are?"

"Ted Winters, Ma'am," Ted replied.

"My best friend," Ann said. "He lives with us out on the farm. And this is Barak—my horse's mascot, I guess you'd call him."

"Welcome Ted, and Barak. Can you come in for coffee and home-made pie, just out of the oven?"

"Well—" Ted hesitated.

"And I probably even have a dog biscuit for Barak," she added as an extra incentive. "Ann, your room is already fixed up. Took your things up personally. It's the first one on the right, head of the stairs. So there's no reason for the two of you not to sit a spell and enjoy some home cooking. That stuff they serve out at that track ain't fit for man or bea...dog," she added, giving Barak a pat. "I promise I won't keep you long."

They both laughed. Then Ted gave in gracefully. "Well, okay. Just a minute, though. We all have to get up pretty early tomorrow." She ushered them into the kitchen, including Barak, and sat them down at a long, roomy table, explaining there were three other boarders with her at the moment, all of whom worked at the track.

While she served them pie and coffee, she talked non-stop. A habitual gossip, there was not much she didn't know about the happenings at the track. Ted and Ann found her highly entertaining, but true to her word, she sent Ted and Barak on their way before an hour had passed. He did not leave empty-handed. In his hand was a lunch bag containing two pieces of pie to share with Scotty for "later."

Ann found her room meticulously clean, complete with little touches of femininity that showed the thoughtfulness of its owner. She smiled, visualizing Mrs. Barton, or Momma Millie, as she liked to be called. She quickly unpacked her clothes and got ready for bed. While she was sure she was too excited to fall asleep right away, she drifted off hardly before her head hit the pillow.

14

DERBY WEEK

The next morning, Ann awoke in the unfamiliar bed and looked around, not sure where she was. Then it all came flooding back to her. Derby Week! Across the street was the track where Lightning awaited her. Her lifelong dream had become a reality. Bolting out of the bed, she pulled an old sweatshirt over her head and slid into her jeans. Padding barefoot, lest her boots make noise, she headed for the communal bathroom. She was about to leave when she noticed her appearance in the mirror. Her hair hung in long curly ringlets nearly to her waist. *That's no good,* she thought. Grasping it in three thick ropes, she plaited it into a long braid. Satisfied, she slipped a rubber band around the end. Moments later she was back to finish dressing and hurry down the stairs.

As she passed through the kitchen on her way to the back door, she noticed a brown paper sack sitting on the kitchen table with her name scrawled across it in bold letters. She smiled. How thoughtful of Mrs. Barton—Momma Millie. She'd have known Ann would want to head to the track extra early, before she served breakfast to the rest of the boarders, and she made sure she had something to eat. Ann snatched up the sack, surprisingly heavier than she expected, and opened the door, closing it quietly behind her.

It was still dark outside, though off to the east the first streaks of light pierced the sky. She jogged across the street and covered the short distance to the back gate in no time. There, a sleepy guard checked her pass and waved her in, hardly noticing her. Familiar now with the route, she made her way quickly to their barn, where she found Ted coming out of Banshee's stall, pitchfork in hand.

"Horses are already fed," he told her, stifling a yawn. "You're awful bright-eyed this early in the morning."

She smiled. "Just excited. Lightning's first workout on the big track." She stopped by his stall and gave him his customary morning hug. Barak leaped up for his pat, sniffing the bag in her hand.

"Yeah, your first workout. Scotty's over at the washroom. Should be back any minute. What's in the sack?"

"Don't know yet. Momma Millie left it on the table for me," Ann explained, opening the sack. "Oh, yum, it's ham biscuits. Lots of them." She took out one and handed the open sack over to Ted, who immediately grabbed a couple and popped one in his mouth before returning it to her.

"Ah," he sighed. "My favorite. Thank you, Momma Millie. I'm going to like walking you back each night."

Just then, Scotty appeared from the other end of the shed row. "What are you two munching on?" Mouth too full to speak, Ann swung around and passed the bag over to Scotty, who dove in and came up with two biscuits. Biting into one, he said, "Delicious. Bless that woman."

The three hungry people devoured the contents of the sack in no time. Even Barak popped out of Lightning's stall, straining at the end of his rope to beg for crumbs. Each of them broke off pieces and tossed them to the eager dog, who gobbled them up and came back for more. Finally Ann said, shaking the empty bag, "Sorry, Barak, all gone. Good, huh?" She gave him an affectionate pat.

"Well, Ann, since you're here already, let's get a saddle on Lightning and go warm him up. I'd like to work him while it's still early, before it gets too crowded out there. We have no idea how he's going to react to this new track. The fewer horses out there, the better."

She got his saddle out of the tack stall and set it across the door before entering his stall. The big black colt nickered softly, nuzzling her. She offered him a piece of carrot before sliding her arms around his neck. "Miss me?" she crooned in a soft voice. How she loved to stroke his sleek coat while she breathed in his distinctive horse smell that mingled with the sweet smell of straw. Early morning in the barn was always the best time of the day to her.

Reaching over the door, she took the brush from the tray that hung there and proceeded to brush Lightning until his black coat gleamed with vitality. After that, she picked out his feet and removed the overnight tangles from his thick mane and tail. Making a quick decision, she braided his long mane into several thick plaits. Then she eased the saddle onto his back and tightened the girth. Scotty handed her his bridle, which she slipped over his head. Once ready, she led him from the stall and joined Ted, who sat aboard Banshee, all set to accompany her to the track. Before she mounted him, she took her long braid and tucked it under her cap. No sense in calling attention to herself. Around the track the term "exercise boy" still meant just that. She hoped she would go unnoticed in the early morning light.

Scotty nodded approvingly. "Good idea," he said. "Today I just want him to get used to the new surroundings. I want you two to take them out and walk them along the outside rail once, before letting him out in a collected canter for the second lap. Then come in for more instructions."

They both nodded, then with Scotty trailing on foot, made their way through the rows of barns until they came out to the track. Stepping onto the sandy loam, Ann felt a thrill jolt through her. This was it. She looked up at the stands in the distance, the first rays of sunlight hitting the twin spires, the rest of the huge building still in shadows. A sense of awe overcame her. How many famous horses had thundered down this great track to make their way into history books? Now it was Lightning's turn. One week from today, hopefully, he would get his chance. She felt humbled and very insignificant as she turned left along the outside rail.

Leaving Scotty behind, they made their way down the track, and as Ann walked Lightning beside Banshee, she could feel the coiled energy beneath her. It was like sitting on a powder keg. *He won't be easy to control today,* she thought. She made a face in Ted's direction.

"Full of himself, huh?" Ted sympathized.

"You know it. Boy, does he want to go! Hope Scotty lets me breeze him even a short stretch. He needs it. But Scotty's so conservative, he may not."

Only a handful of horses were out this early. No one seemed to pay any attention to them. They were just two more horses using the track for their workouts. A couple being breezed sprinted past them along the inside rail. Lightning turned his head in their direction, but Ann held him in check. "Not now," she told him. Reluctantly he responded, only swishing his tail in disappointment. It was not easy to hold him to a walk, especially as they passed by the grandstand for the first time. The big colt looked at everything, prancing in his eagerness. Racing fit, he did not like the restraint. Again and again Ann asked him to be patient, though inside she herself felt the same desire to let loose and fly down the track. *Soon,* she kept telling herself. *Soon we'll get our wings.*

After what seemed like forever, they passed Scotty for the first time and eased the two horses into a light canter. "I know what you want, but you'll have to be content with this," she whispered in his ear. His ears flicked back and forth, acknowledging her voice. Still his huge strides ate up the track, even at a canter. This time they were much quicker returning to Scotty. Ann looked eagerly down at him, waiting for the next instructions.

"Yeah, I know," he sighed, seeing her expression. "I guess it wouldn't hurt. You can breeze him a half mile. No more. And not at top speed, either. Think you can do that? Hold him in? He looks awful full of himself this morning, new track and all."

"He is, but he'll listen to me," she replied with more conviction than she felt. What if he got away from her out there? She wouldn't think about it. Scotty had given her permission to breeze him. She would show him she could follow orders.

Because the gelding seemed to have a calming effect on Lightning, Ted took Banshee back out until they got to the far turn. However, as soon as Ann turned the big colt, all composure was gone. By now he knew what counter-clockwise meant. He was in full stride almost immediately. Somehow Ann managed to hold him in, barely. Though she reveled in his speed, Scotty's words rang in her ears as she fought for control. He needed to save that speed for the race Monday. Still, they had gone about a quarter mile before she felt him respond to her voice and hands. As she passed Scotty at the half-mile pole, she had him under wraps. Letting him continue on down the track, she slowly eased him up until he was cantering. She turned him, taking him to the outside rail so she wouldn't be in the way of others who were breezing their horses. As they passed under the shadow of the stands, Ann took him wide along the rail, letting him canter slowly. In no hurry to return to Scotty, she reveled in the feeling that she was riding her beloved horse on this famous track. Perhaps they were stepping in the very same footprints left behind by past great Thoroughbreds.

The track was filling up. Other horses had come out since they started. Some were being breezed, but now Lightning was much more receptive to Ann, having gotten to stretch his own legs. He dropped down to a trot as she stroked his sleek neck, murmuring to him in a low voice. With her attention no longer solely on him, she became aware of the other horses working out. The track had become a busy place. She kept Lightning away from the others, partially so that he would listen to her better, but also so that no one would notice that she was a girl rider. They'd all know soon enough. For now, she wanted to enjoy her secret.

Ted rode Banshee up to her, and for a time they rode along in amiable silence. Then a magnificent steel grey horse flew past them, his powerful strides eating up the distance with deceptive ease. They both were immediately drawn to the spectacle and pulled their horses in to watch.

"Isn't that Royalair?" Ted asked excitedly. "He must have arrived late last night from Illinois."

"Yes, that's him," Ann replied. "Isn't he stunning? I'm surprised he isn't one of the favorites."

"Never won an important race, that's why," Ted explained.

"Only 'cause he's untried. By the looks of him, I'd say he should be one to watch, though." They continued on around the track. By the time they got back to Scotty, Lightning was not even breathing hard, his sleek coat dry.

"Did you see him?" Ted asked Scotty.

"Him who?"

"Royalair, of course. Wasn't he something?"

Scotty grunted, "Yeah, I suppose." But his eyes twinkled. "Don't worry. I'm keeping track of these Derby colts."

Ann grinned. "Nothing gets by Scotty," she said.

"Darn right. This is serious stuff. Speaking of which, Ann, you did a good job keeping him under wraps today. Wasn't sure you could."

She beamed. Scotty was very stingy with his compliments. "Thank you. I actually had my doubts, but he's getting better."

"You mean we might make a racehorse out of him yet?" Ted teased.

"Exactly," Ann replied.

Later, after the horses had been cooled out and put away, Scotty said, "Think you fooled them. No one seems to have noticed you're a girl."

"Yet," Ann said, "which is why I'm going to dump this sweatshirt and borrow one of Ted's—if I may?"

Ted rolled his eyes. "I'm surprised you'd even bother to ask. Is anything sacred?"

"Well, we were going to take Barak for a walk and see who else has arrived. I just think it would be better if I wasn't seen in this shirt, in case anyone might remember it from this morning," she replied sweetly.

"What a lame excuse," he muttered, throwing a look at Scotty, who only shrugged. "Like it's so dirty that they'd even remember what color it is."

"My point exactly," she said triumphantly. "I need something clean to wear."

"Okay, okay. You'll end up with them anyway. Don't know why I bother to argue. But hurry. I want to see the other Derby colts."

Ann mumbled something in reply, which he missed because she was already in the tack stall, rifling through his stuff. "There, now I'm ready," she grinned when she returned.

"Well, at least it isn't one of my new ones," he conceded, picking up Barak's leash. They were about to head out when a familiar figure came down the shed row.

"I was hoping I'd find you two here," smiled Rusty. "I came to see your horses."

"Great. Here he is," Ann said, slipping under Lightning's stall guard and going to her horse. Rusty's eyes widened at the sight of the beautiful black colt.

"Wow, he's gorgeous. And big, too," was his comment. He came forward to stroke the horse, but Lightning only moved away, submitting to Ann's ministrations by lowering his head. "He seems quiet, too," was Rusty's false assumption, seeing his reaction to Ann.

"Only for Ann," Ted grinned, but did not elaborate.

"Here, why don't I bring him out for you to really see?" Ann suggested, doing just that. Lightning stepped out into the sun, his coat gleaming black from his recent bath. He pranced at the end of his lead, shaking his long thick mane, now freed from its braids, until it flared out and the forelock fell across his eyes. He was the picture of athletic fitness. It was plain his workout of that morning had only whetted his appetite for more. "Easy," she told him, smiling at his eagerness. "I'll come back in a little while and take you out to graze."

"When are you going to race him?" Rusty asked.

"His first race is a maiden on Monday," Ann replied.

"Really? You haven't raced him yet?"

"Nope—this is his first," Ann replied vaguely. She put him back in his stall. "Well, that's it—except for Banshee there." she pointed to his stall. "He's here as our outrider horse. Lightning's all we got. We're only a one-horse stable right now."

"Well, he's pretty impressive. Looks more like a Derby horse than a maiden."

Ted jumped in before they'd be caught having to explain their presence at the track. "Speaking of Derby horses, Ann and I were just about to go see some more of them. Want to join us?"

"Sure. A couple more arrived after I met you two last night. Did you see Royalair work out this morning?"

"Yep, pretty horse. I—we were working Lightning earlier when he came out on the track. He's fast." She'd almost slipped and given herself away, but fortunately Rusty failed to notice. Obviously, he just assumed that Ted was Lightning's exercise boy. She wasn't sure how long they could keep up the masquerade, but the less attention she drew to herself, the better it would be. Besides, she rather enjoyed her secret.

Two barns away from theirs, Rusty turned down the shed row, announcing, "The two stable mates from Maryland, Solitaire and Celtic Glow, are down here. They pulled in last Thursday." He led them to a group of stalls with a big sign hanging out front that read "Dun Roman Farms" in fancy old-style Gothic letters of blue and gold. Each stall in their entourage had a smaller, identical Dun Roman sign along with a stall sign that gave the name and pedigree of its occupant, also in Gothic. Hung in front of each stall were a gold-embossed blue blanket, a blue bucket, and a leather halter with nameplate. This made it easy to find the two Derby colts.

Only one groom seemed to be around, and he was lazily sweeping the area in front of the stalls. It might have been from habit, because the whole area taken up by Dun Roman was so immaculate that not a blade of straw seemed to be out of place.

"We came to see the Derby colts," Rusty said. Without speaking, the groom waved them on, a disinterested expression on his face. No doubt he was probably already bored with the curiosity seekers.

The two colts were very much alike, although Solitaire was a slightly darker bay than Celtic Glow. Neither had any white on them to speak of, and while they had reasonably good conformation, neither was particularly impressive at first glance. But as Thoroughbreds did not run on their looks alone, Ann and Ted figured they'd have to reserve judgment until after they saw their workouts.

Several barns over they came to a huge contingent of what appeared to be misplaced partygoers. In the center of the group stood a large, red-faced man wearing a cowboy hat and boots, his jeans held up by a thick hand-tooled belt sporting a huge shiny silver buckle. He was holding up a can of beer as he toasted a plain brown colt being led by a groom, also dressed in similar attire. Those around him were busy saluting the colt along with the owner.

"The Texans are here," Rusty clarified, as if he needed to explain. "Fred Canaday always does everything bigger than life."

"So I guess this is Capital Gain then," Ann said.

"He's not very impressive. Know anything about him?" Ted asked Rusty.

Rusty looked appalled. "Don't say that in front of them." Then he smiled. "You know, everything is bigger and better in Texas."

"Guess we'll see soon enough," stated an equally unimpressed Ann, catching Ted's eye as she said it. He winked back at her. Fortunately Rusty was still looking at the colt and missed their exchange.

"In the meantime, the media loves them. They make good copy, I guess."

"Well, they sure look like they're having a good time," Ann conceded. "Maybe for them that's what it's all about. Just being here, being part of the experience."

"Yeah, Ann, like us," Ted said, grinning. "As a first timer, I have to say, this is fantastic. I've always wanted to come to a Derby, and now I'm here."

"You're right," Rusty agreed. "This is my first one, too. Always had to stay back at the farm before. We all need to make the most of it, don't you think?"

They agreed. "What other horses have arrived?" Ann wanted to know.

"The California colt, Calculated Risk is supposed to pull in this afternoon," Rusty told them. "Any one hungry?" When they both nodded, he continued, "Let's go over and I'll introduce you to the track cafeteria."

"What about Barak?" Ann wanted to know.

"We can grab burgers and sit outside."

"Sounds good."

But as soon as they settled at a table, it began to rain. Laughing, they ran for the nearest shelter—the overhang coming off the kitchen. Several other stable boys had taken refuge there as well, and since Rusty knew most of them, he introduced everyone all around. A lively discussion ensued, so that by the time Ted and Ann left to return to their barn, they'd made several new friends. They were also included in the nightly ritual—an impromptu gathering usually held around the outdoor tables. After agreeing to join them, the two returned to Barn 39.

Upon arriving, they noted Scotty's absence immediately. "Must have found some of his old cronies," Ann said as she plopped down in a lawn chair. Ted went over to tie Barak up to Lightning's stall before grabbing an empty chair.

"Darn rain," he muttered. They sat there for over an hour, watching the rain as they talked. They heard the sounds of the afternoon races going off, but neither was inclined to venture forth into the wet to watch. They just sat lazily, watching the rain form miniature rivers in the dirt between the shed rows. At one point, Ann even dozed off. That was how Scotty found her.

"Can't find anything to do?" he asked.

"Not if it means going out in the rain," Ann replied, yawning herself awake.

"My, my," he chuckled. "Too bad. I think they're unloading Calculated Risk over in the next row, too."

Ted and Ann jumped to their feet. "They are?" Ann said excitedly.

"Scotty, will you watch Barak?" Ted asked, grabbing Ann's hand and pulling her down the shed row. "Can't miss this."

"Sure." Scotty just shook his head. *Kids!*

The golden chestnut was indeed being unloaded from the horse transport when they got there. As he stepped out into the daylight, the rain miraculously stopped, and a thin watery ray of sunlight showed through. Calculated Risk stood there for a second in all his magnificent glory, a great golden statue. There was a visible gasp from the audience gathered to greet him. Here was the West Coast champion, winner of all the major Derby prep races held in California. He stood before them, a brilliant red-gold figure of flawless conformation, with a wide blaze and four white socks. He was tall, well over sixteen hands. According to the news reporters, here was the horse that could upset Roan Rambler, the favorite. He certainly looked the part.

Then the spell was broken as he moved down the ramp and walked majestically to his stall. The stall door was hardly closed behind him before news reporters descended upon the owners and trainer, seeking a story that would make good copy. Ann and Ted watched from a distance.

"I guess that's what it's like when you're a favorite," she said.

"Aren't you glad they don't know about us yet?"

Calculated Risk stood there for a second in all his magnificent glory, a great golden statue.

"Yep, I'd hate to have to deal with that around Lightning. I'm not sure he would handle it very well."

"He'd better learn," Ted smiled.

"Huh?"

"Ann, you two will have to get used to it after he wins," he said and winked.

"Think so? You're pretty confident."

"Because I know you and your horse. You aren't having any doubts, are you?"

"No, Lightning can do it. It's me I'm concerned about. Sometimes I almost wish you were riding him."

"Me? You don't really mean that. He's your horse and he runs best for you. Actually he runs only for you, come to think of it. Why would you not want to ride him?"

"It's not that. Of course I want to ride him. Just sometimes I get scared. This morning when I was out on that track it hit me. I've never run in a race before. What if I screw up and keep Lightning from winning?"

"Not possible. That horse is smart enough to run his own race without your guidance. Besides, that's what Monday's race is for. You and he will get to know the track and what it's like to run with strange horses."

She smiled faintly. "You're right. Up to now I haven't given the competition a thought. But seeing them in the flesh, I've begun to realize what we're up against. It's intimidating."

"Then don't think about it. Hey, it's stopped raining. Didn't you want to take Lightning out and graze him a bit?"

"Yes, if we can find some grass."

"Then let's go look for some before it starts raining again." Since being with her horse always restored her confidence, she instantly agreed.

Lightning was eager to get out and stretch his legs. The idea of eating some tasty shoots of grass instead of dry hay appealed to him. Ann led him to a small empty area away from the biggest crowds while Ted held Barak's leash and took in the scene around him. Everything was tranquil at the moment. He valued these brief moments, as he knew Ann did. There would not be many of them this week—especially after Lightning raced Monday.

15

FIRST RACE

The rain resumed before dinnertime, this time coming down steadily, with every intention of continuing through the night. That evening Scotty found pleasure in resuming his friendships with some of the other trainers, while Ann and Ted joined Rusty and the other stable boys for their nightly gathering. The talk naturally turned toward the upcoming Derby and each horse's chances. Those like Rusty, who had a Derby colt in their barn, eagerly defended their charges, while the others picked a favorite to champion. Needless to say, the talk was lively. New to the group, Ann and Ted just listened, occasionally catching each other's eye as both enjoyed their anonymity. Since morning came soon at the track, the group broke up early. On the way back to the boarding house, Ted and Ann discussed what they had heard.

"Seem like a nice bunch," Ted said.

"Yes they do. But won't *they* be surprised when they hear we have a Derby colt in our barn," Ann said.

"Sure will. I hate to deceive them, though, but it can't be helped."

"Still, I can understand their loyalties to their own colts, even those who haven't a chance."

"Speaking of chances," Ted said with a sly grin, "what do you think of my chances for another piece of that pie tonight?"

Ann laughed. "Maybe it's a good thing you're not riding," she teased him. "You'd never be able to hold your weight around Momma Millie's cooking."

The following morning, Scotty told her there would be no breezing today. The rain had not let up, leaving the track very muddy, with lots of puddles. While Scotty did not want Lightning risking a chance of hurting himself, he also had planned to work him long and slow for the next two mornings. That way he would be really keen to race by Monday afternoon. Ann, her hair once again tucked up under her cap, followed his orders. *Once around the track, and no one can tell which sex I am anyway,* she thought, amused.

By afternoon the rain had finally tapered off, so Ted and Ann chose to watch some of the racing from the rail along the backstretch. When they got back, they noticed an increase in the number of reporters infiltrating the backside of the track. With the last of the Derby colts arriving that afternoon, the race card was complete. Reporters seeking interesting stories to feed their fans were now in abundance. Ann found herself grateful that they had not been declared yet, so she would not have to face the interrogation, though she couldn't help but perceive how eager the other people connected with Derby colts were to discuss their own. As Sunday came to an end, she felt a reluctance to turn in that night. This would be the last easy, somewhat lazy day for them before the pace stepped up.

She woke Monday morning with a start. Today Lightning raced in his first maiden. Chills ran up and down her spine as she hustled to throw on some jeans and a sweatshirt. She needed to get to the track quickly to work Lightning. It wouldn't do to be late this morning.

She got to the barn as the first rays of sun were just beginning to cross the sky. As nervous as a cat, she saddled her horse and was about to lead him out when Ted stopped her. He pointed to her hair, and she gasped and hastily pulled her thick braid up under her cap. She'd almost forgotten. *That would have been awful,* she thought, *to be discovered today of all days.* Glancing at Ted to make sure she looked all right, she swung up on Lightning and rode alongside him and Banshee out to the track. If he noticed on the way that she was unusually silent or particularly tense, he made no comment. She was grateful, for at the moment she could not have carried on a conversation about anything—even about the weather. She attributed her nervousness to the upcoming race, but that did not make her sick feeling go away. Try as she might, especially for Lightning's sake, she could not shake off the gloomy, frightened feeling that came over her when she thought about the next time she would step out onto this track with her colt.

Scotty's instructions were simple: just work him slowly the wrong way until he warmed up, then let him canter a couple of times around the track, then end with bringing him down and cooling him out. With his words ringing in her ears, she started off, feeling better once she was moving and had something else on her mind. The nervousness gradually left her as she concentrated on following Scotty's directions. It was comforting to have Ted alongside her.

They rode along the outside rail. Occasionally horses passed them at speed, going the other way. Several were Derby hopefuls, but Ann paid no attention today. Instead she focused on Lightning and on keeping him under wraps. She could feel his eagerness to run and told him softly, "Pretty soon, big fella, pretty soon." He only shook his head, but remained soft in her hand. Though he'd never raced before, she sensed he knew what was coming. How, she couldn't tell, though she suspected he fed off her own case of nerves, as sensitive to her as he was. In any case, he was ready, continuing to dance beneath her as he waited impatiently. Though he failed to do more than canter, he was shiny with sweat and still keen to run by the time she returned to Scotty.

Scotty only grunted his response. "He's ready. Let's get back to the barn," was all he said, taking the reins from long habit and leading him off the track, as if Ann needed extra help holding him. Lightning shook his head at the unexpected restraint, causing Scotty to drop his hold, as if it were a hot poker. "Well, excuse me, old man," he grumbled. "Better get used to it, though."

"He will. When the time comes," was Ann's only comment. She thought ahead of the age-old tradition of the trainer leading his charge into the winner's circle. *Yes, Lightning will be ready,* she thought, *but will I?*

Though she tried to stretch out Lightning's bath and took extra time walking him, she still finished much too quickly. With very little to do, time seemed to hang endlessly ahead of her. Ted suggested walking over to the kitchen for breakfast, but when she got there she found she had no appetite for food. Her stomach was filled with nerves, making it impossible to eat anything. Ted and Barak ended up consuming her share, the dog eagerly devouring the food offered before Ann could change her mind.

When they returned to their stalls, Ann dropped down into a chair and stared distractedly out at the familiar scene before her, idly scratching Barak when he came to lie at her feet. There she stayed most of the morning. Ted tried to stay with her, but she kicked him out, telling him to go find Rusty and their other friends, rather than be subject to her dismal disposition. Finally he did, as did Scotty, who left to seek out his buddies from the past. There she sat, finding some comfort in the black-and-tan dog at her side.

Lightning's race was the second one on that afternoon's race card, a maiden for horses who'd not yet broken a first. A little after noon, Scotty reappeared and suggested she start to get ready. Because the official jockey room was strictly for men, she had to change into her jockey silks right there in the tack stall.

Ann opened the box containing the silks her mother had made. She stared down at them with a kind of awe, fingering the beautiful blue and gray silky material, tracing the letters S and H almost reverently. For a few seconds she was frozen in time. Thinking back to all the great horses that had run under these colors, she wondered if she was worthy. But she knew Lightning, and she also knew better than anyone what he could do. He would carry the Stormy Hill colors to the same greatness of his illustrious ancestors, perhaps even beyond. All he needed was the opportunity. Today he would earn that chance.

A smile came over her face. She picked up the jacket and quickly slipped it on. Staring back at her in the small, cracked mirror Scotty had brought along was not some small, scared young girl, but rather a jockey. Suddenly her nerves were gone. Miraculously she was transformed. *This is where I belong,* she thought, *on Lightning, racing for glory, racing into the history books.* Hastily she donned the rest of her outfit, complete with her new, shiny, high black boots. Lastly, she turned to her hair. Once again she would disguise her gender, as she had each morning exercising Lightning. Both she and the Jockey Club committee agreed there was no reason to announce the fact to the world until they had decided whether she could have a license to ride. Taking her thick black braid, she pinned it tightly on her head before jamming the helmet down on top of it. This time when she looked at herself in the mirror, there was no doubt. A jockey stared back at her. Grinning, she opened the door and stepped out into the aisle, right into a pleasant surprise. Her parents and Jock had arrived while she was changing. As soon as they saw her, they all began talking once.

"Hmm, looks like your silks fit," her mother said with a critical eye.

"Sure do—perfectly. Mom, I can't thank you enough. They're beautiful."

"Glad I could help the cause."

Jock whistled, then said, "You look like you're ready to do some serious riding."

"You bet I am. I'm going to go out there and make them see we belong in the Derby, the same as the rest of those colts."

"Boy, that's a big change from the grump you've been all morning," Ted teased.

"Oh that? Nerves, that's all."

"I'll say. Snapped your head off if you even looked in her direction," Scotty grumbled.

She smiled pleasantly at him and Ted. "Don't listen to them," she told her folks. "I just had a slight case of the nerves. I'm fine now."

"I hope so. We have a race to run," was Scotty's only comment.

"And we're ready, right, Lightning?" She stepped over to his stall door and gave him a big hug. The black colt rubbed his head against her contentedly, leaving behind a big smear across her sleeve. "Oh, darn. Lightning, that was not nice," she admonished him. The horse only shook his head, letting his long forelock fall across his large eyes.

Jessica immediately grabbed a towel from a rack and dipped it into his water bucket. She tried unsuccessfully to remove the stain. "Water isn't working. Wish I had my cleaner," she said.

"Oh, I'm sure I'll be a lot dirtier than this after the race," Ann said, shrugging it off. Then as an afterthought, she plaited Lightning's forelock to hold it in place.

"It's almost time. Let's get this boy up to the saddling area," Scotty said, sending them all into a whirlwind of activity. Jock took care of getting Banshee ready for Scotty to ride. Michael took care of locking a very unhappy Barak in the tack stall while they were gone. Ted, acting as groom, led Lightning off to the proper stall, while Ann trailed behind. It seemed strange not to be leading her colt, but protocol had to be followed. Jockeys never led or saddled their mounts. Normally they did not appear until it was time to take directions from the trainer and mount up at the call. While she had no doubt she could trust Scotty and Ted, she felt odd nevertheless.

When she got to the saddling paddock, she immediately looked around at the crowds, praying no one would recognize her gender and cause a commotion. There were plenty of reporters present, since the Derby Trial would be run later that afternoon, with several of the Derby colts on the card. This alone drew great interest, bringing many of the sports writers to the paddock in search of stories. If it got out that one of those colts could possibly be running in this race, and was being ridden by a girl to boot, they would be all over her for an interview. Fortunately, everyone appeared to be so involved with the other entries that she went unnoticed. An unknown colt running his first race was hardly of interest to the press.

In the program, Scotty had listed Lightning's jockey as "A. J. Collins," which gave away nothing. Since Ann's full name was Ann Jessica Collins, it was perfectly legal. No one would suspect the truth from the name. She deliberately kept herself surrounded by family so she wouldn't be closely scrutinized, but even those near her failed to detect anything unusual.

Before she knew it, Scotty was giving her a leg up onto Lightning's back, and she found herself being led by him out of the paddock as everyone called "Good luck" and "See you in the winner's circle." The next thing she knew, they were parading toward the starting gate. It was comforting to know that Scotty was beside her on Banshee.

There were nine horses in this, the second race of the day. Lightning had drawn post position number five, right in the middle of the pack. She would soon find out how he handled starting with strange horses on either side of him. In the meantime, she glanced around her. Excitement had replaced nerves as she sensed the thrill of finally getting to race Lightning, if only in a minor race. At last they were part of this famous track. Her dreams were coming true.

"Try to break with the pack," Scotty was telling her. "Try to get to the rail if you can. But make sure you're not blocked." He stopped. "Are you even listening?"

Suddenly she was aware that Scotty was speaking. Forcefully she pulled her attention back to his instructions. "Yes, yes, of course," she mumbled distractedly.

"Doesn't seem like it. I thought you were miles away just now."

No, only yards, she thought as she turned in the saddle and faced him.

"Okay? It's a short race, so take him to the front early if you can, but don't let him get away from you. It may only be a maiden race, but there could be one or two fast horses in there that could challenge him. Trouble is, there are also beginners like him entered, and you never know what they'll do the first time on the track. You'll want to stay as far away from them as you can, so they don't interfere with his race. And he'll still need something extra for the finish, so try to hold him back until the homestretch. Remember—they are watching *you* to see how *you* handle yourself. They already know our colt is fast. Got it?"

She nodded. They had come to the gate, and the first horse was being led in. Reluctantly she waved goodbye to Scotty as she waited her turn to be led into the gate. Lightning was restless. While he had never raced before, he knew what the starting gate meant, and he was eager for what was coming. When it was his turn to be led in, he shook his head in an effort to rid himself of the restraint. Ann talked softly to him until he finally walked in. The gate clanged shut behind them. The others loaded easily and they were ready. *This is it,* she thought as she sat down, tightened the reins, and got set to ride.

With a clang, the gates sprang open. Lightning bolted from the gate like a rocket. Too late Ann realized she'd forgotten to grab mane at the start. He was so quick that she was almost left behind. As she struggled to regain her seat, the black colt got the bit in his teeth and launched himself out onto the track. He'd broken even with the colts on either side of him. Now as he leapt forward, his long strides quickly outdistanced them, shooting him into the lead.

Scotty's instructions ringing in her ears, Ann tried to pull him back so he'd save himself for the final stretch run. She gathered her reins to get Lightning's attention, but the black colt would have none of it. All he wanted to do was run. Having shaken off his competition, the powerful horse surged ahead, pounding down the wide-open track, running for the sheer joy of it. Since they had arrived four days ago, he had only been allowed to breeze once. The rest of time, Ann had held him down to only long, slow workouts. His eagerness to run had built up in him and now that energy drove him down the track, heedless of the rider on his back.

Try as she might, she couldn't get Lightning to respond to her voice or her hands. Though she was thrilled by his speed, she knew she had to pull him down. It could not look like a rout. She had to show the committee that she did have control over her horse. Relying on the bond she alone shared with him, she continued speaking in her soft voice, asking him to slow, easing him with her hands as she gently tried to regain his mouth. She had no idea how far back the rest of the pack were, nor did she dare glance back to check. All she was aware of was that the poles were flying past her and the rail was merely a blur. After what seemed like forever, she felt a slight lessening of his speed. Encouraged by his response, she renewed her request as she tried to break through his headlong plunge down the track.

Lightning was slowing, imperceptibly at first, but Ann could feel him begin to yield to her pressure. *Is it too late?* she wondered as they rounded the turn leading into the homestretch. Now she could hear the rest of the pack faintly in the background as they surged forward to overtake the fleet black colt. Yet even as she took him down another notch, she knew they would never catch him. Down to the wire they all raced, Lightning still ahead by many lengths, though his lead was shrinking with each stride. Ann continued to hold him back so that they were only a respectable four lengths ahead as they crossed the finish line. Lightning had won his first race.

16

The Decision

"Waiting is the worse part," Ann moaned as she sat slumped in a chair in front of the colt's stall. As soon as she got back, she had ducked into the tack stall and changed quickly. Her filthy silks lay in a discarded heap on a tack trunk. Scotty and Michael had been summoned before the committee soon after the race, and now everyone awaited their return with the news of their fate.

Once the necessary work of cooling Lightning down and putting him in his stall was done, there was nothing more to do. They all found themselves without plans, scattered before the stalls in various lawn chairs, each watching hopefully for any sign of Scotty or Michael.

"Ann, Honey, you should feel pretty excited," her mother said. "After all you two did win your first race."

"I am," she responded. "I mean, I will be as soon as we know the answer. Right now that's all I can think about." Yet her mind drifted back to the moment when she brought Lightning back to the winner's circle and was immediately surrounded by her family, their faces beaming as they showered her with congratulations. *What a moment,* she thought, smiling as she remembered. Her elation was so great that she could barely contain herself when Scotty came out onto the track to take Lightning's reins. For once he didn't balk about it, allowing those familiar hands to lead him into the spotlight where the winning photo was quickly dispatched. Then Jock stepped forward to take over while Ann weighed in, a requirement she almost forgot about in her excitement. This time it was only a short formality, nothing like the ceremony that would surround the Derby winner on Saturday. Soon it was over, and they were on their way back to the barn area.

There had been only a couple of reporters standing about, looking rather bored as they waited for the big race of the day, The Derby Trial. Fortunately for her, none of them showed much interest in the winner of his first maiden race—even if he'd taken it with a four-length lead. *Maybe it didn't look unusual from the distance of the stands,* Ann thought. But she knew different. If she hadn't been able to pull Lightning in out there, his lead would have been much greater, and *that* would have caused a stir. That much she knew. He had out-classed those colts, yet he had done nothing that couldn't be dupli-cated by the other Derby colts. Would the committee see it that way? He was far more superior then the average Thoroughbred. He was a stakes horse.

Her thoughts were interrupted by Barak's bark. The dog pulled at the end of his rope, eagerly jumping up and down. They all looked in his direction, hoping to see Scotty or Michael coming down the aisle. Instead Rusty came trotting toward them, his face beaming.

"Word is you guys won the last race and I had to miss it," he said breathlessly. "Congratulations."

"Oh, thanks," Ann replied for them as she introduced Rusty to her mother and Jock, and explained to them that he was a stable boy with the farm running Time Tester, one of the other Derby colts.

"This is so great. So tell me all about it," he continued, bending down to pat the hound, who'd wriggled all over to get his attention.

Though Ann hardly felt like talking, she briefly related Lightning's race, trying to sound as excited as Rusty expected her to be. By his rapt attention in her words, she assumed he had not caught on that there was anything out of the ordinary going on.

"Wow, I knew he was a winner the first time I saw him," he said. "Wish I could have seen it, but we had a colicky horse emergency this morning. I had to stick around and keep an eye on him."

"Is he okay now?" a concerned Ted wanted to know.

"Oh, yeah, or I wouldn't have left him. I did want to get over here as quick as I could."

"We appreciate you coming," Jessica told him graciously. "Perhaps you'd like to join us later for dinner. I brought Ann's favorite—fried chicken and fresh biscuits."

"And pie?" Ann perked up.

"Of course. Apple, this time. Used up the last of the cherries on Friday's pie."

"Just as good. Whoopee! Now that's a winner's celebration, Mom."

"Then I'll have to see about getting back here," Rusty said. "Right now I was going over to watch the rest of the races. The Derby Trial is coming up. The two Maryland colts are running. Ted, Ann, you want to come?"

"Yeah, we might later," Ted replied distractedly, again glancing down the shed row for signs of Scotty or Michael.

"Me, too, in a bit," echoed Ann.

"Right now we're waiting for Ann's father and Scotty to get back," Jessica clarified quickly, without further explanation. "These two will probably want to join you after that. Then you all can come back here for a bite to eat."

"Sounds good. Well, I'm off then. See you later." Rusty strode off in the direction of the track, humming to himself.

"Whew, I'm glad Michael and Scotty didn't get back while Rusty was here," Ted murmured.

"I know. He's such a great guy, but this is a family thing," Ann said. "I sure didn't want to explain it to him—at least until we know what's going on."

"Yeah," Jock said. "If it's favorable news, they'll all know soon enough."

"It's got to be," Ann said. "I've been replaying the race in my mind over and over, and I can't see anything they could criticize, do you?"

Ted shook his head. "He listened to you out there. That's all that matters."

"He almost didn't," she said, grimacing.

"They don't have to know that. From what everyone saw, he ran a clean, controlled race."

"Then what's keeping them? I can't believe it takes this long to make a decision." She looked at her watch for at least the thousandth time.

"Maybe it's a good thing, Dear," Jessica offered.

"Why is that?"

"Well, perhaps there are a lot of things to discuss if they let you race."

"Like what, Mom?"

"I don't know, but it will set a precedent. For instance, where do you change, for one thing? The jockeys' room has always been a men-only facility."

Leave it to Mom to think of that, Ann thought as she sighed. "Why can't I just change in our tack stall, like I did today?"

"I suppose." Jessica's thoughts were interrupted as Ann suddenly gave a shriek. Scotty and Michael were in sight, and as they drew closer, Ann could see grins on both of their faces.

"What?" she questioned expectantly, ready to burst from excitement as the reality began to take over. They would not be smiling if it were bad news!

"You're in," Scotty said, smiling broadly.

"Honey, they agreed to let you run Lightning," her father clarified.

She froze, not knowing whether to leap in the air, let out a whoop, or hug everyone at once. In the end she tried to do all three, ending up hugging Ted and Jock simultaneously as she poured out her joy. "We're in! We're in!" she kept shrieking happily. "We're going to the Kentucky Derby! Lightning"—she stopped long enough to run over to his stall and give him a big hug—"Lightning, did you hear? We're in the Derby!" The big colt only nuzzled her, enjoying the attention, while Barak barked frantically at all the excitement.

"I guess that was good news," her father said with a chuckle.

"Oh, my, yes," Ann breathed. "What did they say?" She slipped back out of the stall, but pulled her chair up to the stall door so she could continue to stroke the colt as while she listened to Scotty relate details of the meeting.

"Right from the get-go, they couldn't deny that he had the speed to be considered for the Derby," he said.

"I'll say," Ann interrupted. "If I hadn't gotten him back to me, no telling how much he would have won that race by."

"I think that fact was what convinced them that you could handle him in the Derby. Did you know that at one point he was ahead by more than twenty-six lengths?"

"N-no, really? I knew we had a big lead, but I had no idea we were that far in the front. Twenty-six lengths? Wow!"

"Of course it looked like the rest of the pack just caught up by the homestretch."

She smiled. "And I was doing all I could to reel him in like you told me. I almost didn't."

"You and I know that, but of course I didn't let on to the committee. Better they think you were always in charge."

"Oh, sure." She grinned. "With Lightning, anything's possible out there—right, Ted?" Who better than Ted to vouch for her, as he'd spent more time beside her on the track than anyone.

"I'll say," he agreed.

"So, Ann, the decision was to let you race—but there are some stipulations."

"Such as?"

"You'll be granted a conditional license, which only applies to Lightning and any races he's in."

"That's fine. I have no desire to race any other horse."

"At least for now," her father agreed. "What if down the road you should change your mind and want to race others, especially our own future horses?"

"Isn't that what we have Ted for?" she grinned, nudging him. "Honestly, I can't imagine I ever would. I'm just thrilled I can race Lightning."

"You will also be on probation at first," Scotty added.

"Which means?"

"They could revoke your license at any time, if it's warranted."

"What would warrant that?"

"If Lightning poses a threat to other horses on the track and you can't control him. Of course, in that case he'd probably be banned from racing as well. Let's hope that never happens."

"For sure. I know he's not easy to handle, but I don't think he'd ever challenge another horse like he did at first with Si'ad. All he wants to do now is run. He'd be more apt to interfere or foul another horse if one gets in his way. I'd be more afraid of that."

"Me too," Scotty agreed. "Although he's had a lot of training since those early days. Maybe he's over all that. But then we'll know Saturday. It won't be as easy a race as today's was. You won't be able to run away with that race. We'll need a better strategic plan if we're going to win the Derby."

"The Derby! I still can't believe I'm actually going to race in it." She sighed. "It's been my dream for so long."

"Well, believe it. Because you are," Ted told her.

"I know. Isn't it wonderful?" She reached back and grabbed some of Lightning's mane, pulling his head down to her. "Lightning, you and I are in the Derby," she repeated unnecessarily. The black colt only blew through his nostrils at her, covering her with slime and making everyone laugh as she wrinkled her nose. "Now was that nice?" she asked him. He only shook his head and nuzzled her again for the carrot he knew would be forthcoming. Of course she gave in and pulled one out of her pocket for him.

"Lightning, you and I are in the Derby."

"If that isn't the most spoiled horse," her father said.

"The most spoiled Derby horse," Ann corrected. "Scotty, I just had a thought. Will I have to continue to pretend I'm a boy?"

"For now it's wise. Your dad entered you as "A. J. Collins" again for Saturday."

"You mean we're already entered?"

"Sure thing, "Michael said. "As soon as we got the go-ahead, I made out the final entry. He's in. They agreed with me to leave the name as is. Has anyone noticed when you exercise him each morning?"

"Not so far. I just stick my hair under my cap, and everyone seems to think I'm one of the boys. Of course I try not to get too close to anyone either."

"Then go with it. If the secret gets out, we'll deal with it then."

"There are a couple of girls making it into the ranks as exercise girls," Scotty noted, "but none seem to be here. I think only at some of the smaller tracks."

"Then Ann will start a revolution," her mother said, smiling.

"She just might," Michael agreed, "especially if Lightning is successful. She just might."

"Do you think that's one concern of the Jockey Club?"

"Yes, I do, Ann," Scotty said seriously. "Up to now, it's always been a man's world exclusively. There are some who don't want to give that up. Old traditions die hard. You could be setting a precedent for the future. If you're successful, other girls will want to race, too."

"I never considered that," she said thoughtfully. "And we will be successful. We're going to win, right, fella?" Lightning only shook his head to dislodge a pesky fly, which she took as a yes.

"So, getting back to your question," her father said, getting her back on track, "continue to keep your hair covered when you exercise him each morning. If someone guesses, we'll handle it then. On Saturday, you'll have to change again here in the tack stall, like you did today."

"Which reminds me, Ann," her mother said. "Where are your silks? I need to take them home and get them clean for Saturday."

"Where I left them. On the trunk," Ann pointed. Her mother scooped them up and put them in a bag, muttering under her breath about her daughter's carelessness. Ann only grinned behind her back and pretended she didn't hear her.

"If you kids want to see the Derby Trial, you'd better hurry," Scotty put in. "It's nearly time."

Taking Jock with them, Ann and Ted scampered toward the distant track. They sought a spot along the rail in front of the stands, where crowds were already pushing forward to get a good look as the horses paraded past them. It was difficult, but they were able to slip in near the corner against the rail. From there they could just make out the finish line off to their right.

"Which Derby colts are running?" Jock asked them.

"The two from Maryland—Celtic Glow and Solitaire—plus Orbit, from Virginia," Ted replied. "Don't know anything about Orbit. We tried to see him, but he was out of his stall each time we went by."

"All I know is that he's a bright red bay," Ann put in.

"Then could that be him?" Jock said as the horses came past them. "The one with the pink and white silks?"

"I think so." She studied the horse in question, a handsome bay with lots of white, bearing the colors of High Venture Farms. He was full of himself and was giving his jockey and outrider a tough time keeping him under control.

"He's going to burn himself out before he ever gets to the post," Jock decided. "Is he always like that?"

"From what I've heard. He's a real handful," Ted said.

"Then I hope we don't draw next to him," Ann said.

The horses moved on down the track to the starting gate and were loaded without a hitch. As the gates burst open, they broke together as a pack, surging forward toward the first turn. By the time they reached it, they'd sorted themselves out. Orbit rushed to the front with the rest of the field strung out behind him. He maintained his lead through the far turn, where he burned himself out and soon fell victim to the fresher horses, several passing him with ease. As they came into the homestretch, it was anybody's horse race as at least six horses were bunched up in the lead. They stayed that way for nearly a furlong before Celtic Glow and Solitaire broke away from the pack. They battled all the way down to the wire, with Celtic Glow edging out his stable mate at the end to win by a head.

"Well, that was exciting," Jock said as they made their way back to the barn area. Celtic Glow had won the Derby Trial in an impressive time, though the heavy favorites Roan Rambler and Calculated Risk were not entered. "He might be one to watch."

"They all are—even Orbit," Ann replied.

"Why would you say that? He looked very disappointing out there."

"Which means his trainer will come up with a different strategy before he runs again, don't you think?"

"You're right," Jock said thoughtfully. "He'll have to, if he wants to be competitive on Saturday. Maybe that's why they ran him today. Let him get the feel of the track and see what they need to work on."

Ted nodded. "And that's where Ann has an advantage, too. She and Lightning know what to expect."

"To a certain extent. But today the stands were nowhere near as full as they'll be on Saturday. They say there's nothing quite like coming around that bend and being hit by that wall of noise on Derby Day."

"How do you think Lightning will handle it?" Jock asked.

"We'll find out Saturday, won't we?" was Ann's ambiguous reply.

On the way back to the stable area, they met Rusty and some of the other stable boys. Rusty waved to his friends, then joined up with them, talking excitedly about the race they'd just witnessed.

"The Derby's going to be a fast pace, if the Trial was any indication," he said.

"Think your horse can handle it?" Ted remarked.

"Of course," he said loyally. "He's pretty fast."

"Guess his owner's wouldn't have entered him if he wasn't," was Ann's response. "But you may have even more competition."

"What do you mean?"

They'd reached their stalls by then. Ann walked up to greet her colt. Then with a flourish, she said, "Meet the latest entry for the Kentucky Derby!"

"What? You're kidding, right?" Rusty looked shocked.

"Nope. Dad just entered him, didn't you, Dad?"

Michael nodded. "Sure did. Paid for it with Lightning's winnings actually. We were only waiting until he had his first race. Just to make sure he'd handle the track and all," he explained, leaving out other pertinent details. "So, I guess it's no longer a secret, huh?"

Ann looked abashed. "Sorry, but Rusty's our friend. We had to tell him. After all, everyone will know by tomorrow we're harboring a Derby colt."

"She's right, Michael," Scotty defended her. "No sense in keeping that part a secret anymore. Once he's entered, it becomes public knowledge."

"Oh, gosh," Ann moaned. "That means the reporters will know, too. Here I thought we could stay anonymous like we've been. Do you think we'll have to suffer all those interviews?"

"Probably some of the reporters will want a story. What do you think, Scotty?"

"Well, Michael, there's no stopping the press. But as we aren't the favorites, hopefully we won't draw as much attention."

"Does it matter that much?" Rusty asked, confused.

"Reporters make Ann nervous," Ted replied, grinning at her. She poked him back. "No, really they do," he continued, a teasing glint in his eye.

"So when they come around, I'll let you handle it," she told him. "You're the big mouth around here."

"How true. Strike one for Ann," Jock said with a laugh.

They both looked ready to tear into each other, so Michael diffused them with a suggestion. "Before you two get into another argument, how about we eat? Your mom made a wonderful supper, and it would be a shame for it to go to waste."

"Now you're talking." Ted did an about-face and headed for the food piled on a folding table next to the tack stall. The next few minutes were silent as they all savored Jessica's culinary skills. Everyone agreed she'd outdone herself this time.

"Maybe you're all just hungry," she said with a shrug. "Save room for the pie." A chorus of affirmatives greeted her, and it didn't take long for them to put away the whole pie.

As soon as they were finished, Rusty left to return to his barn. Jessica gathered up the few scraps that were left and said, "Get together your dirty laundry for me to take back home. Ann, I got yours from Mrs. Barton, and I left you some fresh clothes. Now I just need yours—Ted, Scotty." They hastened to comply, though not without some banter at Ted's expense over Ann snatching his clothes to wear.

When that was done, Michael said, "Well, we best be going. Chores await us." At Ann's disappointed look, he added. "What? You're not having enough fun without your boring parents around?"

She giggled. "Yes, we are. I mean, not that I don't want you two around but—well, this *has* been an amazing experience."

"And it's only going to get better," her mother added. "Enjoy every minute, Honey. You've certainly earned it."

"And so did you, Dad. Finally you'll been able to put Stormy Hill back on top. We've got a Derby colt at last. Now if we can only win it."

"Don't think about that," her dad said. "Just enjoy the moment. Go out and ride your best ride on Saturday. That's all your mom and I expect of you. Anything can happen in the Derby. Just ask Scotty. Some things are beyond your control, so don't worry too much. If it's meant to happen, it will. In the meantime, you and Ted go and have fun this week. We'll see you Friday afternoon."

"Thanks, Dad. Guess I needed a pep talk." She gave her father a big hug. "I'm getting nervous just thinking about the race. I've dreamt about this all my life."

"I know you have. But you'll do fine." As he made ready to leave, he added, "Oh, I think we should take Barak back home with us. Lightning seems fine now, and you three will be so busy from now on. He'll only get in the way."

"I suppose so," she said, hugging the dog before handing him over to her father. She gave them each another hug, and then turned to Jock. "I wish you could stay, too. But it's wonderful of you to handle the chores so Ted could come."

"I appreciate that," he said. "And I don't think Dad minds a buffer to keep you and Ted in line."

"Actually, they've been behaving themselves most of the time," Scotty cut in. "And I've got to say, at the risk of giving Ted a bigger head than he's already got, he's been a great help. Kind of glad you talked me into bringing him."

"So am I," Ted grinned. "Thanks, Pal. It's been a heck of ride so far."

"And it'll get better," his friend told him. "Remember—I was there once, too. Tag and I had our moment."

"And before we relive those days all over again, I think we better get out of here," Michael smiled. With that they were off, a reluctant Barak in tow.

Before Ann had time to miss them, Ted was suggesting that they go join their friends for what had become a nightly ritual. They found several of the stable boys, including Rusty, gathered at the outside tables next to the track kitchen. A couple were just finishing their dinners. Ted and Ann were immediately hailed.

"What's this Rusty tells us you've got a Derby entry in your barn?" a short, sandy-haired boy named Freddie asked. "Been holding out on us, huh?"

"The decision was made only after he won his maiden this afternoon," Ann said, brushing it off.

"I see," said Max, a stable boy connected with Overflow, a long shot from New Mexico. "So now that you're in, what do you think of your chances?"

Ted smiled casually, "Probably same as everyone else's I guess. You know the Derby."

"Yeah, yeah. Anything can happen," said Chip, a tall lean boy with a bad complexion, who tended to be gruff at times to hide a severe case of shyness. "We all know that. But really, what are your chances? After all, he's in your barn."

Ann only shook her head. "His first race was today, and he won by four lengths. That doesn't tell us much. He's fast, but so are all the colts—or they wouldn't be entered. Guess you'll have to wait until Saturday."

Rusty, always the pacifist, jumped in. "Well I, for one, think it's pretty exciting. Max has Overflow, I've got Time Tester, and now we have another horse to root for. Let's hope one of our horses wins."

"Don't forget Jake, who just arrived from California with Turnabout," said Max. "They got in last night. Met him out at Santa Anita earlier this year. Real nice guy. He's going to try and join us later."

Ted's ears perked up. "Santa Anita, you say? Ever know a trainer who went by Old Ben?"

"Naw, but Jake might. He spent more time at that track than I did."

"I'll ask him then," Ted said nonchalantly, without explaining further. Ann caught his glance though. It would mean a lot to Ted to find out something about the old trainer who played such an important part in his early life.

Unfortunately, Jake failed to show before the group broke up. They sat around for a little while longer, mostly talking about the upcoming Derby, rehashing each horse's chances until it was time to turn in.

On the way back, Ted mentioned Jake to Ann. "Hope I get to meet him soon. Wouldn't it be great if he knows Old Ben? Or at least has heard about him?"

"Yeah, that would be great for you. I know you'd love to hear how he's doing."

Ted nodded. "I owe everything to that old man," was all he said, but those words spoke volumes.

17

ANTICIPATION

When Ann brought Lightning out onto the track the next morning, she was surprised by the increased activity. Several of the Derby colts were being worked, and the railbirds were in great abundance. She watched as Time Tester and a horse she did not know breezed past them. She said to Ted, "Rusty's colt looks good this morning."

Ted nodded as he pointed to a big, golden chestnut colt coming up behind them. There was no mistaking the California favorite, Calculated Risk. He was as thrilling to watch in motion as he had been posing before his stall when he arrived the previous Saturday. His coat had a burnished copper hue, heightened by the early rays of dawn. It was as if wherever he went he was bathed in a golden halo. She knew Scotty was watching his process very closely. His record of being undefeated in all his California races made him the bookies' favorite choice for an upset against Roan Rambler.

Thinking about the favorite, Ann looked around but did not see the distinctive red roan. He might be on the far side of the track—unless he'd already been worked or hadn't made an appearance yet. The track was awful busy this morning. Since Lightning had raced yesterday, Ann doubted that Scotty would want her to breeze him today. She was somewhat relieved about that because of all this traffic, but she knew she couldn't avoid it. He would just have to get used to it.

Fortunately, Lightning was easier to handle this morning. Most likely the race yesterday had taken the edge off. That and the fact that this was the fourth morning straight she'd brought him out here to exercise. He could be falling into the routine, recognizing the distinction between the two trips to the track. He was smart enough to catch on to the difference. She bent over and stroked his black neck, already shiny with sweat. Her confidence in him welled up as she anticipated the upcoming challenge against these other colts. She grinned over at Ted as three more horses passed them going in the other direction at a full gallop. Reading her thoughts, he grinned back at her.

As dawn cleared the sky, a light mist rose, bathing the horses and track in a near-mystical beauty. Right at that moment, there was no place in the world she'd rather be than on her beloved horse, cantering along the Churchill Downs track. And she knew without words that Ted felt the same.

When Scotty called them in, they both came reluctantly, neither wanting to break the perfection of that one moment in time. Yet only minutes later they were laughing and teasing each other as they bathed their horses.

Ted accidentally got her with the hose as he sprayed Banshee, and she responded with a well-aimed sponge right in the center of his back. It quickly escalated into a full-scale, no-holds-barred war. The end result left them soaked to the skin and had Scotty muttering something about "teenagers" before he made a hasty retreat to the safety of his colleagues. His parting remark was, "You better make sure both those horses are cooled out before you put them away."

Chagrined, they agreed, but they burst into laughter as soon as he was out of sight. Ann tried unsuccessfully to wring out her long wet hair, which had come loose from the braid, before turning the hose on her head and washing away the dirty, soapy mess. Then she ducked into the tack stall and grabbed a towel to wrap her hair in. She also snitched one of Ted's sweatshirts for a quick change into something dry before returning to walk out her colt.

Ted, on the other hand, ignored his wet condition in favor of finishing the task of scraping Banshee free of excess water. As Ann went by him, blatantly refusing to acknowledge his presence, he grumbled, "Isn't that one of *my* sweatshirts you're wearing?"

"Well you got me wet. It was dry. So I took it," she rationalized, placing Lightning between her and Ted, who might have retaliation in mind. However, they couldn't stay mad at each other for long. It was too perfect a day. They were both where they always wanted to be, and they knew it. They walked along, not minding what was generally considered a boring chore. This morning belonged to them.

By the time Lightning was dry and nearly ready to come in, Ann decided she wanted to find him some green grass to eat, so they took the horses in search of a grazing spot. The one they found was already in use, but there was plenty of room for two more horses. As she entered the area, she thought she recognized the horse.

"Isn't that Turnabout from California?" she asked the groom who held the chestnut's lead rope.

The dark-haired boy nodded. "Yeah, he's a Derby colt, all right."

"Then you must be Jake," Ted guessed excitedly.

Again he nodded. "How did you know?" he asked.

"We met a friend of yours—Max—from New Mexico. His stable's running Overflow," Ann explained.

"Oh, yeah, Max. We were all at Santa Anita together a couple of weeks ago. He's a great guy. Ran into him the other night when we arrived, but only had time to say hi. How's he doing?"

"Fine," Ted replied. "He mentioned you were coming. I guess he thought you'd join a group of us who kind of hang out each evening."

"I wanted to, but got too busy with my chores." He shrugged. "You know how it goes, this being Derby Week and all."

"Yep, that we do," Ted agreed.

"I'll get over there tonight if I can." Then he looked expectantly at them.

"Oh, I'm sorry," Ann said, realizing Jake didn't know who they were. "I'm Ann and this is Ted. We're over in barn 39. We've been here since Friday."

"And your horse is?" He stared critically at the black colt Ann was holding. As with any true horseman, he could see that this colt's quality was above that of the average Thoroughbred.

"Stormy Lightning. A late entry," Ann told him proudly. "We're from right here in Kentucky."

"A looker," he commented. "And Kentucky-bred. Nice combination."

Ted could contain his curiosity no longer. "Max said he knew you out at Santa Anita?"

"That's right."

"Did you ever come across a trainer there by the name of Old Ben?"

"Old Ben, hmm. Sure did. Funny old coot. Full of stories of the old days. Used to hang out with a couple of the other old has-beens. They were all a bunch of characters, as I remember."

"How is he?"

"Poor guy up and died a couple a months ago."

"Died?" Ted realized he'd been holding his breath, and at the news let it out with a big whoosh.

"Lung cancer, I think it was. Always smoked like a chimney." Suddenly aware of Ted's stricken reaction, he said more sympathetically, "Did you know him?"

"Yeah. Taught me everything I know about racing," he said sadly. Ann, comprehending what a blow the news was to Ted, went up to him and placed her hand on his arm supportively.

"I'm sorry. I didn't mean to sound so calloused. He really was a great old guy. You must be good then if Old Ben took you under his wing. That old man forgot more than most people ever know about the racing world."

Ann thanked him with her eyes for trying to make Ted feel better. "Oh, he's good. You should see him with Si'ad, his stallion at home. That horse'll do anything for him."

Ted had the courtesy to blush. "Si'ad's as good as any horse here," he said loyally.

"Except Lightning, of course," Ann countered, rubbing her horse's neck.

"Hah! He got his speed from his father, you know."

"But Lightning's still faster," she argued. Then, seeing that Ted was about to take a swipe at her with his lead rope, she nudged Lightning, who accommodated her by bending his left foreleg so she could vault up on him.

"No fair," Ted yelled. "You can't hide up there." Then he leaped on Banshee's back, trying to inch closer to her. But Ann only laughed as she whirled Lightning away. The colt shook his head at being pulled away from the succulent grass.

"Just try and get me, Ted Winters," she said, laughing. "You're not on Si'ad now."

"I told you, this morning was an accident," he fired back, easing Banshee ever closer, jousting for position. Each time he got near, Ann only nudged Lightning in the other direction. The game went on that way for several minutes, finally ending in a draw.

Meanwhile Jake stared at the two, aghast. "Can you two do that?" he asked.

"What do you mean?" Ann smiled back, having thwarted Ted one more time.

"Ride him like that? Isn't he a Derby colt?"

"Yes, but what does that have to do with anything? I ride Lightning all the time," Ann said without thinking.

"Aren't you his groom?"

"Sure—that, among other things." Then she realized suddenly how it looked to an outsider. "Oh, I see." She had no idea what to say without giving herself away.

Ted, realizing her dilemma, jumped in to clarify. "Ann hand-raised him on her parents' farm," he explained. "That horse will do anything for her. He's really a big baby in her hands."

"Oh," Jake said, apparently accepting that. "Well, I'd better get this one back to his stall before they come looking for me. It was nice to meet both of you. See you tonight?"

"Count on it," Ted replied, sliding down from Banshee to shake his hand. "And thanks for telling me about Old Ben." Just the thought saddened him again.

"You were lucky to have learned under him. That old codger was quite a trainer in his day." Then he waved to Ann, still sitting atop Lightning.

She regretfully slid off her horse. "Guess I'd better walk him back to the barn, too," she sighed. "Don't want to shock any more people."

"Don't worry. It'll be my secret," Jake assured her. "Very impressive, though. Too bad girls aren't jockeys. I get the feeling that if you can ride him bareback, you'd be good at it."

"Thanks," she mumbled, ducking her head and quickly becoming preoccupied with Lightning's lead rope. "Gotta run. See you later."

As soon as they were out of earshot, Ted said, "If he only knew."

"He'll know soon enough," she said, sighing. "Gosh, I hope no one lets it out at least till race day. This place is already crawling with reporters. I don't think I can go through that."

"At the moment he's still a long shot. Maybe that'll keep them from showing much interest in him."

"I don't know. Someone is bound to come looking for a story. Hope Scotty's around when they do. He can deal with the press better than me."

Then a thought struck Ted. "Do you think he'll recognize you when you exercise Lightning in the morning? If he does, I hope he won't give you away."

"I don't think so. But Jake seems pretty observant. He's bound to recognize me on Lightning if he spots me out there. Still, he said he would keep it quiet."

"We'll have to wait and see. He may not get close enough to notice, since he's only Turnabout's groom."

"Seems like a nice guy though. Imagine running into someone who knew your old friend."

"Yes, wasn't it? Too bad Old Ben died. I'd have loved to see him again, let him know what happened to me. If it wasn't for him…" He let the thought hang in the air as sadness settled over him.

"Let him know you turned out okay?" Ann said sincerely. "I'm sure he knows, wherever he is."

"Yeah, maybe."

By the time they got back to the stalls, they found Scotty had returned also. He eyed them critically. "I see you two still seem to be intact," he observed. "Why don't you put the horses away and let's grab some lunch? I'll just tell Jay next door where we're going."

"Sounds good to me," Ted agreed, putting Banshee in his stall. He checked his water bucket and added another flake of hay before slipping into the tack stall to change to cleaner clothes. As he did, he noticed the pile of extra sweatshirts and T-shirts Jessica had left behind the day before. *If Ann keeps swiping mine, will we make it till Saturday?* he wondered with a grin.

He was still grinning when he exited his makeshift home. "What's the grin for?" Ann asked him as they started over to the track kitchen.

"Oh, nothing," he said mysteriously. Sometimes it was better to leave well enough alone.

Fortunately Scotty interrupted with, "Now that Lightning's officially declared in the Derby, I don't want him left alone."

Ann turned to him, suddenly concerned. "You don't think anyone would try to do something to him, do you?" she asked.

"I'm sure he's perfectly safe. He's not considered a threat by anyone but us." He grinned to put their minds at rest. "But it *is* the Derby. And I've been talking to other trainers. Everyone's got guards on their colts. So, 'better safe than sorry,' as the saying goes."

"Shouldn't one of us stay back with him then?" Ted wanted to know.

"That's why I asked Jay next door to keep an eye on him," he said. "He's going to be hanging around the rest of the afternoon anyway. I've known Jay a long time. He's very reliable. He'll watch him as if he was one of his own."

"That's good. You're right though, Scotty," Ann said, relaxing visibly. "We can just make sure one of us is always around. We've come too far to get careless now."

"I don't care about watching the races this afternoon," Ted volunteered. "I'll sit with him."

"Neither do I," Ann said. "I'll stay with Ted—and Scotty, you can go watch or visit with your trainer friends, if you want."

"Sure?" he asked. "This is your time, too."

"I'm sure," Ann said emphatically. "I'd rather hang out with Lightning. 'Sides, we've already seen several races." Then she laughed, "And I get to see an awful lot of that track each morning."

"Yeah, I guess you do," Scotty said, smiling. They arrived at the kitchen's ordering window. "Three cheeseburgers, please, with fries, and—what do you want to drink?" They made their requests. The food was served quickly, and they grabbed a table. As they sat, Ann noticed Rusty and some of the other stable boys sitting at a table nearby. She waved and sat down beside Scotty.

"If you two want to join your friends, that's fine," he said.

"Naw. We'll see them tonight," Ted replied.

"Maybe not," Scotty said. "Tonight is the trainers' party. I figured you'd want to go with me."

"Isn't it just for trainers?" Ann asked

"No—everyone who's involved with one of the colts is included. Along with the usual prominent people."

"You'll get to hobnob with the rich and famous," Ted teased.

She made a face at him. "So will you," she countered.

"How so? Someone's got to stay back and watch Lightning."

"I've already got that figured out," Scotty told them. "There'll be lots of security around here to see that the Derby colts are kept safe. But Jay's got two grooms who will also be sticking close.

"From now on there will be parties every night." Catching the look on their faces, he added, "What? It's Derby Week. For most people, that's what this week is all about. Nothing but one big party."

"Do we have to go to *all* of them?" Ann wailed. The thought made her nauseous.

Seeing the expression on her face, Scotty relented. "No, not if you don't want to."

"Oh, good."

"But tonight is important."

"So you want us to go."

"I'd like for you to go. Neither of you have ever been to one of these parties. They *are* a lot of fun. You'll see."

"But I won't know anyone. And I'll have to wear a *dress*," she moaned.

Ted laughed. "Dress. Yeah, that's the real reason," he teased. "Come on. I'll be there. You'll know one person."

"No fair," she cried. "You *want* to go."

"Why not? As Scotty says, it'll be fun. And there'll be lots of food."

"Yeah, that's the real reason *you* want to go." She poked him. "Okay, okay. You twisted my arm. I'll go."

After they finished eating, while Scotty went off to join some of his old friends, Ann and Ted talked about it some more back at the barn.

"Surely you've been to these parties before?" he asked her.

"Oh, yeah, but I was much younger, just a kid. No one pays much attention to a kid. And we didn't have a Derby entry then."

"What difference should that make?"

"Well, people are bound to come up and talk to us. What would I say?"

Ted smiled. He knew she was shy. "They won't all be strangers," he told her. "You do know a lot of the owners, don't you? I mean through Scotty and your folks?"

"Oh sure, I know who they are. But it'll be different if I have to carry on a conversation with them. And what do I say about Lightning? What if I let slip something that implies I'll be riding him?"

"Just stay with Scotty and me. We'll do all the talking."

"I guess it's okay. They know I raised him from an orphan. After all, Dad's name is down as owner. Everyone can see we bred him. That will lend credence to why I'm here with him, I guess."

"It worked with Jake."

"Yep, that's right." She looked pensive. "Maybe it won't be so bad after all."

"And there's bound to be lots of good food," he added.

"The food again. That's the Ted *I* know. Always thinking with your stomach. I can't wait to see you all dressed up in a suit."

"How do you know I own one?" he grinned. "Maybe I'll just show up in a clean T-shirt."

"Like Scotty would let you. Sorry. I saw Mom pack one for each of you in that garment bag hanging up in there." She pointed to the tack stall. "You're stuck, too. You have to wear it."

He was about to reply when a single reporter approached them. He waved to get their attention and walked right up to them, assuming they would welcome him. "You the folks who have a Derby colt in your stable?" He was short, bald, and appeared to be sweating a lot, as it had turned quite warm. He looked very uncomfortable in his suit jacket. His shirt was wet from perspiration, and his tie was pulled loose. He had an arrogant air that turned both of them off from the start.

"He's entered," Ted pointed toward Lightning's stall.

He looked down at what appeared to be a wrinkled racing form and some loose sheets of paper. "And which one is this?"

"Stormy Lightning," Ted replied.

He glanced at his notes some more, and then brightened in recognition. "Oh, yeah, the long shot," he said, his manner changing to one of almost boredom. "What can you tell me about him? Didn't you just enter him yesterday?"

Ann only nodded, irritated by his tone.

"Looks like he's only been in one race," he went on, annoying them further. "What makes you think he's good enough for the Derby?"

"You'd have to ask his trainer," Ted said, trying hard to be polite. "He's not here right now."

The reporter dismissed the suggestion, apparently bent on getting a story anyway. "So is he fast?" he persisted.

"He's fast," was all Ann would offer.

He took another look at Lightning, who was nonchalantly eating his hay. "Nice looking horse, though. I'll give you that. Who'd you hire to ride him Saturday?"

"Hasn't been decided yet," Ted said quickly. *If he wants to know so bad, let him look it up,* he thought angrily. This reporter was really beginning to rub him the wrong way. He could feel Ann tensing beside him, and knew she felt the same.

"Better not wait too long. All the good ones have already been taken at this late date anyway."

Ted said nothing.

"Who's his trainer?"

"Scott MacDougal," Ann stated simply.

"Don't know him. Well, gotta go see about some of the other horses so I can put this story to bed. Here's my card. If you think of anything else, let me know." He was gone as quickly as he showed up. No "Thank you for your time," no "Good luck." Nothing.

"Of all the arrogant, obnoxious people." Ted grimaced, crumpling the card in his hand and depositing it in the trash.

"As if we'd tell him anything with that kind of attitude," Ann said. "The nerve. He just wrote Lightning off as if he wasn't even in the race."

He could tell though that she was hurt by the encounter. "Don't let it worry you. Just think about how stupid he's going to feel when you win Saturday."

She smiled weakly. "You think so?"

"I know so. That's the best strategy ever. No one will be expecting it, because he's such a long shot. Then you'll come racing down to the finish line and they'll all go 'Who's he?' as you win the race."

She could almost see it. She smiled gratefully. "You're right. I shouldn't get upset over these reporters. Next time I'll just tell them to go talk to Scotty. He knows how to handle them. But they do rile me with their know-it-all attitudes."

"I don't think they are all like that. We just got lucky with this one. That's all."

18

POST POSITION

The party was not so bad after all, as Ann found out. Always one to avoid calling attention to herself, she tried at first to shrink behind Scotty and Ted when they entered. Held at a nearby hotel, the party was sponsored by an organization that had rented their largest room. But even it proved too small as they entered the packed space. It seemed everybody who was anyone in the racing world was in attendance. Right away Ann realized she'd be lucky if she was noticed at all in this mob, and she began to relax.

Scotty was surprised at how many people he did know in the crowd. He seemed to delight in going from group to group, greeting those he remembered from the past. It had only been three years since Tag had run, and being a second-generation trainer for the same farm helped his image. The Kentucky racing world was a tightly knit group where, as a farm that had been in the same family for five generations; they would be well accepted, regardless of their personal fortunes, or lack thereof. Scotty was received as if he'd never been gone for three years.

Each time he stopped to talk to a group, he introduced both Ann and Ted. As all the old families recognized the Collins name, they welcomed Ann with the usual greeting—"So you're Michael's little girl. All grown up I see"—and the like. Ann got to the point where she

169

thought she would scream if she heard it again. She kept making faces at Ted until he suggested they go check out the banquet table. Scotty, absorbed in a lengthy conversation about how the weather could affect the running of the Derby, let them go with a wave.

The long table was laden with all sorts of goodies. Ann and Ted piled their plates high and escaped to a table in the far corner, from where they could people-watch at will. Ann kept Ted entertained with a running who's who, complete with little-known quips about each person who passed within their line of vision.

Ted was surprised at her wealth of knowledge about people in the horse world. "And I only thought you were interested in the horses," he said, chuckling.

She waved it off. "Oh, you know, I grew up around all of this. It's a very small world, where everyone knows everyone else's business. With Dad's feed and tack store, he knows all the gossip—whether he wants to or not."

"I can see that. It's nice of Scotty to introduce me as one of the family, though."

She was surprised to hear him say that. "Why wouldn't he? You are." Sometimes Ted's old insecurities about his background could surface when least expected. "Come on, Ted. You haven't been thought of as 'help' to us since—I don't know—at least the third day after you arrived?"

That made him smile. "Only the third day?"

"Seriously. You're like an adopted son to Dad and Mom. If you don't know that by now—" She playfully slapped his arm. "No more said about it, okay? It's a done deal. We're stuck with you, like it or not."

He had to grin at that. "Okay, okay. I won't mention it again."

To change the subject, she directed his attention to the shifting crowd. "Oh, my gosh. Look who just came in."

"Who?"

"The Garrisons—and they have Greta with them." Their neighbors had broken away from the crowd and were making their way toward the buffet table. "How fast can we get out of here?" she yelped.

Too late. The elder Garrisons spotted Ann at the table and descended on her without hesitation. "Ann, my dear, how wonderful to see you again," Mrs. Garrison gushed. "Greta, Honey, look who's here?" She acted surprised that they would have been invited to this party, when in reality it was they who were the newcomers to the sport. "Oh, and, Ted, isn't it?" Remembering vaguely that he worked for them at various times, her greeting was mainly out of politeness. Ann smiled to herself, thinking how Ted actually had more right to be there than the Garrisons. They weren't running any of their horses at this meet.

"Oh, Ted," Greta cried, "I had no idea you'd be here. How wonderful." She looked like she had every intention of sitting down beside him and drawing him into a long conversation. Ann felt him stiffen beside her and thought fast.

"Yes, nice to see all of you again. However, we have to go find Scotty and bring him some food." She still had her plate, half piled with food that she was too full to eat, though Ted had finished all of his. Taking her plate, she rose. "I know if I don't, he'll be too busy reminiscing with old friends to take the time to eat himself. Coming, Ted?"

Ted shrugged. "Nice to see you again," he said noncommittally as he followed her back into the crowds. Once out of sight, he burst into laughter. "Very slick move, Ann."

"Yes, wasn't it? Sometimes I get positively inspired."

"Boy, she's the last one I'd want to get stuck with here." He grimaced.

Ann sympathized. "And that's just what she had in mind, too. Let's go find Scotty. I'm ready to get out of here and head back anyway."

"So am I. Going to eat that?" He eyed the plate still in her hand.

"No. I was really looking for a trash can."

"Hand it here." He made short work of several items before tossing it in a nearby receptacle.

"Good thing you're not riding Lightning after all," she teased. "He'd never get around the track with you eating like that." She was well aware of Ted's ability to consume vast amounts of food, then burning it off without gaining an ounce. This was not the first time he'd finished what she couldn't eat herself.

"Well, since *you* are, I just thought I'd better help you keep your weight down."

"Right." She smirked at him. Then, seeing Scotty in the crush of people, she swiftly made her way over to him before the crowds cut him off from view.

"You two about ready to go?" he asked.

They nodded. "Just coming to look for you," Ann said.

"Then let's depart. I think I've talked to everyone I wanted to see."

"Oh Ted," Greta cried, "I had no idea you'd be here. How wonderful."

"I don't think you could have possibly missed anyone," Ted assured him. "Do you really know everyone, or does it just seem that way?"

He smiled. "Actually a lot of them knew my dad when he was alive. He was the one with the reputation, not me."

"Yet," Ted added. When Scotty gave him a questioning glance, he clarified. "I think things are going to change shortly."

"I hope so, Son, I hope so."

They returned first to the stalls, where Jay's grooms assured them all was well. There had been no unusual visits from unauthorized personnel while they were gone. They thanked them, offering to return the favor.

While Ted and Scotty slipped into the tack stall to change their clothes, Ann went over to pat her horse. "Careful, fella," she told him. "I'm in my good clothes, so you can't rub against me right now. I may need to wear this dress again." Not comfortable being dressed up around the horses, she was eager to get back to the rooming house and take her dress off before she got it dirty.

Ted volunteered again to walk her back across the street. On the way, she commented to him, "You know, it really was an okay party, as parties go."

"I actually thought it was a lot of fun. Interesting to see how the other half lives."

"You mean the half that doesn't soil their hands out in the barn with their horses, but rather watches the help do it?" There was a twinkle in her eyes as she said it.

"Exactly. They don't know what they're missing."

"How true. I think even if someday we were rich and could hire help, I'd still want to be right here in the trenches, getting dirty with my horses, don't you?"

He nodded. "I couldn't wait to get out of that suit and back into my jeans again. Guess I'll never be fit for company."

"That makes two of us. I can't wait to get this dress off and get back into my real clothes." She'd worn her hair loose that night, but now she pulled it back into a ponytail to get it out of her face.

They reached the porch steps of the boarding house and were about to say goodnight when Momma Millie opened the door. She immediately asked Ted if he wanted to come in for a snack.

"No thanks," he said. "Not tonight. We had entirely too much at the party."

"Of course Ted ate all of his and half of mine," Ann said, laughing. "Tell the truth. That's why you're full."

"Well, then I'll just have to send some snacks with Ann tomorrow morning."

Ted's eyes widened. "Oh, Momma Millie, you'll spoil us," he said in gratitude.

She smiled, touched by his words. "Can't have you two wasting away to nothing," she said.

"I don't think that's likely to happen to Ted," Ann said. She sometimes wondered if his healthy appetite was a direct result of his not getting enough to eat when he was a child. The neglect he'd suffered then had left scars, but only she knew how deep some of them ran. Once again, she was so glad he was having this opportunity to be a part of the whole Derby experience. It meant so much to him.

After he left and she retreated to her room, she thought again about Ted's reaction to Scotty's introduction tonight. Did he really feel that he was still little better than hired help? What would it take to convince him he was one of them? She herself saw him as much a brother to her as Jock. And she was sincere when she told him that her parents considered him as one would an adopted son. On the other hand, memories of those past rejections could come back to haunt him at the least expected times. At those times Ann wished she could help him, though she knew just being his friend was enough. That night she fell into a troubled sleep.

§ § § § §

"Did you see this?" Scotty returned back from a quick breakfast at the track kitchen waving a newspaper agitatedly. "Looks like we made the sports page, but you're not going to like what they wrote."

Ann had finished her morning chores. Lightning was cooled out and put away in a clean stall with fresh water. She and Ted had just polished off the "snack" that Momma Millie had sent over with her that morning, a considerable mound of sausage biscuits and a thermos of coffee. Scotty, on the other hand, had had a desire for eggs so had opted to go over to the kitchen for some. Now he was back, still waving the paper in irritation.

Ann caught the newspaper as he was about to fling it into a chair. "There. Read that column." He pointed to the offending column, written by a well-known track writer notorious for his rapier-like wit. She scanned down the page, noting that there was a rundown of each colt entered in the Derby and what, according to him, his chances of winning were. The second-to-last paragraph caught her eye. She read aloud:

The thirteenth and final entry into the Derby field on Saturday is a last-minute entry, a Kentucky-bred colt by the name of Stormy Lightning. While there's no denying his outward appearance, we are reminded that Thoroughbreds do not run on looks alone. This black colt is basically untried, having only broken his maiden with a win two days ago. Another drawback will be an unknown apprentice jockey in the irons. While he will be going off as a long shot, I wouldn't waste my money on this one, folks. There are some owners who get a thrill seeing their horses in this prestigious race, and it looks like this could be one of them. As the only Kentucky-bred and Kentucky-owned horse in the field, it looks like this year the "Kentucky" Derby will go to another state.

When Ann finished reading, she angrily threw the paper down. "That awful reporter who was here while you were away yesterday. What an obnoxious creep!"

"Arrogant," Ted cried. "Insinuated we weren't worth his trouble because we weren't some big-time outfit!"

"What did he say to you?" Scotty wanted to know. After they told him, he calmed down a bit. "Okay, now I understand. Unfortunately, we do have to deal with those types. I'm sorry I wasn't here to handle it. But you two did right. Don't tell them anything. They can read the racing form. The less they know about us, the better."

"But, Scotty—shouldn't we ask for some kind of rebuttal?" Ann wanted to know. "What he said was insulting."

"Naw. Let it go. I know it hurts, but this way we'll fly under the wire. The more we seem like a non-threat in that race, the easier it'll be for you, Lass. You'll have enough to worry about anyway. This race is nothing like the one you ran Monday. There you had things pretty much your own way. Lightning ran to the head of the pack and stayed there. No one challenged him. It won't be like that this time. You got the cream of the crop out there, and experienced jockeys. They're not going to give you the race, no matter how fast we know our colt is. If none of them think you're a threat, they won't be looking for you. That's to *our* advantage."

"But—" Ann started to argue, but Ted cut her off.

"Scotty's right, Ann. What he says makes sense. Think about it."

She thought for a minute. "Well, I guess I see your point. Still, I hate to have those things said about him, and us."

"Then make him eat his words. Go out and win Saturday," Scotty challenged.

"Okay, I will," she said, looking more confident than she felt at the moment.

"Here's something that will cheer you up," Scotty said, changing the subject. "There are more parties tonight and tomorrow night—"

They both groaned.

"But you'll be happy to know that neither of you have to go—unless you want to, of course." He was greeted with another round of groans.

Ann sighed. "Not if it means I have to dress up again," she said.

"Same goes for me," Ted said.

Scotty smiled. "Then I take it as a 'no'?" After they nodded, he continued. "But we'll all be going to the owner's party Friday night. Even your parents are coming in for that one. Jock has volunteered to stay back and watch after Lightning."

"Lucky him," Ann said, although it was well known that Jock hated parties, so no one was surprised.

"Well, I'm glad that's settled. Now this afternoon it's your turn to go watch some races if you want," Scotty said. "I'll just stay here."

"You're sure?" Ted asked.

"Yep. Some of the guys are coming by anyway. You two go and have some fun with your friends for a change."

They did just that. They found several of their new friends, including Rusty and Jake, and they all headed for a spot along the rail in front of the stands where they could get a good view of each race. There they joked and kidded with each other as they tried to guess which horse would win. Their guesses, based on the knowledge they had gleaned from their time spent on the backside, had some merit. Some of the horses had been observed during their morning workouts. Others were known by the stable running them or by tips from their grooms. It was fun to speculate on the winners. In the end, they all figured that had they been betting they would have broken even or possibly been a little bit ahead.

"Enough to pay for a round of these cheeseburgers," Jake joked as they ended the afternoon at the track kitchen.

Rusty speculated. "Doesn't sound like it's enough to give up our day jobs and become bookies."

"It's still fun anyway," Chip said. "What say we do this again, maybe Saturday?"

Ann looked at Ted, but before they could say anything, Jake jumped in. "Well, I don't know. Three of us have Derby colts running. We're probably gonna be too busy to watch any races."

"Won't you get to see the big one?" Chip asked.

"I hope so. But I'm not sure where I'll be watching it from," Jake said.

Well I know where I'll be for that race—right in the middle of it, Ann thought, smiling. Ted caught her smile and returned it with one of his own. If anyone noticed their glances, no one said a word.

"Guess we'll just have to see," was all Rusty said.

The rest of the day passed uneventfully, except for the increase in traffic around the barns. As Derby Week progressed, they all noticed the heightened activity, as well as a tightening of security. By now all the gate guards knew her and Ted, though they were asked to show their passes each time anyway. She did not mind if it kept the undesirables out. But it did remind her each time of the magnitude of this event. Not just the horse world, but other circles came together for this, the oldest sporting event in the country.

Having grown up on a Kentucky horse farm, Ann had always accepted the Kentucky Derby as a ritual that took place the first Saturday in May every year. Her family couldn't even imagine not attending. Box seats in the famous old grandstand were carefully hoarded by the farms that were lucky enough to have one. They were almost impossible to get, because often families passed them on as a legacy to their children. That was how Ann's family had come by their box. It had belonged to a Collins for several generations now. Michael would never even consider giving it up when the payment came due, no matter how broke they might be at the time. His dream had always been that one day he would sit in it to watch his colt win the Derby. How many times had she heard him express that desire during her childhood? Could this be the year? It was all up to her to make her dad's dreams come true. And her own.

§ § § § §

Thursday it rained. Ann found her morning workout with Lightning distasteful for the first time all week. For one thing, it poured the whole time. For another, the track seemed crowded with horses, as if everyone wanted to get it over with on this miserable day so they could return to the shed rows and dry out. She was almost happy Scotty decided not to breeze him as she watched others flying down the track, mud slinging in all directions. She fervently hoped the rain would be gone by Saturday. As it was, she returned to their stalls covered in mud and slime. The only upside was that when she looked at Ted, she saw he was just as filthy.

Fortunately it was a warm rain. During the horses' bath, she and Ted managed to spray as much water on each other as they did their horses—only this time there was no malice as they attempted to remove as much filth from themselves as they could. The end result left them far more recognizable—a least that was Scotty's comment after seeing them. But it also meant another raid on Ted's fast disappearing pile of clean clothes.

Ann relented at his reaction to her thievery. "I'll ask Momma Millie if I can run some of these things through her washer," she offered. That seemed to appease his sense of justice for the moment.

True to her word, she returned to the boarding house later that morning, dirty laundry in hand, and made a bargain with the kind woman. When Ted walked her back to the boarding house that evening, Momma Millie presented him with a pile of fresh, clean clothes, for which he was grateful. Her kitchen also smelled of hot cherry cobbler, an irresistible temptation. Once again he could be coerced to stay for a piece.

The next morning, not long after the horses were put away, Scotty announced that it was time to go over to the office to pick their post position. When they got there, they found the room crowded with trainers, owners, and others connected the Derby colts. The noise level was high, as excitement permeated the air. A favorable post position could mean the difference between a good start and a poor showing. With the best three-year-olds of that year's crop entered, even the slightest edge was significant. A race could be won or lost at the starting gate.

As serious as having a good post position was, there was still a lot of good-natured ribbing among the trainers, who'd all known each other for years. The better ones had earned the respect of their peers, even when they had horses running against each other. The Derby was no exception.

Ann and Ted felt a little out of their league, in awe of it all. They took a seat by Scotty while the person in charge described the rules and process by which each colt would be assigned his post position the following day. It was quite simple. The numbers were placed in a hat, and each trainer would pull the number to be assigned his entry.

First to be called up was Orbit's trainer, who reached into the hat, then made a face as he pulled out number nine and held it up for all to see. Grumbling amiably as he made his way back to his seat, he nevertheless slapped Regg Conti on the back and wished him better luck as he went up to draw for Calculated Risk. Seconds later the trainer from California let out a whoop of joy as he held up number one. His disclosure at having snagged the choice spot was quickly followed by jeers and groans, as those yet to pick voiced their reaction. As Calculated Risk was the favored second who could possibly upset Roan Rambler, a good post position could be the winning factor.

Next to go was Neal Wyatt, Rambler's trainer, who withdrew another low number—three. As he held it up, there was a crescendo of noise as speculation flew about the room. With the favorite being just two horses away from the rail, he was in a very good position to offset the California colt's advantage.

The drawing continued. Each number that was drawn received its own battery of comments, some favorable, some not so. The brown colt, Pinch Hitter, so named because his owner had a baseball franchise, drew the number two spot. Known for having a lot of early speed, the colt from New York would probably break quickly, which could prove very interesting since he was sandwiched between the two favorites.

Time Tester would race from the number four gate, a fact that did not escape Ann and Ted, who remarked to each other that they were glad for Rusty's sake. The horse was considered a possible threat with the right racing luck.

They waited to hear how Max and Jake's charges faired. Turnabout would run from number seven and Max's horse, Overflow, drew an outside position of number twelve. Others came up to draw until there were only two trainers left to pick. Ann had been keeping track of the numbers as they were pulled, so she knew the two numbers left were number five and thirteen. She held her breath as Royalair's trainer went up to the podium. It seemed to take forever before he raised his number for all to see. By the pleased expression on his face, she already knew he had number five in his hand. A sigh went through her. Then Scotty went up as the last trainer, but it was only a formality as he pulled out the remaining number thirteen and showed it to the audience. It was dutifully recorded and he returned to his seat.

"Lucky Thirteen," he muttered as he sat down beside them.

"I hope so, this time," Ann said with a grimace.

The room began to empty as clusters of men filed out, each discussing the results of the draw and what it would mean to his colt's chances. Ann and Ted straggled silently behind Scotty, somewhere near the back of the crowd. Nothing was said until they returned to their stalls.

"What bad luck," Ann said as she lowered herself into a lawn chair.

"Yeah, really," Ted agreed.

"I don't know, kids," Scotty contradicted. "Maybe not."

"Why would you say that?" Ann wanted to know, surprised.

"Well, you two are both green to this racing. Perhaps it's not so bad that you'll be breaking from the outside. At least you'll avoid the traffic jam to the first turn."

Ann appeared to ponder the merit in his words. "But won't that put him in the back of the pack?"

"Several of those colts are quick out of the box. Pitch Hitter for one. With him breaking between Calculated Risk and Roan Rambler, I rather expect those jockeys will be busy fending each other off, looking for a good rail position. The rest are going to be pretty bunched too. I think our best strategy may be to let them go and rely on Lightning's early speed to come from the outside and get yourself a spot somewhere in the middle at least down the backstretch. I'm hoping you can pull him in once you find your place. The less traffic he has to deal with the better, far as I'm concerned."

"And if I can't hold him? You know how strong he is. I barely got him back in Monday's race."

"Well, he can't go wire to wire at top speed, Lass—not in a race like this one's going to be. I know he's headstrong, but he'll listen to you."

"I hope so."

"Getting cold feet?" he asked sympathetically.

"I'm not sure. As it gets closer to the time I'm—well, I'm just nervous, that's all. It's not that I don't want to ride him. I do. I've always wanted to be his rider," she added fervently. "But, Scotty, what if I let him down? What if I screw up?"

Scotty knew exactly how she felt. She was, after all, still a child—and for all her talent, she was facing the unknown out on that track. Did they expect too much of her? Lightning was a big, powerful horse with fantastic speed, and he adored her beyond reason—would do anything for her, in fact. Still, for all his training this past year, he was not that far removed from his wild period. His experiences during the time he was away from them had nearly destroyed the mild, gentle colt she'd raised and turned him into an almost savagely independent stallion. Were they wrong to try to reform him into a racehorse? Worse, would he endanger the other colts in tomorrow's race, should he revert to his wild side? Did they trust too much that the strong bond between him and Ann would make him obey her out there? Would he choose to run with the heart of his Thoroughbred ancestors—or the wild forebears of his desert-bred sire? These thoughts concerned Scotty, but as he looked into her troubled face, he knew he could express none of them to her.

Instead he put an arm around her narrow shoulders and said softly, "Lass, you could never let us down. When the time comes, you and your horse will run a brilliant race. You two will give everything you've got. We all know that. And if by chance you don't cross that finish line first, you will have the satisfaction of knowing you gave it your all. This I believe with all my heart. And I know your parents feel the same. We all couldn't be prouder of you."

A tear slid down her cheek as Scotty's words sank in. She reached out and hugged him. "Thank you. And I know in my heart it's true, but sometimes I get scared."

"That's only human. I understand. Now enough of this serious stuff. Why don't you and Ted go find some fun? If this race goes the way I think it will, this may well be the last day of your obscurity in the racing world. Enjoy it while it lasts."

"You don't mind?"

"Of course not. Kind of like to have a few moments to myself here in the sun. Might even take a catnap." He smiled at the thought. "Your folks and Jock will be here soon enough. Don't forget—we have the owner's party this evening."

"How could I forget?' Ann muttered, making a face.

"Aren't you excited?" Ted teased. "Hey—another chance for you to wear a dress!" She made a fist and threatened him with it, but he only ducked off, realizing that putting some distance between them might be a good thing at the moment. She chased after him squealing, until they were lost from Scotty's view. He smiled. Leave it to Ted to lighten the moment. *She'll be fine,* he thought, *just a case of pre-race jitters.*

19

DERBY JITTERS

Ann and Ted spent part of the afternoon wandering about the barn area, watching the excitement build as crowds gathered in front of each Derby colt's stall. Everywhere they went they came across legions of reporters, all vying for that big story to take home to their readers. There was a palpable feeling of excitement in the air as Derby Week wound toward its climax. While it could be felt all over Louisville, nowhere was it felt more than right here on the backside. Ann and Ted were swept up in the anticipation, too. It was understandable for Ted, who was witnessing his first Derby. However, for Ann, who had grown up attending every Derby practically since birth, it was a different matter. The only one she'd missed had been the previous year, when Lightning was still missing. Then she'd been unable to face the spectacle that had been her dream since he was born; now here she was a day shy of having that dream a reality. Best of all, she was going to be in the saddle for the momentous event. Could anything be better than that?

At each barn, they watched in awe as reporters and fans alike gathered around the participants. The crowds ebbed and flowed, almost taking on a life of their own.

"I'm so glad we're considered the underdog," Ann said. "I sure would hate to have all that fuss around Lightning. He's not big on crowds."

Ted laughed at her understatement. "Then he'd better get used to it. Like it or not, there'll plenty of people surrounding him tomorrow when he goes to the post."

"Yeah, I know. I'm a little concerned about it, too, though I haven't said anything to Scotty."

"Oh, he knows. He'll want you to stay close to Lightning to keep him calm."

"And who will keep me calm?"—but she was smiling as she said it. Still, she feared those pre-race jitters she remembered from Monday. And that had been only a minor race.

"We'll all be there for you." Then, to take her mind off thinking about it, he said, "Come on. Let's go see what's up with the favorite." He led her off to Roan Rambler's barn.

There they found Neal Wyatt holding court in front of an appreciative audience, his booming voice carrying above the crowds as he extolled the virtues of his champion. In his element, he seemed to revel in the interest the crowds found in his colt, and expounded with all the arrogance of a strutting peacock.

"He acts like his colt has already won the Derby," Ann whispered as they stood off to the side and watched the show.

Ted grinned. "I'd hate to be in his shoes tomorrow if that colt doesn't win or makes a poor showing, wouldn't you?"

She nodded. "And it could just happen, if we have any say in it. After all," she said, grinning, "anything can happen in the Derby!"

"You got it," Ted said, pleased with the return of her confidence. Then he added, "I guess that's 'cause none of these colts has ever run a mile-and-a-quarter before. No one knows for sure whether they can keep up that speed."

"You're right. It's awfully early in the year to run a three-year-old for that distance."

"But Lightning can."

"Yes—he can." She smiled.

They went on through the barn area, enjoying the ambiguity of having a horse in the race that wasn't considered a contender. Each day they read through the papers, but very little was being said about their horse, for which they were all grateful. After that first belittling write-up, they thought perhaps the reporters were shying away from their barn, figuring there wasn't much of a story there.

"Do you think Scotty has had much company this afternoon?" Ann asked.

"I'm sure nothing like these guys. Rather him than us. He can handle it," was Ted's response. Ann agreed.

As they walked along the backside of the track, they saw huge crowds gathered for the day's races. Today was the running of the Kentucky Oaks, the filly equivalent of the Derby. While fillies were allowed to run in the Derby, few did, preferring their own race. In the past only Regret had beaten all her male counterparts to win the big one. None, however, were entered this year.

"Maybe one day we'll have a filly for the Oaks," Ann mused.

"Probably one of his kids," Ted said, referring to Lightning.

"No doubt. And you'll be riding her," she added, grinning, unaware then of how prophetic her words were to become.

Not long after they returned to their stalls, the rest of the family arrived. They'd fed all the farm horses before leaving Stormy Hill, and they'd arrived just in time to get ready for the owner's party that night. Everyone was planning to go—except Jock, who, true to form, elected to sit with Lightning while they were gone.

Like the other party, this one was held in a local hotel, in the main ballroom that had been deemed large enough to hold the huge crowd expected to attend. As they made their way the short distance to the hotel, they couldn't help but notice how Kentucky Derby fever had spread across what seemed like all of Louisville. The city was alive with celebration. For many people, it was not about the horses so much as a chance to party to the extreme.

Upon arriving, they quickly realized that the massive crowd had taken over more than just the ballroom as clusters of people spilled out into the lobby, the hallways and even out to the pool area. The air was charged with enthusiasm for the upcoming race. They felt it the minute they walked in. This was even bigger and grander than the party they'd previously attended. Ann was overwhelmed and stuck very close to her family.

"Don't worry," Ted assured her, "I'm right here." She flashed him a grateful, though tremulous smile.

Michael was in his element. Well known among most of the Kentucky horse breeders, certainly those in and around Lexington, he was immediately accepted into their circles. Going from group to group, he greeted each as he introduced his family in turn. Ann soon tired of the smile she painted on her face with each introduction, but she could not deny her father's pleasure at being back among his peers. A product of generations of Kentucky horsemen, he belonged here as much as anyone in this room. Though it had been over three years since he'd run a horse under the Stormy Hill colors, the farm's past record spoke for itself, and he was accepted as one of them. Their financial reverses were treated as a minor setback, something not even worth mentioning. He had a horse running now, and that was all that mattered.

When Ted suggested they go find the food table, she welcomed the diversion. Her father said "Have fun" and waved them away. They struggled to get through the crowded room as they sought out the food. As before, the long buffet table was piled so high with delicious goodies, it threatened to collapse under the weight. Once again Ted piled his plate high with food as Ann wondered where he put it all. His lean frame showed very little gain since he'd arrived a year ago. She herself only picked at her plate, unable to swallow as she sat in awe of her surroundings. In the end she passed the barely touched food over to Ted, who once again made quick work of it.

This time they caught a glimpse of the Garrisons first and immediately ducked into the crowds before they were spotted. Giggling at their deception, they found themselves out by the pool area. The throng was thinner here, so they stayed awhile, breathing in the marvelous smells of blooming azaleas, tulips, and of course roses, that permeated the night air.

"Run for the roses," Ann reminisced as she bent down to smell the deep red flowers.

"You're going to do fine tomorrow, you know," Ted told her, taking her hand and leading her to a nearby stone bench.

"You do?"

"Yes, I do. And now is the perfect time for my 'Ted talk.'" He looked so serious that the grin that was threatening to light up her face didn't materialize.

"Okay, then. Let's have it," she said instead.

"Since the day that horse was born, you've had complete faith in him. He will do whatever you ask of him in that race. He has an incredible heart, and he loves you. Whatever happens out there, you won't let him down."

Her lower lip trembled as she fought to hold the tears back. "I know you are right, but—well, all my life I've had this dream. Especially after Lightning was born. Way before anyone else saw his potential, I knew it was there. Then when he was returned to me—us—last year, I saw that dream take hold. But having it and the reality of it are two different things. Tomorrow I get to live my dream—and I'm scared stiff!"

"I know, I know. Just don't let him know."

"How?" She suddenly seemed very vulnerable.

"You'll know when the time comes. You did on Monday, didn't you?"

"But Monday I wasn't racing in the Derby," she wailed.

"Then just think of it as another horse race."

"Easy for you to say."

"You're right. I wish there was a magic formula I could give you. I just know you'll do fine once you're out there, on the track. Trust your horse. Lightning would never put you in danger if there was any way he could avoid it."

"How do you know that?"

"He's just like his sire. And I know Si'ad."

She smiled then. "How could I forget? We're so alike, you and I. You understand me better than anyone else in our family."

Ted had no answer for that. Instead he said, "Speaking of which, think we should go find them? They may want to stay a bit longer, but you should probably turn in. You've got a full day coming up."

"Yes, I'm ready to call it quits, but I don't think I'll sleep a wink tonight."

They made their way back through the crowds and found Ann's parents and Scotty, who were ready to leave as well. On the way back they stopped at the stalls, where they found Jock comfortably dozing in front of Lightning's stall. He roused himself upon their arrival, and after asking if they'd had a good time, he left to go back to the farm, where he would tend to the morning chores before returning the following afternoon.

The black horse was lying peacefully stretched out in his stall, so Ann tried not to disturb him. She quickly motioned to her parents to leave. They dropped her off at the boarding house before making their way to their motel just down the street.

She thought she could make it up to her room unseen, but Momma Millie spied her before she got too far. Before she could plead exhaustion, the woman called out, "Just want you to know we're all excited about your race tomorrow. Imagine me having the daughter of a Derby colt owner right here under my roof." Ann thanked her, but the kind woman went on. "I even got tickets for it so I'll be up there in the stands rooting for your horse." Ann stifled a yawn. "Oh dear, I'm sorry. You must be tired, as early as you get up. Please go on to bed now. Don't mind the rattling of an old woman."

"That's okay," Ann assured her. "But I *am* pretty tired. Thanks for everything, though." She made her way up to her room, where she quickly changed and collapsed on the bed, asleep the minute her head hit the pillow.

§ § § § § §

Derby Day! Ann knew it the minute she woke up. This was the day she'd awaited all her life. She dressed in haste and slipped out the door while it was still dark. In her hand was another bag full of ham biscuits and a note that said simply "Good luck." Ann smiled to herself at the kindness of the old woman. What would she say if she only knew that she, *Ann,* was riding in the Derby? She hoped she wouldn't give the poor thing a heart attack when she found out.

She was fairly skipping as she made her way past the sleepy guard, who only grunted as he checked her badge and went back to dozing. He had a long, busy day ahead of him, so she said nothing and kept going.

"Sure am glad to see you so early," Scotty greeted her, eyeing the sack in her hand. She handed it over, which immediately drew Ted from Banshee's stall. She watched, amused, as they devoured the ham biscuits one by one. As Scotty returned the bag, he said, "Here—saved you a couple."

She smiled, for she had little appetite at the moment. "What's it to be today?"

"Horses are fed. I want them out on the track as soon as possible. Want to beat the rush. All the colts will be working early, so the rail-birds will be out in force. Like to avoid the traffic, if possible."

"I'm ready. Let's do it." She turned toward Lightning's stall, training saddle in hand. She was greeted by a lively whinny as the big horse swung his head around and half-reared. "Whew! What's this?" she asked, taken back.

"Oh, I forgot to tell you. He's feeling good this morning."

"I'll say! What's up, fella? You sense something in the wind?" She entered the stall, but had a tough time holding him steady to get his saddle on. He kept circling, refusing to settle. Finally Ted slipped in and held him so she could tighten the girth.

"He sure is full of himself today," he said. "Think you can ride him?"

"Are you kidding? Just watch me," she snapped back.

"I'd hate to see you eat some dirt out there," he teased.

"I can stick to him just fine, thank you."

"Maybe you should have eaten something. Give you energy. You're going to need it," he said, grinning.

"Maybe I would have if someone hadn't made a pig of himself," she countered, eyeing the now-deflated bag sitting on a chair. Ted had the grace to look somewhat ashamed at his greed.

Seeing this conversation heading in the wrong direction, Scotty quickly changed the subject. "Right now we've got a horse to work. Let's go, you two," he said.

Ted swung up on Banshee as Scotty gave Ann a leg up on the fractious colt. Lightning danced about, eager to be on his way. Ann had her hands full as they walked the horses out to the track, the sky above them still dark, though the first streaks of dawn were visible off to the east.

As Lightning stepped onto the dirt, he half reared and let out a buck. A lesser rider might not have sat such a stunt, but Ann, used to his antics, held on grimly. "Feeling that good, eh, fella?" she told him, stroking his neck to calm him. He'd already broken into a sweat, a thin sheen splashing his long neck. She grinned over at Ted. "Going to be an interesting morning," she said. Ted sent her back a look of empathy. Si'ad was prone to such moods himself.

"Now that he's over his little temper tantrum," Scotty grunted, not quite as forgiving, "shall we get on with it?" He gave them their instructions, including a short breeze when he was warmed up. He stressed the word "short." "If he feels at all like getting away from you, scratch it altogether. The last thing we want is for him to burn himself up now. I just want to tantalize him with a bit of a run so he's fired up for this afternoon."

"I don't think that will be a problem," Ann replied. "He knows what's coming."

"I imagine you're right. Off you go."

Few horses were out this early. As Ann moved along the outside rail, a shiver of anticipation slid down her spine. She smiled over at Ted, who returned her grin. *This is the best time of day,* she thought, looking around. The mist was rising, enveloping and caressing them. Steam already rose from her horse. "Can you feel it, Lightning?" she asked him, easing him into a light canter. "The next time we come out onto this track, it will be for all the marbles. The Kentucky Derby! The run for the roses! Oh, Lightning, you and I—we made it." She wanted to throw her arms around his neck in happiness, but settled for a light pat instead. Beneath her she felt the strength of his coiled muscles bunching and stretching as he moved. He was as fit as he'd ever be. Scotty had trained him just right. He was ready—ready to go out and make his mark in history.

She took him over to the inside rail and breezed him according to Scotty's directions. When she asked him to pull up, he did so reluctantly, still capable of so much more, but willing to listen to her for once. She rode back to Ted and proceeded to cool him out. It was with great reluctance that she finally left the track at Scotty's motioning. By now the sky was streaked with light and the track was filling up fast. Most of the other Derby colts were taking their turns on the track, so it was time to return to the barns. With one final glance back at the famous old twin steeples, she walked her horse through the gate to where Scotty awaited them.

"He did well today," Scotty said approvingly. "I was afraid he might give you trouble after the way he started out."

"No, he was good. He's learning to be a racehorse."

"I would hope so. But we'll see," was all he said.

They walked back in easy silence. There was nothing left to say for the moment. All the preparation, all the waiting, all the speculation was over. In a few hours it would all come down to two short minutes ending in either fame and glory, or obscurity. It was out of their hands now.

Jay, from next door, came up to greet them as they returned. He was waving a track sheet, the first of many that would circulate around the backside that day.

"They say the track is going to be fast—lightning fast," he said unnecessarily, for the headlines screamed the news in bold lettering.

"For a Lightning colt," Ann responded.

"With a field like we have today, records could be broken," he went on, interpreting the paper for them.

"Enough," Scotty told him, though not unkindly. "Let's get these horses cleaned off and cooled out. There'll be plenty of time to talk later." He gently pointed them to the work at hand. It did not do to upset Ann unnecessarily. Though it wasn't Jay's fault, since he had no idea she was riding, bringing these facts to her attention only made her more stressed. She would have to deal with her pre-race nerves her own way, but the less said about it the better.

While Jay went on back to his own charges, Ted and Ann got to work bathing their horses. There was no horsing around today. Instinctively Ted knew Ann was not in the mood. Nor would it improve her humor. As they walked the horses out, she became more and more withdrawn. Anything he said to her was received with a grunt, until he quit trying to converse altogether. Knowing her silence had nothing to do with him, he continued to walk beside her in silent support. It was the best he could do. She understood.

Once the horses were put away, there was nothing to do but wait. The empty hours hung over them. Ann tried to sit in a chair but kept turning about restlessly until at last she rose and announced. "I'm going for a walk." When Ted started to rise, she stopped him. "Alone. Don't worry—I'll be fine. I just need some time to myself. I won't be long," she assured them. Ted sat back down, a worried frown on his face—but he didn't argue.

She was grateful neither of them objected. This was something she had to do alone. The restlessness within her had to be overcome her way. She didn't dare approach Lightning, lest he sense her nervousness and react in kind. So the best thing to do was to walk it off.

Her steps took her along to the backside of the track where, since it was still early, many horses were now being worked. She tried to watch, but her thoughts were so distracted that she found herself unable to focus. Before she realized it, she'd drifted over to the shadow of the ancient grandstand. Quiet now, it would soon be overflowing with excited fans, many making their annual pilgrimage to the great event. *A wall of noise,* she thought when she passed it again.

Passing through the famous tunnel, she came out by the clubhouse. As she stepped into the middle of the grounds, she was struck by an overwhelming feeling of tradition. The red bricks were empty now, except for a few workers sweeping up the last remains of yesterday's crowd. The sun had not yet poked its head over the roofs of the grandstand, leaving much of the area bathed in shadow. Soon this too would be crammed with people. But for now she relished the solitude as she looked around at the familiar old buildings. Wooden, painted dazzling white, they had stood for many decades. They were a large part of the institution that was the Derby. The very color of the place hit her—the brightly colored flowers, tulips of yellow and red, azaleas in full bloom, the pink dogwoods, and roses, of course. Red, the color of the Derby. *Run for the roses,* she thought again. It was all part of the custom, the lore that was the Derby.

She walked farther, until she was standing in front of the statue of Aristides, the first winner of the Kentucky Derby, some nearly one hundred years ago. There in the midst of the clubhouse garden stood the bronze likeness, frozen in time, as if he had just crossed the finish line. Red tulips set him off in all his glory, a tribute to all those winners who had come after him.

It drew her eyes upward, where they took in the plaques along the walls, each bearing the names of the past winners and the year they won. As a rite of passage, she walked along, reading each name reverently, slowly nodding as she paid tribute to the past greats. Some names were merely obscure now, long forgotten with time. But others stood out, remembered as much today as they had been when they made history on one memorable Saturday in May. War Admiral, Whirlaway, Citation, Count Fleet, she read. And there was Swaps, winner of the famous duel with Nashua. They were all there. Would Lightning's name be added after today?

She stayed a bit longer, soaking up the tradition, the pageantry, and the spirit that was the Derby, enjoying the calm before the storm. But already her meditation was interrupted as the first early visitors began to trickle in. By now the sun had peaked over the roofs, bathing the clubhouse in light. No longer alone, she made her way back through the tunnel. To the bored attendant checking her pass, she was just one more nameless person passing by. She relished the anonymity. If they won, it would be the only thing she would hate to surrender after today.

As she slowly walked back to her shed row, the warmth of the sun penetrated her light jacket, promising a near perfect day for the race. She stared out at the now-familiar track, where only a handful of horses still worked out. Even they were winding up their training schedules. How well she knew that piece of dirt, having been here a week now. It was so comfortable, like the one at home. Why was she so filled with anxiety then?

It's this eternal waiting, she thought. *Everything's done—now it's just wait.* She hated it. *Let's get on with it,* her internal voice screamed. *I've waited all my life for this one moment, and I'm tired of waiting.* She got back to the barn and plopped into an easy chair, not speaking to either Ted or Scotty. Sensing her mood, they both went about their business in silence. If she needed time alone, they would give it. They both understood the tension that ate at her. They themselves wished the time would pass more quickly. It was much easier to have something to do.

Time crept so slowly that it seemed to have stopped altogether, and Ann continued to sit, wrapped up in her silent, withdrawn world. She did not even acknowledge Lightning, for she feared her frame of mind would rub off on him. But she was very aware of him, occasionally thumping about his stall, eager to get out and run. In the distance she could hear the first couple of races go off, the cheers a far greater crescendo than those earlier in the week.

She could picture the infield filling up with people, some who'd never even get to see a horse, so blocked by the crowds were they. By now the grandstand was filled to capacity, awash with color from the sea of outfits women had bought especially for that day. And the hats—each head adorned with one more lavish than the last. Yes, she saw it all in her mind, as she had seen it so many years in the past, sitting up there in her family's box seats. Not this year.

I'm not ready! her mind screamed. For one brief moment she wished she could go back to a time when this was all still ahead of her. She remembered telling Ted last night how the dream and the reality were two different things. She'd lived the dream so long. Her mind replayed that awful stormy night Lightning was born, soon to be an orphan. Oh, how she'd fought to save him. Even then she knew he was something very special. He'd become her horse that night. She reminisced over the days that followed, even after he was long out of danger. In her mind she could see the graceful colt scampering across his pasture as fleet as the wind, but always returning to her whenever he saw her. As gentle as a kitten for her, he would do anything she asked. Breaking him was easy, and she knew riding him would be, too. Then came that awful night he was stolen from her. That was the blackest time in her life, when no day passed that she didn't wonder where he was or if she would ever see him again.

One year ago today he'd miraculously turned up, a magnificent stallion standing glorious atop the hill behind their farm. Having skipped the Derby last year for the first time ever, she'd been drawn by circumstances to that spot where she'd first spotted him. Her memory flashed back to that first ride—and what a ride it had been! No restraint to hinder him, they'd run wild and free all the way back home. She'd never forget it. It was at that moment she knew they had their Derby colt. It took a while to convince her dad and Scotty, but eventually they saw it too. From then on, everything had led to this point in time. Now here he was, on the brink of greatness. She knew her colt was fast. Soon the world would know it, too.

20

POST PARADE

Ann was drawn from her reverie when she saw her parents standing before her. Her mother held a garment bag in her hand. "I'm sorry. Were you taking a nap?" Jessica asked her daughter.

"I guess," she said groggily. "Have I been out long?"

"I don't know, Hon. We just got here." She held up the bag. "I decided not to take a chance with your silks, so I had the cleaners do them."

"Oh, thanks, Mom," she said, taking the bag.

"You might as well go ahead and put them on," Scotty told her, coming over to them. "It's time."

"Is it already?" She panicked. "I really must have dozed off then."

"I'm not surprised," Michael said. "With all the pressure you've been under lately, you probably needed it."

She stepped into the tack stall, unzipped the garment bag, and pulled out her jockey silks. For a second she stared at the blue and gray silks, tenderly running her hands over the smooth cloth. Thinking about all the hours her mother had devoted making these silks, she was overwhelmed by the love she felt emanating from the fabric. She removed her old clothes and then slowly, almost reverently, began to don her racing silks. First came the snowy white breeches, then the jacket, blue and gray with the letters "S" and "H" and a splash of lightning now added across the back—added especially for Lightning. Finally she donned the high black boots, polished to a glossy shine. She reached over and took her bat from the hook, tucking it in her left boot negligently. She would have no need for it, but since all the jockeys carried them, she felt she needed to conform rather than draw attention to herself.

When she was done, she stared at herself in the small cracked mirror that hung on the wall. Her hair still hung in thick black curls to her waist. She started to restrain it into the usual braid, then stopped. With a touch of rebellion, she caught it up and shoved it under her helmet instead, the seed of a plan forming in her head. All week she'd hidden her gender from others. It had been relatively easy actually, since no one expected to see a *girl* exercising horses in the early morning. Only a very few girls were even hired as grooms currently around the track. And certainly the last thing anyone would expect would be a girl jockey—especially here in the Kentucky Derby.

When the committee granted her a license, no one had said she must not reveal her sex. They had told Scotty that it was probably wise to continue with her disguise—however, more as a protection against unwanted publicity than anything. And that was exactly what they had done. But once the Derby was run, there would be no hiding the fact. After the race, everyone would know that Lightning's jockey was a girl. They and the committee were aware of that. She was conscious of the fact that she and her family would have to deal with it eventually. News like that would spread like wildfire.

So what difference would it make if she let it slip just before the race? It wouldn't matter then. All she had to do was pull her helmet off, releasing her hair, then plunk it back on her head. She could see the stir now. But she'd be out on the track, out of reach of the press. No one could touch her there. With a smile on her face, she opened the door and stepped out into the sunlight.

Everyone immediately noticed the change. It was as if she'd shed her anxiety and nerves with her old clothes, for the minute she donned her jockey silks she had her confidence back. No more stepping on eggshells around Ann for fear she'd bite their heads off. This was the old Ann they all knew.

Jock had arrived, having taken care of the necessary chores back at the farm. He saw her and whistled. "Hey, you look just like a jockey," he teased.

"I would hope so," she said, grinning.

"Sounds like the old Ann is back," Ted said to Scotty.

"Thank goodness. Now we can get on with the race." He went into the tack stall to pick up her saddle and pads, along with the bridle. Jock slid the new leather halter, complete with Lightning's name on a brass plate along the side, over the black colt's head. Acting as his official groom, he led the handsome youngster out of his stall. Lightning pranced out, knowing what was coming, and eager to get on with it. As he stepped into the sunlight, he froze for a split second, standing like a magnificent statue, his black coat gleaming with health. Then he moved forward, his sleek muscles rippling, his tail extended high and full, his long neck arched. He was the picture of a fit, well-conditioned athlete. Just the sight of him made them all suck in their breaths. No one could say that he did not belong in this great race.

Jock grabbed his blue and gray cooler and slung it over his shoulder, then tucked a brush in his back pocket. "Have we got everything?" he asked.

"Think so," his father replied.

"So we're off." Jock led their small entourage down the shed row toward the track. They each fell in line behind him for the long walk to the saddling paddock, with Ann in the middle, where she would be less conspicuous. As it was highly unusual for a jockey to accompany his mount from the backside, she was bound to be noticed. Normally the jockeys stayed in the jockey room, appearing only in the saddling paddock just before it was time to mount up. But since that room was restricted to men only, Ann had no choice but to do it this way.

As they crossed the track, they were joined by other groups bringing their hopefuls up to the saddling paddock for the main event. The previous race had been run. Off to the side, Ann noticed the starting gate being brought up in line with the head of the stretch. The field was large enough to require two gates, side by side. Above each were the words "Churchill Downs." The sight sent shivers of anticipation down her spine. Ted, noting her focus, looked at her and grinned. It was official. The Kentucky Derby had now begun.

Ahead was the grandstand, filled to capacity, a sea of shifting humanity. Ann didn't doubt for a moment that the crowd had reached the magic number—100,000. Even so, she was unprepared for the wall of noise that greeted her as they passed through the tunnel and came out into the less boisterous paddock area. She glanced anxiously at Lightning, but other than a brief snort, he seemed unaffected by the crowd's roar. This helped her relax as they entered the saddling paddock and went to their assigned stall.

Once there, Jock left them, returning to the barn to bring up Banshee for Scotty. He would have him ready for his father when Scotty led Lightning and Ann back through the tunnel, standing by with the rest of the pony horses to lead the colts down the track in the post parade.

Ted took over Jock's duties, slipping into the stall and picking up the brush to flick away any dirt the colt had picked up on his way over. It was more for something to do, however, than because he really needed it. The black colt's coat glistened with a light sheen of sweat. Nerves. Afire with anticipation, Lightning sensed what was coming. Even Ann's soft words failed to calm him as he glanced around, head high in anticipation of the coming race.

Everywhere she looked, she was greeted with a wall of people. Even here in the paddock, she was surprised by how thick the crowds were around each entry. When Scotty stepped in and slid the saddle onto Lightning's back, it was Ann who had to tighten the girth. He was too restless to let anyone else near him. Even so, he kept pushing his nose against her as she whispered calming words into his ear. She reached up and stroked that ear, forcing herself to block out the noise and confusion of the crowds around them.

Early on in Lightning's life, she'd developed a bond with him that only they shared. Quietly, almost trancelike, she drew within herself and returned to that place. Slowly she stroked his head, his neck, and his chest, reaching those spots that had always soothed him in the past. He lowered his head, snuffling against her, enjoying the attention of his favorite person. She continued to communicate in a lowered whisper that only he could hear, as she explained to him how important this race was and how he needed to focus only on victory, forgetting all the distractions around him. It worked. Moments later, when Ted stepped forward to walk him out onto the circle he did so with his head lowered.

Scotty motioned Ann over to a clear spot, where he gave her his last-minute instructions. "It's good he's breaking from the outside," he told her again. "Let him break fast and join the pack somewhere in the middle, not too fast behind the leaders. Don't worry about the inside rail. You two don't have the experience yet to fight for that spot. There are too many good, experienced jockeys out there who'd beat you to it. Just try to stay two or three horses out, and watch those leaders. One or two will tire, so you don't want to be carried out if a horse starts to wobble and drift to the outside. Try to pass on the inside." She nodded, concentrating on what he was saying. "At the top of the stretch, those with energy left in the tank will make their moves. Go with them. Don't get left behind. Ride it all the way to the finish. He'll have the speed."

"Got it."

"Just remember all we've talked about. I'll be with you through the post parade."

Before she could answer, the call came: "Riders Up!"

Ted held Lightning for Scotty so he could give her a leg up. With a quick hug for her father, mother, and Ted, she swung lightly into the saddle, giving each a big grin. It was comforting to be on his back at last. They would draw their strength from each other.

Her family surrounded her at that moment, all wishing her well. She blew kisses all around as Ted shouted above the noise of the crowd, "See you in the winner's circle."

Everywhere about them, jockeys were mounting their colts. Ann glanced around quickly, noting the many colorful silks. Ted led Lightning back to the circle, where she fell in line behind number twelve, Overflow, the colt from New Mexico, another long shot. Briefly she glimpsed Max, beaming with pride as he held the colt's cooler draped over his arm. She started to call encouragement to him, when she remembered he wouldn't—or shouldn't—recognize her yet as Lightning's jockey.

The long post parade began, winding around the paddock and then filing out one by one, disappearing into the famous tunnel that led under the grandstand and out onto the track. Scotty took the lead rope from Ted and continued solemnly after the others, number thirteen, last in line. Behind them, the crowd that had parted as they all passed closed in again. However, at Lightning's warning kick, they remained a respectful distance behind.

Though not dark inside the tunnel, the absence of the brilliant sunlight made Ann blink before her eyes adjusted to the difference. Bubbling with excitement, she reached nervous hands up and pulled off her helmet, letting her hair spill free, tumbling down her back. With a defiant gesture, she shoved the helmet back on her head and hooked the chinstrap, pulling the brim down low to shade her eyes. At the same time, she checked to make sure her goggles were in place, ready to pull over her eyes when the time came.

There, she thought rebelliously, *now everyone will know a girl is riding in a man's sport—in the most famous race in the world.* She was tired of hiding the fact. A huge grin spread across her face. As she rode back into the sunlight, she looked down at Scotty and caught his eye. His face registered one of shock. No. More like surprise.

"Are you upset with me?" she asked simply.

"N-no. It's your choice to let your secret out, I guess. Everyone will know by the time the race is over anyway."

"Yes, they will," she said triumphantly. "In a few minutes everyone will know that a girl rode in the greatest race of all. If we win, the world will know the winning horse was ridden by a girl. And if we lose—if we lose, it won't matter anyhow."

It was at that moment that Scotty knew Ann would be all right out there. Whatever happened, she and Lightning would run as a team and take care of each other. He could stop worrying about whether he'd made the right choice letting her pursue her dream. Ann would be fine.

As they approached the opening leading out to the track, Ann noticed the pony horses, standing with their riders in a line. As each colt cleared the gate and stepped onto the track, he was picked up by his outrider, who would accompany the colt to the gate. At the end stood Banshee with Jock at his head. Scotty picked up his reins and swung aboard, as Jock, the surprised look on his face a copy of his father's, stepped aside with a salute. Although she could not hear him over the din, she interpreted the mouthed words to mean "good luck." Then he was lost in the crowd as they moved forward out onto the track.

They hadn't gone far when she heard it. Above the deafening racket came the sweet strains of "My Old Kentucky Home." A huge surge of emotion passed through her as the University Band struck up the familiar chords. This was, after all, her home. She was a sixth-generation Kentuckian, and none of the other jockeys out there could lay claim to Kentucky. Tears sprang to her eyes as she realized something for the first time. She was not just riding for her family, her horse, or herself. She was riding to keep the *Kentucky* Derby right here in Kentucky, where it belonged. She had every right to feel sentimental at the sound of her state song.

Meanwhile, the news of her gender was rapidly spreading through the stands. Cameras focused on her, zooming in for a close-up. Newscasters, completely taken aback by a rider of which none of them were aware, screamed at their copy boys to get the story, any story. Sportscasters providing live TV coverage were thrown into a tailspin as everyone scrambled for the facts. Everyone recognized a story here, a big story. Unfortunately for them, they were too late. The race was only minutes from getting underway.

Luckily for Ann, she was completely unaware of the excitement she'd caused. Lightning felt good beneath her, his keenness for the coming race keeping her on her toes. She was glad Scotty held his lead rope, keeping him from breaking free. All too soon they would be on their own. She needed to reach him now, before it was time to warm him up. Therefore she put all her concentration into doing just that.

As they paraded past the stands, several other colts were being equally as fractious for their jockeys. Then one by one they were released into a slow canter as they began their warm ups.

"You okay?" Scotty asked her as he released his hold on Lightning.

She nodded. "Never better."

"Good, 'cause from here on out it's all yours. Try to bring him up last to the gate, since you'll load last anyway. The less time he has to stand around, the better for him."

"Good idea."

"Ann, good luck out there." He looked like he wanted to say more, but she understood.

"See you in the winner's circle," she said, parroting Ted's words with a big grin before following the others in a long, slow canter past the stands and on up the track, past the start, and around the far turn. Lightning felt fresh and eager to run as Ann tried to hold him to a canter. She took her time, talking to him, trying to reach into that one place that only she could reach. Only when she was sure he was listening to her did she turn back to the starting gate.

The chaos around the start this time was far worse than the past Monday. This was the big one, and everyone wanted—no, *had*—to get it right. The official starter stood in his box above them, shouting orders his staff hastened to carry out. Several of the colts were proving hard to load. Calculated Risk, in the number one spot, went in quickly, but the number two horse, Pinch Hitter, fought his restraint and managed to kick out, scattering the assistants who scrambled for safety. In the end, it took several men to load him, even as he tried to rear, causing his jockey to hop on the ledge on the side of the stall, lest he get crushed.

The next couple of horses loaded without a fuss. Everyone was breathing easier when it came time to load Celtic Glow. Always fractious in the starting box, today was no exception. The bay colt just planted his feet and refused to move. At last he was practically carried into the box, where he at least stood as if frozen to the spot. His jockey only scowled. Being his regular rider, he was well used to the colt's antics.

One by one the colts were loaded, some easier than others. Ann stood off to the side, trying to calm Lightning until it was her turn. He didn't need to see this, but she had no choice. When the first gate was fully loaded, the assistant starters moved to the second gate. Only one horse would load from that one—Lightning. *Lucky thirteen,* Ann thought as she moved him forward. Immediately the staff moved in to assist, but she waved them away. At about that moment, those nearest to her realized her gender and a stir went through the group. Ann was too busy controlling her horse to respond as Lightning chose that moment to rear, scattering the starters back to a safer spot. Again Ann signaled them to let her try alone. They stayed put, and she eased him forward.

"That's it, boy—just like the one at home," she coaxed him. "You'll be fine." Just when they were all convinced he wasn't going to load and started to move in to assist, the black colt bolted forward and leapt into the box, with one quick-thinking assistant slamming the gate shut behind them. Ann pulled her goggles down over her eyes and grabbed a hunk of black mane so she would not be left behind this time when he bolted.

The Derby field was at the gate!

21

THE KENTUCKY DERBY

Clang!

The gate burst open, releasing the colts. The Kentucky Derby was on!

Twelve horses surged forward! A seething tide of horseflesh leaped out onto the track.

But one gate failed to open—Lightning's! Some mechanical glitch in the system kept his from releasing with the others. Ann was too stunned to respond, as was the starter perched above her on the ledge. But upon seeing the competition getting away from him, Lightning took charge. Furious with his confinement, the black colt reared, striking out and releasing the gate. Suddenly the way was clear before him. Springing forward, he galloped down the track, bent on catching the fast-disappearing cluster of horses in front of him.

Ann was nearly caught off guard, thankful that she still had a handful of mane. That and the instinctive skill that came with riding the often-unpredictable colt kept her in the saddle. Regaining her balance, she bent over his neck and looked ahead. Seeing the rapidly retreating pack many yards in front of them, she almost despaired. There was so much ground to make up. "Oh, Lightning," she sobbed into his mane, "have we lost the race already?"

Up in the stands, there was an audible gasp from the Stormy Hill box as they saw all except Lightning break from the gate. Having no idea that something had gone awfully wrong with the gate mechanism, they had to assume that Ann was having trouble with her horse.

"Where is he?" Jessica moaned to her husband, her heart sinking. As soon as all the horses were in the gate, she'd fixed her gaze at the spot where Ann and the colt would appear. She knew her eyes would be on them throughout the whole race. She'd be running it with her daughter.

"There," Michael shouted excitedly as Lightning burst out of the gate, but his heart sank when he saw how much distance they had to make up if they were even to get back into the race.

"What happened?" Jessica asked, though she expected no answer.

"I wish I knew, Hon—I wish I knew."

Jock was not yet back from returning Banshee to his stall, but down along the rail, Scotty and Ted saw the start. They were going through their own private agony as they watched the race unfold. Scotty was in a better position to observe the break from the gate, so when Ted heard his anguished, "Oh, no—it didn't open," he immediately focused his eyes on the second starting gate—and just in time to see Lightning erupt from the gate, hitting his stride almost immediately.

"Call it! Call it! The gate didn't open," Scotty screamed, to no avail. "It's not his fault!" But even as he cried out, he realized very few people knew what happened. There was no way to restart now. The race was already in progress.

"Scotty," Ted wailed. "He's out! He's going after them! Can he—"

"I don't know, Son. There's so much ground to make up. I just don't know." Ted had never heard such despair in his voice. They both stared bleakly out at the track as the horses came past the grandstand for the first time.

But "quit" was not part of Lightning's makeup. He had only one thing in mind—to catch the horses ahead of him. Hitting top speed within seconds, he ran after the pack, Ann only a passenger now. She let him go. What else could she do? If they were to have any possibility of being in this race at all, she had to trust her horse. She had to rely on not just his speed, for she knew he was fast, but also on his staying power. If he was to sustain that speed, he would have to have the endurance, too. He would have to fall back on the great heritage of his sire. Like those remarkable horses of the desert behind Si'ad, he would have to pull from the depths of his strengths if he was to have any chance at all. There would be no falling in somewhere in the middle of the pack and coasting along to the head of the stretch, as Scotty had suggested. Not this time. *Sorry, Scotty,* she thought, *but this time we'll have to run it his way.*

The horses, still fairly bunched, came past the grandstand for the first time, their jockeys vying for a good position along the rail. Up front, Pinch Hitter and Solitaire ran neck and neck, burning up the track with early speed, each contending for the lead. Just one length behind them came Celtic Glow, Overflow, Calculated Risk, and Time Tester, strung out across the track, refusing to let the leaders get away. When the time for the first furlong was announced, a cheer went up in the stands. They were on a record-breaking pace. Still, the old guard of the racing world had to wonder if they would not burn each other off, leaving the race wide open for one of the more conservative colts to win the race.

However, Ann knew none of this. She and Lightning were at the back of the pack, running their own race. Wrapped up totally in her colt, she was barely aware that they were passing in front of the stands. She had completely blocked out the wall of noise as she concentrated on only one thing: the feel of the powerful racing machine beneath her, his huge strides eating up the distance between him and the horse in front of him. As she passed under the finish line for the first time, he'd caught the flame red chestnut and pulled alongside. By the number eleven emblazoned on his saddle pad, she knew she had just passed Aztec, a long shot from Arizona.

One down, she thought, not dwelling on it but concentrating instead on the next horse, Orbit, three lengths ahead. Lightning began to inch up on him, catching the bay just as they went into the turn. Ann felt elated, though she knew they were a long way from the leaders, with a lot of ground still to make up. And Lightning had to come from the outside!

It was a little quieter along the backside, though the crowds in the infield maintained their own din. Here was where she'd have to make up considerable distance if she was to be in contention by the time they reached the homestretch. But would he have enough left for the final surge? He was running at peak speed now. No colt at three could maintain that speed for a mile and a quarter, could he?

Along the backstretch, the horses began to spread out. Solitaire, having burned himself out trying to stay with Pinch Hitter, began to fade, slipping back as Time Tester surged up to challenge Calculated Risk. Roan Rambler fell in behind them, along the rail, in perfect position to open up when the leaders lost their momentum. His jockey, a seasoned veteran of many Derbies, had him just where he wanted him. Behind him sat Capital Gain and Royalair, their jockeys both ready to make their moves when the time came.

Another cheer went up from the now-distant crowd as the time for the first half mile flashed over the screen. They were still on a record-setting pace. By now everyone knew they were watching what might be the setting of a new record. Excitement gripped the stands as the screen flashed.

In the Stormy Hill box, however, Jessica was hardly making a sound as she watched her daughter's brave attempt to stay in the race. Her eyes never leaving the lone black horse with the blue and gray silks, she held her breath as Lightning continued to eat up the distance with his huge stride. Along the back stretch, he passed other horses one by one as he crept up to the middle of the pack, making up ground the hard way—from the outside. Would he have enough left at the end? Did she dare hope? She gripped Michael's hand so tightly that it began to go numb. Neither of them noticed.

Along the rail, Ted was staring at the screen, since they were now hidden by the infield crowd. He was hardly aware that he was jumping up and down while pounding on Scotty's back, screaming, "Where is she? Where is she? *There!* Oh, gosh, there she is. Scotty, she's made it to the middle of the field! Go, Lightning! Go, Ann!" If Scotty noticed the thumping on his back, he made no protest. His focus was totally on the black horse as he willed him on, praying for enough speed to finish the race. His brain kept telling him no colt had ever survived such a handicap and gone on to win the Derby. But his heart told him this was no ordinary horse.

All the way down the backstretch, Lightning continued to gain ground as he passed horse after horse. Up ahead, Turnabout began to wobble. Lightning was directly behind him, and Ann noticed it in time to pull her colt to the left and go around him on the inside— the first time she'd been lucky enough to do that. It gained Lightning a scant second, but it was enough to put him in sight of the next two horses racing side by side, Solitaire and Celtic Glow, the two stable mates from Dun Roman Farms. Would they veer out as they went into the turn, giving her a chance to pass on the inside, or would she be forced to go around, using up more valuable time?

The decision was taken out of her hands as Lightning aimed for the inside. She started to pull him back, thinking to herself, *no room, no room!* But suddenly, miraculously, a tiny space opened up and Lightning took advantage of it. In a split second, he'd squeezed through with perfect timing, his stride never faltering. Her heart sang as she realized what a big break that was.

Then they were into the far turn, and just in front of them she saw a dark tail—Royalair, the horse from Illinois, the one Scotty had told her to keep an eye on. Making an instant decision, she took Lightning up just off his right side and held that position. Remembering Scotty's advice that his jockey, Roy Gorman, was a brilliant strategist, she decided to take advantage of that information. When he made his move, she'd go with him.

All around her, horses were beginning to stir as their jockeys hustled to make their moves coming into the homestretch. Right before them she saw the number eight horse, Capital Gain, suddenly galvanize into motion as he opened up coming out of the far turn. The dark brown horse sailed past the weakening Pinch Hitter, who fell back as though he were standing still. Royalair's jockey eased his horse past him, carrying Lightning as well. Realizing he had begun his move, Ann signaled Lightning to stay with him, slightly behind and to the outside. There was no room to move up on the inside anymore, so she would just have to stay put and hope Lightning had enough stamina left in him for that final surge to the wire.

Coming out of the turn, she saw the grandstand looming tall ahead, and she recognized the head of the homestretch. Dismayed, she noticed that there were several colts ahead of them, and yet she still had a lot of ground left to make up. As the wall of noise hit them, she prayed that Lightning yet had something left for the stretch run.

Jessica saw Ann and Lightning the minute they rounded the far turn. Grabbing Michael's arm, she screeched, "They're still in it! Our little girl is still there!"

"But will her horse have enough left for the finish?" Michael said. In a field like this, no horse could go wire to wire flat out and still win. He began praying for a miracle, even as he watched Lightning eat up the distance as he moved forward in the wake of the number five horse.

Up front it was still anyone's race, with Time Tester and Calculated Risk being challenged by Capital Gain and Roan Rambler. All the jockeys had gone for their whips as they urged their horses to their top speeds. For several strides there were four horses strung out across the track, each fighting to capture the lead. Several lengths back came Royalair, with Lightning hugging his flank. Then slowly the grey colt began to close that distance.

For what seemed like forever—but was in reality only a few dozen yards—they stayed like that. Suddenly, in the blink of an eye, the field underwent a change. Like falling dominos, the four horses in the lead erupted into several different patterns at once. Time Tester, who had been at or near the front throughout the whole race, seemed to collapse, fading quickly and taking Capital Gain with him. The two fell back, leaving the field open for the favorite and Calculated Risk to battle for the lead, switching places several times. Each time one would draw ahead, the other would make a tremendous surge to put himself back on top. Meanwhile, their jockeys worked their whips furiously, using everything they had to go for the win.

Neither was aware, however, of the drama unfolding behind them—but the crowd was. Suddenly newscasters, announcers, and possibly most of the huge crowd, all became aware of the rapidly gaining grey horse coming up on the outside. And with him came a huge black horse, flying along just at his tail. They were gaining ground with every leap, passing the tiring Time Tester, then the dark brown colt from Texas, leaving them behind as they set their sights on the two leaders.

By now Ann could do no more than encourage her colt. She knew the whip in her boot was unnecessary, would probably do more harm than good. She had never used a whip on him. Never needed one. Lightning would run because of his splendid Thoroughbred heart, because he was born to run, and because she asked it of him. That was enough. She was one with her horse. Only his great love for her would win this race now.

On the rail, Ted and Scotty watched, hardly able to breathe as the scenario opened before them. *Can they do it?* They each asked themselves. They were running out of track, with still so much ground to make up. Could they pull it off?

Ted voiced his concerns to Scotty. "Will he have enough left in the tank?" he asked. "He's got to have run full-out the whole way."

"I don't know. He's a powerful horse. We can only hope," Scotty replied without taking his eyes off the unfolding spectacle.

Fate was with them as a gasp went up from the crowd. Ted strained to see what had happened. Roan Rambler was dropping back, and this time he was making no surge to take the lead back. He was done, his great heart unable to sustain the drive to the wire against his rival, Calculated Risk. As his speed slowed, he was quickly passed first by Royalair, and then Lightning. Now only two horses remained ahead of their colt.

Excitedly, Ted began to hope. "He's going to do it, Scotty," he yelled. "I believe he's going to do it!" Scotty didn't answer. His eyes never left the black colt as he made his bid for the lead. His heart swelled with pride as he watched. She was running an excellent race, given the poor start. No matter what the conclusion, he was never prouder of her than at that moment.

Royalair drove down the track, aiming for the golden chestnut from California. Thinking he was in the clear and had the race won, Calculated Risk's jockey didn't see him until it was too late. The grey blew by him, gaining ground as he surged to the finish pole, the black shadow that had been with him since the backstretch still clinging to his heels.

Ann's heart leaped as Lightning passed the colt from California, his jockey still driving with his whip, though it was doing little good at this point. Calculated Risk could not regain his edge. His momentum was gone.

There was only one horse left now, she realized. But they were running out of track. She leaned down low over his powerful neck, calling on the reserve she believed he still had. He'd run at top speed throughout the race. Was there anything left? So close. She told him, "Just a little more, Lightning. You can do this. I know you can. Show them; show them all you're the best there ever was. You know it and I know it. Now everyone will know it! Please, Lightning, go for it!"

And then, as if he understood every word, the great black colt began to increase his speed. From somewhere down deep inside him he called on his reserves. Unbelievably, Ann felt it as he lengthened his strides and began to draw closer to Royalair. Inch by inch he was closing the gap. Inch by inch he was gaining precious ground. Would it be enough? In all the times she'd ridden him, never had she felt such a force of energy swell beneath her. This was Lightning's finest moment, the moment for which he'd been bred. Everything that had led up to this one instant in time was being fulfilled. His black head was even with Royalair's saddle, and still he came on. Ann caught the look from his jockey as he glanced over and acknowledged her for the first time. In his eyes she saw him recognize her as a threat, and he renewed his efforts with his bat.

Ann needed no whip. Lightning was giving all he had. She could do no more.

Inches. His head came even with the horse's neck. Then his head. All at once they were dead even, with the finish line only scant yards to go. As they crossed under the finish wire, it was too close to call. But Ann knew. She sensed it in her great horse as he thrust his nose out ahead just as he exploded beneath the wire. He had done it! Lightning had won the Kentucky Derby!

All at once they were dead even with the finish line only scant yards away.

22

AFTERMATH

"Photo finish."

As soon as the tote board flashed those words, there was bedlam in the stands. Ann's parents stared at the tote board in disbelief, holding each other tightly, screams frozen in their mouths. All around them the crowds were going wild, but they stood by helplessly, holding their collective breaths, waiting.

Ted and Scotty stood motionless as well, eyes focused only on the track, though Ann and Lightning were long out of sight. Still they could not tear their eyes away from the last spot they'd seen her. Life seemed to hang in balance as they awaited the results. Jock, standing along the rail with the other grooms, was similarly in limbo.

Unaware of her family's turmoil, Ann continued on up the track, letting Lightning ease up slowly as her horse came back to a canter. Still beside her was Royalair, with whom they had fought the final battle, his jockey also intent upon slowing his horse. For a brief moment she felt like she was in a fog. There were just the two of them cantering along, isolated from all the madness going on about her. All she was aware was a wonderful glow settling over her as she realized her dream had at last come true. Her heart swelled with love and pride for the horse that had given his all to make it happen. She stroked his shiny wet neck, talking to him in her soft voice, in a language only he could understand, telling him over and over what a good boy he was. Never had she been prouder of him than this glorious moment.

She was brought back to the present by a huge roar coming up from the crowd behind her. Then she realized Roy Gorman, Royalair's jockey, was speaking to her. "Congratulations," he was saying. "That was a heck of a race you gave us."

"Huh?" She looked over at him, puzzled.

"There, look." He pointed to the tote board in the distance, smiling. Number Thirteen flashed in the winner's spot. It was official.

Suddenly she was beaming. "We won! Oh, my gosh, we won!" She flung herself across Lightning's neck in joy. It was as if she was grasping it all over again, even though she had known it in her heart as they crossed the finish line. But now it was official. Her whole face lit up. Royalair's jockey couldn't help but feel happy for her. Her joy was infectious. She was so young, and a girl yet. She had just made racing history, but the wizened veteran jockey knew beyond a doubt that this child beside him still had no idea what she had just accomplished. She'd know soon enough.

"You not only won—you tied the track record! I knew it was an awfully fast pace we were setting out there."

"Record?" She stared back at the board in disbelief. Their time had equaled the existing record time set for the Kentucky Derby.

"Yep, you did. Thought I had it, too. Ran a textbook race until you came along," he complimented her.

"Thanks," was all she could muster, shyness overcoming her. This was the first time she'd ever received praise from one of her peers.

"That's some horse you've got there. Like to hear the story sometime." He moved on, leaving her to savor her victory alone for a few more moments.

As soon as the results flashed across the tote board, Jessica threw herself into her husband's arms, weeping uncontrollably. "She won! Our little girl won!" she wailed in great, gulping sobs. Michael, who was leaking a few tears himself, just held her, unable to put into words how he felt at that moment, as filled with pride for his daughter as he was.

Soon those in adjoining boxes descended upon them, offering congratulations to the owners of the Derby winner. Having had this box all his life, Michael knew and was known by all his neighbors.

"Must get down to the winner's circle," he apologized to one and all unnecessarily as he led his wife out of the box. Even as they made their descent through the stands, he was repeatedly slapped on the back by more well-wishers. Michael found himself having to push his way through the thick crowds as he struggled to reach his daughter.

Ted and Scotty were also having some difficulty pushing through the crowds to get out onto the track so they could escort her to the winner's circle. Ted was beside himself, repeating, "They did it! Did you see? They did it!" over and over while Scotty, normally more taciturn, was beaming, beside himself with pride over their victory. He burst through the gate, brandishing his pass impatiently at the guard who, recognizing him as the winning trainer, waved him on. There he found Jock standing, holding Lightning's cooler.

"What a race, huh, Dad?" Jock exclaimed, his face, too, radiating his exhilaration over the results. He threw his arms around his father in a giant bear hug, repeating it when he saw Ted behind him. "Congratulations! You got another winner!"

"Looks like it," Scotty replied. "You sure you still want to take him back? It's going to be some party up there." He nodded toward the stand in the center of the winner's circle, where the press was already gathering with the massive camera equipment and crew.

"Not I," Jock said, waving away his chance. "You know I hate crowds. This is your moment, Dad. Your victory. Go enjoy every minute of it!"

"That we will," he told him, slapping his son's shoulder in gratitude. "We'll see you soon, though."

"No, take your time. It's not every day you win the Kentucky Derby. I'll be fine."

Scotty looked around then. "Where is she?" he said to no one in particular. Most of the other colts had already returned, their grooms stepping forward to take them back to the barns to be cooled out. "What's she doing?" he stammered with irritation.

Ted grinned knowingly. "Oh, Scotty, You know Ann. She's just taking her time, savoring the moment." *Doing what I'd do,* he thought, *spending a few solitary moments with her horse before the world descends on them.*

"Well, I wish she'd hurry," he said, though he understood only too well what Ann must be feeling.

That was exactly what was going through Ann's mind as she took him far down the backstretch before turning. She let him canter along easily, "savoring the moment," as Ted had said. She was in no hurry to return. For this one fleeting instant, this victory belonged solely to her and Lightning. Too soon she would have to face the world that awaited her.

All along she'd focused only on winning the Derby. Never had she given a thought to what would happen if she actually accomplished her goal! She was completely unprepared. Suddenly she was overwhelmed by the magnitude of what a win in this, the greatest race of all, would mean. Gone was her anonymity here around the track. She would have to meet *those* people, face TV cameras for the first time. If she'd ever faced any fear about the race itself, it was nothing compared to the apprehension gripping her now.

Slowly she cantered along the inside rail, coming back down the homestretch past the grandstand once more. It was alive with thousands of screaming fans—and they were all screaming for *her.* She turned away, concentrating on riding her colt, blocking the sight from her mind as she made her way to Scotty, beaming and gesturing excitedly to her. Beside him stood her best friends, Jock and Ted, equally as thrilled for her as they waved her on. She relaxed a bit. She would be surrounded by family. She could find strength in them.

The sight of her loved ones brought the joy back to her face. Gray eyes sparkling with excitement, she descended on them with shouts of elation. "Scotty, Jock, Ted! Did you see him? Wasn't he magnificent?" she called to them as Jock stepped forward and snapped a lead rope on Lightning's bridle and handed it to Scotty, who proudly led him toward the Winner's Circle.

"I can't believe what happened. After the gate failed to open, I thought we were through." She was babbling, but she didn't care.

"What? What happened?" Scotty asked.

"I was stunned. I could do nothing. But not Lightning! He reared up and *forced* it open. Can you believe? Bless him, he *knew* what to do. And then he just took off."

"Dad, Lightning's leg," Jock said suddenly, staring down in horror. "It's bleeding!"

Scotty immediately stopped the horse and bent down. Lightning's left front leg was indeed red with fresh blood. Without thinking, Ann started to dismount, but Scotty stopped her. "No—you stay put. Do you want to get disqualified? I'll take care of it."

Concerned, unable to see anything from her position, Ann wailed, "What is it? Is he going to be okay? Oh, my gosh, if he's hurt—" Though he had shown no signs of it bothering him, she feared what running on the cut leg could mean to his future.

After what seemed an eternity, Scotty stood. "It's just superficial," he told her. "He's going to be fine. The bleeding has nearly stopped anyway."

"Are you sure?" She was still frantic about her horse.

"Yes, I'm sure. Jock will soak it when he gets him back to the barn. He'll be good as new before you know it. Must have done it when he kicked the gate," he guessed.

Ann nodded. "Most likely. He just reared up and let fly. If I didn't have a good hunk of mane in my hand, I might have been left behind. Scotty, all the times I've ridden him, I knew he had power—and speed—but today, well...I've never taken him that fast, least I don't think so." She wrapped her arms around his neck in a big hug. "He's an amazing horse."

"That he is. You tied the track record for the Derby you know?"

She nodded. "Royalair's jockey told me when we were cooling them out. I still can't believe he made up all that distance and WON!"

Ted swung over beside her and grabbed her hand. "Yes, you won!" he said meaningfully. "And what a race it was! But we didn't think beyond the winning, did we?" He squeezed her hand, putting into that gesture all the things he did not need to express with words. She knew he understood, that he'd be there for her.

Then they were entering the Winner's Circle, where she saw her parents waiting happily for her. She waved and blew kisses to them, holding up two fingers in victory. They smiled back anxiously as the crowds closed in around them. That made Lightning fidgety, causing him to kick out, dispersing the throng quickly.

Cameras flashed as the huge garland of roses was placed across Lightning's neck. He danced a bit as it slapped against his legs, but Ann whispered to him, and he settled, arching his neck handsomely as his long forelock fell into his eyes. Then her family stepped forward for the official picture while she beamed into the camera. Just before she jumped down to go weigh in, she threw her arms around his powerful long neck and gave him a huge hug, her long hair tumbling down to blend with his thick black mane. The look of utter adoration for her horse did not go unnoticed. Every photographer within range scrambled for the picture that would grace many front pages in the weeks to come.

The moment was broken as she threw her leg over and slid down. She quickly undid the girth and removed her saddle. Hugging it to her, she stepped onto the scale for the weigh-in, and it was official. After handing the saddle over to Jock, she ran to her parents, throwing herself into their waiting arms.

"Fantastic!" her father said. "What a race, Honey!"

"Oh, Darling." Jessica kissed her. "I didn't think I could hold my breath for two whole minutes."

She wiggled free and launched herself at Jock, Scotty, and Ted, practically simultaneously, laughing and crying as she tried to hug all of them at once. Lightning nickered, causing her to pull herself free and return to him. Painfully she looked down at his leg, already clotted, though the red stain ran the length of his cannon bone. "Oh, my poor baby," she murmured, bending over to check it closer.

"It looks worse than it is," Scotty told her. "Jock will take good care of it."

"You know I will," Jock said, squeezing her shoulder.

"Yes, I trust you will," she said.

"Take him on back now," Scotty told his son, who hastened to lead him out and back to the barn. Ann watched anxiously, thankful he showed no signs of limping as he walked away. All at once the TV crew corralled her and chauffeured her up onto the podium. Dragging Ted with her by refusing to let go of his hand, she acknowledged his presence to the announcer by saying, "He's been with me through this whole adventure. He's my best friend," and made sure he was on the podium beside her. She was not about to go through this interview without moral support.

The camera loved Ann. Her shy demeanor personified the essence of the little horse farm triumphing over the big breeders and wealthy owners. Every reporter saw a big story in this win and jumped to capitalize on it. They fell in love with this young girl, whose skill and genuine love for her horse helped pioneer hitherto uncharted territory. She'd run with the boys and bested them at their own game. The fact that she stood there shyly, surrounded by her supportive family, told a story in itself. But they all knew it went deeper than that.

"What made you decide to ride him yourself?" the announcer asked.

"Easy," she replied. "No one else can ride him."

"Really? No one?" He looked rather skeptical.

"Originally Ted here was supposed to ride him," she said, nodding to her friend, "but Lightning wouldn't let him. And Ted's a top-notch rider, too. But it was no go. So Scotty applied to the racing commission."

"That's right. We didn't know until earlier this week if they were going to let her ride," Scotty explained, jumping in.

"Is that why it was kept a secret until the race then?"

"Well, yes, mostly to avoid all the 'chaos,' shall we say. But also for Ann's sake. We knew she wouldn't be able to endure all the publicity before the race and stay focused."

"I'm afraid the cat's out of the bag now." The announcer smiled at Ann, who returned it with a hesitant one of her own.

"I guess," she mumbled.

"How about a replay of the race?" he suggested. "Your horse broke from the outside position and broke late—"

She interrupted him, "No—the gate failed to open," she corrected.

"What?" The announcer squinted at the screen. This interview was filled with all sorts of surprises. Good thing he was a pro—used to handling the unexpected.

"The gate didn't open, so Lighting kicked it with his leg. That's when he got cut."

"Oh, my—that bears looking into. So he actually sprung the gate himself?"

Ann nodded. "That put him in the back of the pack. He had to run pretty much full out to even catch them. I couldn't do anything at that point but just let him go, if we were going to get back into the race at all." She went on to describe the race with as little detail as possible, hoping they'd take the camera off her so she could get back to her family. After her adrenaline rush of the race, she was beginning to feel exhaustion setting in. And she was still concerned about Lightning. Though she had complete faith in Jock, she felt her place was with her horse.

Then it was over. Ann and her family had not told the complete story, but they'd given the reporters enough facts for now. The rest would have to wait. With Michael carrying the huge trophy, the five of them left the winner's circle and began the long walk back to the barn, where Jock and Lightning waited.

"Okay, where are we going to celebrate?" Michael asked, lifting the trophy aloft.

"Dad, would you mind terribly if we didn't go out to eat? Maybe put it on hold till tomorrow. I really don't want to leave Lightning right now. And I'm just so exhausted!"

"Oh, Honey, of course you are," her mother said, putting her arm around her daughter's shoulders. "How selfish of us. One of us will just run out and bring something back. We can celebrate tomorrow."

"I'll go," Michael volunteered. "You see to your horse."

On the way back, they chattered excitedly about the race. When they arrived, Jock was glad to see them. He'd already called for a vet, who waited until they got back to assure them—especially Ann—that Lightning would be fine.

"He'll be up and running in a couple of days, just like new."

Ann stood next to her colt, looking doubtful. "You sure?" The wound looked a lot better now that Jock had cleaned and dressed it. As soon as they all had a look, the vet wrapped it to prevent infection.

"Absolutely. Don't think for a minute he won't be in top form in time for the Preakness."

"Preakness?" Ann mumbled.

"Why, of course," the vet said. "As the Derby winner, he's expected to go on to the Preakness. Don't you want to take a stab at the Triple Crown?"

"We sure do," she said, brightening, her exhaustion suddenly swept away with the realization that she'd get to race him again. She looked up at her father expectantly.

"Already got him entered," he said, laughing at her surprise. "Did you forget what comes next?"

She shook her head as if to clear it. "N-no, but…you know, I've been so focused on winning the Derby, the Preakness never occurred to me."

"Then you'd better start thinking about it," Scotty grinned. "This is only the beginning. We're going all the way, Lass."

"Hear that, Ted?" She hugged him. "Pimlico, here we come!" Then she ducked into the stall and threw her arms around Lightning's neck. "The second jewel. Up for another one, big fella?" she said as he snuffled against her, enjoying the attention.

Jock looked at Ted and chuckled. "Here we go again."

Ted grinned. "I get the feeling that nothing will ever be same from here on in."